THE TURNCOAT

· THE ·

TURNCOAT

Siegfried Lenz

Translated from the German by John Cullen

OTHER PRESS
NEW YORK

Originally published in German as *Der Überläufer* in 2016
by Hoffmann und Campe Verlag, Hamburg
Copyright © 2016 by Hoffmann und Campe Verlag, Hamburg
Translation copyright © 2020 Other Press

The translation of this work was supported by a grant
from the Goethe-Institut.

Production editor: *Yvonne E. Cárdenas*
Text designer: *Jennifer Daddio / Bookmark Design & Media Inc.*
This book was set in Bembo by Alpha Design & Composition of Pittsfield, NH.

1 3 5 7 9 10 8 6 4 2

Library of Congress Cataloging-in-Publication Data

Names: Lenz, Siegfried, 1926–2014, author. | Cullen, John, 1942– translator.
Title: The turncoat / Siegfried Lenz ; translated from the German by John Cullen.
Other titles: Überläufer. English
Description: New York : Other Press, [2020] | Originally published in German
as Der Überläufer in 2016 by Hoffmann und Campe Verlag, Hamburg.
Identifiers: LCCN 2020001400 (print) | LCCN 2020001401 (ebook) |
ISBN 9781590510537 (paperback) | ISBN 9781590510544 (ebook)
Subjects: LCSH: World War, 1939-1945—Campaigns—Poland—Fiction. |
GSAFD: Historical fiction.
Classification: LCC PT2623.E583 U35513 2020 (print) |
LCC PT2623.E583 (ebook) | DDC 833/.914—dc23
LC record available at https://lccn.loc.gov/2020001400
LC ebook record available at https://lccn.loc.gov/2020001401

THE TURNCOAT

· ONE ·

Nobody answered the door.

Proska knocked on it again, harder, more purposefully, holding his breath. He waited, bowed his head, and considered the letter in his hand. He noticed a key sticking out of the door lock; someone must be home.

He stepped slowly away from the door and ventured a look through a cloudy window. Doing so gave the sun a clear shot at the back of his head, but Proska didn't mind. Suddenly his knees, the knees of a robust, thirty-five-year-old assistant, began to tremble. He forced his lips apart—a thin thread of saliva had glued them together.

Before him, two meters away on the other side of the glass pane, an old man was sitting on a chair. He'd completely bared his left arm—a dry, yellowish, half-withered branch of his body—and was filling a hypodermic needle. The fussiness he brought to bear on this task was intolerable. When it was done, he let the empty, used-up vial fall unheeded to the floor. Proska thought he heard a soft, shattering noise, but he only imagined it; the windowpane blocked the tiny sound.

The old man carefully laid the syringe on a low table, picked up a ball of cotton wool, and with flesh-less fingers plucked out a small piece. Trembling, he twisted the stuff into a plug and held it to the mouth of a bottle, which he then slowly raised and inverted. The liquid soaked the plug, which seemed insatiable as its color changed.

Proska let no movement, not the slightest gesture, escape his notice. He'd seen the old man only four or five times before in his life, greeted him only four or five times before in his life. Except that he was a drug-gist, Proska knew nothing about him. His doorplate bore only his name—Adomeit—and nothing else.

The old man rubbed a spot on his arm with the cotton wad and paused for a moment. While he was waiting, he squinted over the metal rim of his specta-cles at the syringe, which gleamed innocuously in the sunlight.

What's this old man going to do? Is he going to stick that thing in his arm? In a vein? Why?

The corners of Proska's mouth twitched.

Adomeit picked up the syringe and brought it close to his eyeglasses. He pressed the plunger briefly, and a thin stream of brown liquid shot out of the needle. The instrument was reliable; it worked as it should. Then the old man stabbed it into his arm so suddenly that Proska, standing outside the window, froze as though paralyzed. He couldn't cry out or raise a hand or run away. While he watched the old man doing something, perhaps some harm, to his own body, Proska himself seemed to feel a sharp, deep pain, a pain as sharp as a tweezed hair and as deep as the wellspring of a human eye. The druggist's index finger pressed the liquid into his blood, steadily, relentlessly.

When the old man yanked the needle out of his arm, Proska felt capable of movement again. He hurried back to the wooden door, banged on it, and waited. But no one came to open it. With great care, Proska pressed the handle down; the door moved, reluctant and creaking, and let him pass inside.

"Hello," said Proska. His voice sounded hoarse.

The old fellow made no reply. Apparently, he hadn't yet noticed the man who had just stepped into his room.

"I wanted to ask you . . . ," Proska called loudly. He left the sentence unfinished, for he saw that Adomeit had picked up the cotton pad and was using it to swab the spot on his arm from which he'd just withdrawn the hypodermic needle. Then the old man got up from his chair and walked over to the window. He thrust his yellow arm into the sunlight and murmured,

"There, lick it off, quick, make it dry." Proska could see a small red mark—the needle's bite—on one of the old man's veins.

"Herr Adomeit!"

Adomeit didn't turn around.

"Good morning, Herr Adomeit!"

The old man looked out the window and rolled down his sleeve. Then Proska cried out, "I said, 'Good morning!'"

The druggist slowly turned, discovered his visitor, and gazed at him with friendly, gray, puzzled little eyes. "Good morning," he said. "You're Herr Proska, right?"

"Yes. I wanted to ask if you might lend me a postage stamp." Proska held up his envelope.

"A letter for me?" Adomeit asked. "Who would write me a letter?"

"No," said Proska. "I wanted to ask if—"

"You have to speak louder," the druggist interrupted. "My hearing is very bad." He sat down on his chair but left his visitor standing.

"Do you have a stamp I could use, Herr Adomeit?"

"Give me the letter. I can't imagine who would be writing to me."

"The letter is not for you!" Proska shouted. "I just wanted to ask if I could borrow a stamp. I'll replace it tomorrow, probably."

"You want a stamp?"

"Yes. I'll get you a new one tomorrow."

"I have lots of stamps," the old man said amiably. "I can give you several. We don't need them anymore over here. And who am I supposed to write to, anyway? I still have a friend, he lives near Braunschweig. We used to be neighbors, just like we're neighbors now. I've known him for sixty years, and in those sixty years, we've said everything two people can possibly say to each other . . . How many stamps do you need?"

"Two!"

"How many? You have to talk louder. I don't hear well."

"I need two stamps!" Proska yelled. "I'll pay you back tomorrow!"

"You can have them," Adomeit murmured, standing up. He opened a dresser drawer, took out an exercise book, and lumbered back to his visitor.

"The stamps are in here. Take what you want."

The assistant quickly leafed through the pages of the notebook and found a strip of ten stamps.

"There they are," the old man said. "Take as many as you need."

He smelled disagreeably like a hospital. Proska felt a slight ache in the left side of his forehead and longed for some fresh air.

"Go ahead, take some," the druggist said, encouraging his hesitant guest.

"These stamps are old. They aren't valid anymore."

"You can take more than two," the old man said. He was attentively observing the movements of his visitor's lips.

"I'm telling you, these stamps are invalid," Proska said, and then, shouting: "Your stamps aren't any good! They're old and obsolete!"

"But they still stick very well."

"Nobody cares about that now. Stamps have to stick *and* be valid . . ."

"All the same, you can take some," said the old man, eager to help.

"But I can't use them."

"How many?"

"I can't use them!" Proska screamed.

Adomeit thrust the ten-stamp strip into the exercise book again, shrugged his shoulders regretfully, and moved back to the dresser. Before closing the drawer, he turned around and asked, "Did you say something?"

Proska shook his head and looked at the unstamped letter in his hand.

The druggist sat down again. "So you have to mail a letter?"

"Yes."

"At your age," said Adomeit, winking behind his eyeglasses, "at your age I wrote letters too."

"This letter is to my sister."

"My mother's been dead a long time."

Proska screamed, "This letter is for my sister!"

"Sister, yes. Sister? You have a sister?"

"Yes. Of course. Nothing unusual about that." Proska wanted to leave, but something was forcing him to stay in this room. His headache kept getting worse; it seemed like a jackhammer was hard at work behind the left half of his forehead.

Adomeit scratched the arm he'd stuck the needle into and rubbed the spot of the injection with the heel of his hand. "Why are you writing to your sister?" he asked. "Family members don't usually have very much to say to one another. Is your letter long?"

"Fifteen pages!" Proska screamed.

"Good God, fifteen pages."

Proska felt his knees start to tremble again. He stroked his low, wide forehead, patted his straggly, sun-bleached hair, and shut his eyes.

"Are you tired?" the old man asked.

"Maybe so. I've been doing a lot of hard thinking. That kind of thing always takes a toll."

"You should try not to work so much," said the old man.

Proska screamed, "I've been thinking!"

"Thinking? So, thinking. But that doesn't do any good." The old man pressed his fingers together and smiled.

"Maybe not," said Proska listlessly. Then, suddenly, he raised his head, gave the old man an unusually long, hard stare, and asked him, "Why did you stick that thing in your arm?" He slid his eyes over to the syringe for a second. "That thing over there. I watched you do it."

"Do you still want the stamps?"

"Why did you?" Proska shouted so loud that he flinched at the force of his own voice. "Why did you stick that needle in your arm?"

"The needle?" The old man clicked his tongue. "The needle's sharp. You don't feel any pain. Once the medicine's under your skin, it swells up a little around the puncture. But the swelling goes down fast."

"Why do you do it?"

"Do you want to try? It's really easy. You hold the thing like this, look . . ."

The druggist grasped the syringe and held it with the needle pointing straight up in the air.

"Why are you giving yourself shots?" Proska bellowed. He was furious at the old man, though he had no reason to be; he clenched one hand into a fist and struck his own thigh. He had big red hands.

Adomeit laid the syringe on the little table, gave his visitor a friendly smile, giggled for a while, and then raised his head like a roebuck that's just heard a suspicious sound. "Herr Proska, I'll tell you just why I give myself shots. That was what you wanted to know, right?"

"Yes—if you don't mind."

"Good, I'll explain the reason as precisely as I can. But for God's sake, don't get angry." He scratched the site of his recent injection, glanced briefly through the window, and turned to Proska with a sly twinkle in his eye.

"Just don't get angry. So: I like sitting by windows. I suppose you do too, don't you? And sometimes when you look out, I suppose thoughts come to you too, don't they? Memories? Or not? And when you see the stupid old roads and the woods with their comfy hiding places and the pretty spot behind the big juniper tree, I suppose nothing occurs to you, right? And if a girl goes down this road into the woods, you don't think anything about that either? Maybe you just calmly spit into the wind or peel yourself an apple. Even when you know that a girl could mean more to you behind the big juniper than on the boring road?

"Look, I'm an old man, a lame fox every hen can outrun. But I have memories, you know? Some people can live for twenty years on memories. They carry them around wherever they go, they fasten them to a watch chain and put them in their safest pocket. I can't do that, I hate it! But memories come to you even if you don't summon them—there they are, whether you can use them or not. At least, that's the way it is with me. If I look out at the street, and . . . do you understand what I'm saying? People shouldn't remember! Very few can learn from what happened, and I'm not one of them. So that's why I send memories to the devil, and to make sure they don't come back, I shoot that stuff into my arm. You can understand that, can't you? Now you're mad at me."

Proska tilted his square head to one side and cleared his throat.

"Did you say something? You have to talk louder."

"No!" Proska screamed. "Said nothing, thought nothing."

"I'm not finished yet either," said the druggist. "Memories aren't good for much. They're as heavy as sugar sacks. You drag them around long enough, sooner or later they'll bring you to your knees. I don't like memories. Every day is different; nothing repeats itself."

Sweat covered Proska's forehead. His headache throbbed against it. "May I sit down?" he asked.

"Now? Why? You have to go already?"

"I asked if I could sit down!" Proska shouted.

"Yes, yes—here, on the bed. Just sit, go on, make yourself comfortable. I'm not finished yet, but I won't be much longer. And you're not mad at me after all, are you? No, you're not. Look, I too was a soldier once. I was in a war, not this last one, but there were lots of corpses back then too. And I also shot a man, a handsome young man. He had black hair and a pretty nose like a girl's—small, thin, slightly turned up. What they call a snub nose, I guess. What good does it do me to remember all that? Does it do *any* good? Look, when it happened, I was lying full-length on the ground beside a kind of lane in the woods. My chest was resting on my arms, my chin on my hands. The needles under me were damp and soft, their smell practically enough to make me tipsy. You know what pine needles smell like up close. A jaybird shrieked somewhere above me, big, lonely clouds drifted across the sky, and everything was quiet and peaceful and beautiful. Then, all of a sudden, a man was coming down the narrow path, calm as could be—a young fellow, a handsome Russian enemy. He couldn't see me, so he had no idea someone was lying there with eyes fixed on him like a buzzard watching a field mouse. He came closer, and that was when I saw the big silver medal on his chest, silver with a blue border. Ten steps away from me, he stopped, stood in place, and rubbed one of his lovely, dark eyes. Some bug had obviously flown into it. I let him rub his eye in peace, but when he finished and started coming even closer to me, so close he was sure to spot me any second, I pulled the trigger . . . Now do you know why memories do so little good? Look, maybe he was a very unhappy man. Maybe he's grateful to me today. What's the point of remembering such things? Those who can learn from them should do so. Those who can't should focus on what's affecting them today, right now; that's more important."

Adomeit stopped talking and looked at the syringe. His eyelids narrowed and formed two slits. He felt he'd said more than he really wanted to, and that made him angry.

Proska stood up and screamed, "What did you aim at?"

The druggist murmured, "The silver medal."

Both men were silent for a while, their eyes meeting and then turning away to scan the room.

Suddenly the old man's face changed. He said, "Maybe I have some other stamps after all."

He pulled out a drawer, rummaged in it at length, found a well-worn notebook, and hissed, "There it is. Many things hide from us, don't you think? Have a look! Some new stamps are stuck in there somewhere."

Proska took the little book in his hands and leafed through it. He found four stamps. He cried, "These are valid! Can I have two of them? Until tomorrow?"

"Yes, yes," said the druggist. "Take them. Your letter will reach its destination. Best wishes. And goodbye."

Proska stood still in the front courtyard for a few moments; the cool air soothed his headache. Behind a wire mesh fence, an old cherry tree was in bloom, compelled by the spring. A dovecote hung above Adomeit's window, but there was no movement in any compartment; the pigeons were cooing elsewhere. Proska moistened the back of both stamps with his tongue and stuck them on his envelope. Then he walked to the gate in the low, whitewashed fence, slipped outside to the street, and stood there looking around for a long time. But since he saw no girl heading for the forest and its soft hiding places, and no man or child either, he opened the slot in the yellow mailbox, raised his letter to his eyes, gazed at it with a seriously pensive expression—exactly as if he were charged with coming to an important, one-time decision—and then suddenly flicked the envelope into the mailbox's slender, gloomy maw. The slot flap fell down; something definitive had taken place. Now the letter wasn't his anymore, he no longer had any claim to it. He had given something away—forever.

Proska crossed the desolate street, climbed up the stairs to his low-ceilinged room, and stationed himself at the open window. Outside there, thirty meters away, hung the mailbox, fastened to a wall. The sun beat down mercilessly on the box, which threw a shadow as sharp as a knife.

What will she do once she's read that letter? What will Maria do? She'll press her hands against her chest and try to calm her pounding heart. But that won't be possible. Reading the letter will make her think of me. She'll curse me. Maybe I shouldn't have written to her—it would probably have been better not to. That letter will kill her hope like a well-aimed shot. She'll fall onto the chair, she won't be able to cry, despair will choke her hard and long. She'll take off her apron, read the letter a second time, and then, after she's calmed herself down a little . . . But she can't, she won't be calm. Nobody could, not with such a letter in hand. But I had to write the letter; despair drove me to it. One day despair chased me to the cupboard, forced me to take out pen and paper, obliged me to sit down and write. Let Maria turn me in! She's my sister, she'll know what has to be done. I'm braced for anything, ready for anything. Today is Tuesday, a sunny, warm spring day. She'll get the letter the day after tomorrow, so Thursday, around ten in the morning. Then she'll decide everything, assuming there's anything at all left to decide. It's my fault that she's alone—it was me, six years ago, who . . .

With weary movements, the thirty-five-year-old assistant Walter Proska cast about the room for the only chair, pulled it closer, sat on it, leaned his elbows on the windowsill, cradled his chin in his big hands, and stared at the mailbox. He heard swift, slapping wing beats; the pigeons were coming back. The man breathed deeply, several times, in and out. As he did so, a mild, pleasantly dizzy sensation took hold of him. For a second, in a flash of imagination, he was falling from somewhere, from a wall, from a roof, from a tree or a cliff. Then the scene changed, and he imagined he was bent over a well and breathlessly, intently listening to it, to the deep, comforting landscape of silence. And while he listened down, so to speak, projecting his hearing into the stagnant world of the past, while he seemed to glimpse his low, wide forehead, his muscular neck, and his sun-bleached hair in the distant mirror of the well water's surface, in the mirror of what had been, of what he'd lived through and withstood, the images stored in his memory emerged from the fog of time. Walter Proska, the assistant, suddenly heard a train whistle blow . . .

· TWO ·

At the Prowursk station, the little locomotive got a drink. An iron trunk was swung out over its red-hot body, a hand wheel was turned, and then a thick stream of water shot into its opened flank.

Proska heard the rush of water and stepped over to the broken window of his compartment. All he could see were a tiny white station house with a number on its facade, a deserted platform, and two woodpiles, for the village itself lay a good half hour away from the station, on the other side of a deciduous forest. A soldier was patrolling the area alongside the train. Since the weather was hot, he'd unbuttoned his collar. He carried his assault rifle slung to his back as casually as an African mother carries her nursling. When he reached the end of the little convoy, which consisted of the locomotive, a supply car, and a mail car, he did an about-face without raising his head and slouched back, retracing his steps. This sequence was repeated several times. The landscape gave the impression of a huge, abandoned hearth; no wind, no gentle breeze could be detected, nor any rustling in the thin shrubbery.

"Will we stop here a long time?" asked Proska, when the sentry drew even with him.

"Until we go on!"

"I thought the locomotive just needed water."

"Ah," said the sentry grumpily. "So that's what it needs?" All of a sudden, he raised his head and looked down the mud road that led to Prowursk. Standing by the window, Proska looked in the same direction and saw a girl who was waving to the train and rapidly coming closer. She wore a little leaf-green dress and a wide belt around her waist, which was as narrow as the neck of an hourglass. Stepping quickly, she reached the platform and headed directly for the sentry. Her red hair had a dull sheen, her nose was short, her eyes green-blue. Her feet were inside a pair of cloth shoes. "What do you want?" growled the sentry, staring at her naked legs.

"Mister Soldier . . . ," she said, trembling. She put down the earthenware jug she was carrying and laid a folded raincoat on top of it.

"What do you have in the jug, milk or water?"

She shook her head and brushed back her hair. Proska admired the outline of her breasts.

"I suppose you want a ride?" the sentry asked.

"Yes, just a short way. To the Pripet Marshes. I can give you money, or—"

"Get out of here, and be quick about it! We're not allowed to take anyone with us. Really, you ought to know that. Didn't you ask me for a ride once before?"

"No, sir."

"You're a Pole, right?"

"Yes."

"Where did you learn German?"

At that moment, the little locomotive whistled twice, once long and once short. The sentry left the girl standing there, gave Proska a sullen look, and walked toward the front of the train. Cursing, he clambered up into the supply car, sat on a crate, and began to smoke. His assault rifle dug into his flesh, but he didn't unsling the weapon, because he was too lazy. The heat shimmered above the parched earth.

The locomotive started with a jerk, groaning, and the narrow-gauge train slowly went into motion.

The girl gathered up her things and walked along-side the train. She looked imploringly at Proska, moved very close to him, and whispered, "Please take me with you."

And the assistant couldn't resist her eyes, her hair, her slender, naked legs, and the provocative outline of her breasts. He pushed the compartment door open, braced one foot against the board, and reached out a hand. She passed him jug and raincoat, jumped up on the footboard by herself, and let him help her into the compartment. He closed the door and turned around. She stood in front of him, looked him over, and smiled.

"I'll get off right before we reach the marshes," she said, as though apologizing.

He remained silent and stared at her strong teeth.

"Your comrade will be angry," she whispered.

It wasn't easy for him to keep his hands in his pockets.

"Will he shoot me?" she asked with a smile.

He smiled too, pulled a pack of cigarettes out of his pocket, and said, "Have a cigarette. It'll calm you down a little."

"I don't smoke."

"Well then, at least we can sit down."

They sat down. His knees were a few centimeters from hers.

The sun shot a beam of light into the compartment. Proska watched the dust motes dancing up and down. He and the girl fell silent, listening to the little locomotive groan, and on the other side of the broken window, the landscape slipped by: meadows and burnt fields and small birch groves and—very seldom—a little straw-covered shack, above which a column of smoke sometimes stood motionless in the dry air. No one was working in the fields; in the meadows, a few cows stood around, staring obtusely into space; every now and then, following a lazy habit apparently meant to shoo away flies, their tails would slap their bony hindquarters.

"Do you live in Prowursk?" Proska asked.

"Yes, I was born here."

"I wouldn't have thought such girls grew in this place. Does your father have cows too?"

"My father was a forester. He's dead."

"Did he die long ago?"

"Two years."

"In the war?"

"I don't know. Two years ago, a soldier in Prowursk got shot. The local police came to our village at dawn. They searched every house for men and weapons. We live on the edge of the village, so they came to us first. My father didn't have time to hide himself properly. He crept into the wardrobe, and when the military police came, I led them through the house and showed them everything, and they were almost on the point of leaving. But when we came back to the room where the wardrobe was, my father had to cough, and one of the policemen pulled out his pistol and fired four shots into the wardrobe, two above and two below."

"This will all be over soon," said Proska. She laid her hands on her thighs and kicked her feet up and down.

"Are you married?" he asked.

"No. You're not supposed to get married before you're twenty-eight . . ."

"Why not?"

She gazed at him for a long time. Then she slid to his side, took his head in her hot hands, and breathed on his forehead. Proska put an arm around her shoulder, but she immediately jerked away from him and sat in her former place.

"I wanted to read your forehead."

"So, you know how to do that?" he said. "What does it say?" He struck his head with the flat of his hand. "What can you read there?"

She drew in air; her breasts rose. She looked at him mysteriously, and he thought he could dive into her green-blue eyes, suddenly, like diving into a pond.

"Everything will turn out fine," she said, "or then again maybe not."

He laughed. "Is that what it says?"

"Verbatim," said she.

"Then you're a real little prophet. And people love to believe prophets like you. What's your name?"

"Wanda."

"And how old are you?"

"Twenty-seven. And you?"

"Twenty-nine."

"And your name is . . . ?"

"Walter," he said.

"Walter and Wanda. If your comrade doesn't shoot me dead, we'll meet again." She smiled mischievously.

"Nonsense," said Proska. "He won't do anything to you."

They stopped talking and looked past each other and tuned their ears to the rhythm of the moving train: *hmm-tmm-tmm, hmm-tmm-tmm, hmm-tmm-tmm.* And he thought that a good many words have something in common with this rhythm, words of profound melancholy, words of peaceful longing and bygone love. *Hmm-tmm-tmm, hmm-tmm-tmm*: It sounded like cover-let, or yes-ter-day, or mis-e-ry, or take-my-word, or one-last-kiss.

It grew unbearably hot in the compartment. Sweat broke out on Proska's forehead; his gums craved liquid. She looked at his assault rifle, which was hanging barrel-down on a hook. "Have you ever fired that?" she asked.

He didn't answer. He stood up, stepped to the door, and thrust his head through the window opening. The airstream lashed his face and blew his blond hair back. The cooling-off did him good. He could feel her watching him, and he thought, *If only we'd stopped for a night in Prowursk! She has exceptional breasts. And that red hair and those green-blue eyes sure go well together. In two hours it'll be dark. I hope . . .*

He turned around and asked, "Do you know how long it will take the train to get to the marshes?"

"About four hours. If nothing happens."

"What can happen?"

"Mines," she said with a smile.

"How do you know that?"

"People in the village talk about them sometimes."

"In Prowursk?"

"Yes. How they hear such things, I don't know, but they *do* discuss them."

"The heat probably spreads rumors," he said. "Or the hypocritical sky or your wimpy trees. How often do people talk about a train wreck?"

"Every day," she said.

"Does a train get blown up every day?"

"No. But when it happens, it gives people something to talk about for a week. And then it happens again."

He sat next to her and pressed his thigh against hers. "When's the last time a train got blown up around here?"

"Five days ago." She turned to him, put her soft arm around his shoulders, puckered her lips, and said, "I'm tired. The heat makes me lazy."

Proska looked past her ear at the broken window. They were traveling through a mixed forest, which had already reconquered half the railroad embankment and continued to send out advance parties of small birches, spruces, and willow shrubs against it. The little locomotive blew its whistle once, briefly, and seemed itself to have no idea why.

"The heat makes me thirsty," said Proska. "I'd like something to drink right now. A cold beer, or . . . what have you got in that jug? Milk or water?"

She shook her head and removed her arm from his shoulder. "Nothing to drink. My brother's in that jug."

He looked at the earthenware vessel and said, "And what can that possibly mean?"

"You don't believe me?"

Proska pinched her upper arm; she seemed to feel no pain.

"Now the prophet turns into a magician," he said. "Marigolds grow especially well in the marsh. Why wouldn't a brother thrive there too? Do you intend to plant him?"

She acted serious and smoothed the skirt of her little leaf-green dress over her knee and avoided looking him in the eye.

"My brother's ashes are inside this jug. We had him cremated in Lemberg. He was a railroad man, and the train he was on blew up. I'm traveling to Tomashgrod—that's where my brother's wife lives. She asked me to bring her his ashes."

"Was your brother's train running on this line?"

"I don't know."

Proska put his arm around her and stared fretfully at the inexpressive earthen jug. Now he felt as though he were under surveillance, and the more he strove to suppress the feeling, the more stubbornly and intensely it fixed itself in his brain. He felt a certain sympathy for Wanda and gently stroked her neck with his big, strong fingers. He moved his head closer and kissed her hair.

"This will all be over soon," he said sincerely. "I think it will all disappear overnight, just the way it came. You'll open your window—not tomorrow, but one fine day—and the sun will shine in your eyes and wish you good morning. The blackbird will perch in your garden, and you'll listen to it and find out that everything has changed. You think it will happen like that, Wanda? You can't imagine it, can you? In any case, you're only twenty-seven, you still have a whole year."

Silence fell between them. Some old spruce trees that lived in somber dignity at the foot of the embankment looked in on them imperturbably for a moment. He drummed his fingers on her collarbone and then suddenly let them slide down and touch her right breast. She immediately withdrew from his embrace, moved away from him, and smiled menacingly. And that smile stood there like a magical barrier, like an insurmountable obstacle between them.

"I'd like to sleep now," she said.

"You can put your head on my shoulder," he said.

"Too dangerous for me, I think."

"If you keep your coat off that jug, I won't do a thing to you."

"I don't understand," she said.

The assistant pointed to the container and said, "I have the feeling this thing is watching me. It seems—at least to me—to have eyes. It's like I'm under constant observation. Do you understand what I'm saying?"

"If that's really how you feel . . . ," she said, and then she stretched out on the bench seat and laid her head in Proska's lap. She looked up at him, a friendly look, and began to breathe deeply.

After a while, he asked her, "Are you asleep already?"

"Yes," she said. "I'm dreaming of you and our next meeting."

"Is your brother there too? I mean, can you see this jug anywhere near us?"

"No, we're alone. We're all alone—and it's wonderful. No one's watching us. We love each other. But your rifle's here, looking at us. It's not saying anything, though. Can your rifle keep quiet?"

"If it has to. Go to sleep, Wanda. Sleep and dream—or wait, I can make it even more comfortable for you."

As well as he could while remaining seated, he pulled off his uniform jacket, then folded it, raised her head from his lap, scooted to one side, and shoved the folded jacket under her head as a pillow.

"Thanks a lot," she whispered.

He said nothing and stared at the jug. He thought, *If it wouldn't hurt her, I'd throw this stupid thing right out the window. I never had such a traveling companion before. If they blow up the train, her brother will go swirling around, and if she's lucky enough to survive, she can wipe him off the vegetation. Maybe a finger off a birch, maybe a toe off a spruce trunk.*

A shiver ran down his spine. He stood up, took a couple of steps through the compartment, and stopped in front of the jug, which stood in a corner, slightly vibrating with the swaying movements of the train. It was a simple, probably homemade vessel with a solidly attached side handle. The opening was sealed with greaseproof parchment paper; thin but durable cord had been wrapped around it, the ends conscientiously knotted.

He cast a quick glance over at her, and when he determined that she wasn't opening her eyelids and was really trying to sleep, he resolutely snatched up the raincoat, unfolded it, and threw it over the jug. She appeared not to notice any of that. As he spread out his arms and stepped to the window, it seemed to Proska that he felt at once freer and braver. The sun greeted him through the treetops; on the forest floor, a rabbit ran wildly in circles and then dashed away. The little locomotive rumbled as it hauled its load through the mixed forest. Proska thought about the wooded surroundings of Lyck, the small Masurian city where he was born. It smelled just like this; the Borecka Forest, especially where it bordered Lake Sunowo, had once made the same impression on him.

The assistant spotted a squirrel, looking up at the train with dark, glistening eyes.

Her hair is the color of its fur. I'm going to call her "Squirrel."

He turned away from the window. She was lying peacefully athwart the seat, her legs crossed, one hand in her lap, the other on her mouth. He cautiously moved close to her, took the hem of her dress between two fingers, and pushed the fabric up a little. Then he bent down and kissed her suntanned leg, just above the knee. He looked at her face; her eyes remained closed, her lips twitched. When he straightened up, she said, "Not on the mouth."

"I thought you were asleep," he said.

"Whoever kisses me on the mouth is in for some bad luck."

"Really?"

"Watch out!"

"I don't care, I'll take my chances if—"

"Don't do it!" she said with a smile.

He lifted her head and kissed her. She returned his kiss and threw her arms around his muscular neck and then affectionately pushed him away.

"It'll be dark in an hour and a half," he said. "We have to see each other again."

"You covered the jug with my raincoat."

"Yes, I couldn't stand it anymore. It was making me uncomfortable."

"Take it off again, please. It will be dark in an hour and a half."

Proska apathetically did as Wanda asked, lay down on the other bench seat, waved to her, and attempted to fall asleep. But sleep obeys no orders, and the harder the man tried to surrender his senses and forget all his surroundings, the smaller his chances of success became. He squinted in her direction and called softly, "Squirrel?"

"What do you mean?" she asked.

"You can't fall asleep either, Squirrel."

"What's a squirrel?"

"You, for example."

"What am I?" she asked weakly.

"A little reddish-brown animal with curious eyes and tiny, pointed ears. You play in the trees, you're friends with an old, crotchety hazel bush. And you tease the young branches and challenge them and let them bounce you into the air. But in the winter, my little squirrel, you go to sleep, and if you get hungry, you just reach into the nut storeroom behind you . . ."

"You kissed me on the mouth," she said.

"Now do you know what a squirrel is?" he asked.

"You kissed me, so bad luck's on the way."

She said that with mild seriousness, in a voice he hardly recognized. He grew uneasy and stood up.

"Do you think something's going to happen to the train?"

"I warned you . . ."

"So why aren't you afraid? You don't care if all of a sudden . . ."

He took his rifle off its hook, balanced it in his hand, stroked the breech, and pulled a magazine out of his haversack.

From the seat where she lay, she was watching him. "What do you mean to do?" she asked.

"Just in case," he said, and he rammed in the magazine.

"How many cartridges are in there?"

"Enough." Leaving the safety catch off, he stood the weapon in a corner and thrust his head through the window opening.

"What do you see?" she asked.

"Nightfall."

"Is that really something you can see?"

"It's acting very fearful, and you have to pay close attention if you want to figure out which directions it's creeping up on us from . . . What would you say if I had to fire my rifle?"

"Why do you want to know that?"

"It would be your people, after all," he said, lighting a cigarette.

"In a minute they'll attack us."

He moved close beside her. "Get up," he said.

She lay unmoving.

"You have to get up, Wanda."

"But I'm so tired. It'll be dark soon."

Seized by an odd disquiet, he asked her curtly, "Who'll attack us in a minute? What's this prophetic babbling supposed to mean?"

"The mosquitoes. There are so many mosquitoes in these marshes!"

He laughed, and his laughter felt like a liberation.

"You Poles should keep more little birds, you know. Then there would be fewer mosquitoes. But birds die very young in your country. And the few I've seen are lonely, they fly around looking sad. Their songs have stuck in their throats."

"It was different before," she said.

"I know," he said.

All of a sudden, the little locomotive blasted out a hoarse, long-breathed whistle and reduced its speed. The man seized his assault rifle and braced its butt against his hip.

"It's still a long way to Tomashgrod."

"I can imagine," he said. "I guess we're in for it pretty soon."

Now the train was moving at only a walking pace.

"In the daytime," he said, "they hunker down in their nests like owls and don't dare leave. But as soon as night starts to fall, they wake up and get lively. They crawl under night's skirts and pick out a position in the dark and make little slits and shoot through them like it was broad daylight."

"Who are you talking about?"

"The boys who blow up the trains."

"You mean you think they shouldn't?"

"Be quiet."

He slowly opened the compartment door, bent down, and glanced up the track. Then he turned back to her and said in a rush, "You have to disappear, right away. Quick, quick, it's the military police. They'll probably check the whole train . . . Hurry up! Lie flat on the embankment and wait. I'll give you a sign when the coast is clear. Here, you have to get out on the other side."

She sprang up immediately and dashed to the door. "The lock's jammed," she said despairingly.

He raised his foot and kicked at the latch with all his strength.

"All right, Wanda, go, get out now! If they find you here, we'll both have a very bad time."

She jumped out, landed flat on the embankment, scooted down a little farther, and lay on her stomach.

The little train traveled on for another fifty meters, and then its brakes squealed.

While he swiftly pulled on his uniform jacket, Proska thought, *I have to hope she can run the distance to the train. It can't be more than fifty meters. She'd better not bail out on me. But she can't, she left her coat behind, not to mention that blasted jug. I can't look at that thing anymore.*

He wrapped the jug in the raincoat and shoved the bundle far under the train seat. As he was standing up, a policeman clambered into the compartment. "Well," he said. "Everything as it should be? May I see your marching orders?"

Proska handed him a crumpled piece of paper covered front and back with stamps.

"Where are you headed?" the MP asked.

"Not far from Kiev."

"And where are you coming from?"

"I was on leave in Lyck."

"And where might that be?"

"In Masuria, seventeen kilometers from the Polish border."

"From the former border," the policeman corrected him, flicking on the quadrangular pocket flashlight that hung on his chest. He aimed the light beam at the shabby scrap of paper. He checked every stamp, pointed with a scarred index finger at a signature, and asked, "That says 'Kilian,' right?"

"Yes, exactly right. That's my captain's name. He signed the pass. I'm bringing him a package from his wife."

"You can just send that package right back. The captain's dead."

"Killed in battle?"

"Indeed. A Kalmuck got him right between the eyes."

"When was this?"

"Four days ago. I had work to do near the front. They carried the captain two kilometers to the dressing station, but he couldn't be revived."

"So what should I do with his package?"

"What's in it?"

"According to his wife, wrist warmers and earmuffs. He mostly suffered from frozen ears in the winter."

"It's practically summer now," said the MP. "If you think you'll be able to use ear warmers yourself next winter, then just keep them."

"Thanks, the only part of me that gets cold is my feet."

The policeman looked up at the sky. "The moon's so curious today. I think it's going to have something to look at."

"You think the train's going to get blown up?"

"Keep your head away from the window," the policeman said. He switched off his flashlight and disappeared.

The assistant rushed to the other side of the compartment. His eyes scanned the embankment, but Wanda was nowhere to be seen. He waited for a moment, and then he called out, "Squirrel! Don't you hear me? You can come! Wanda! Where are you? Come here, now!" She didn't come. She didn't step out from behind a tree, as he hoped she might, or stand up from the shoulder of the embankment, as he wanted her to.

The train jerked into motion.

"Wanda!" Proska called, more loudly than before. "Why don't you come?"

The train gained speed.

"We'll meet again!" he called. "It won't be long!"

He'd been holding the door open, hoping to make it easier for her to jump in, but now he slammed it shut and sat down.

She forgot the jug and the raincoat. She was probably more scared than she was willing to admit. I'll hand over the jug in Tomashgrod.

Proska stood up, pulled the bundle with the jug out from under the seat, and set the vessel down on the floor in front of him. Moonlight shone on it. He thought it was blinking at him.

"Don't be afraid," he murmured. "I won't throw you out the window. It would be easy for me, but I won't do it. I'll treat you humanely, even though you're not human anymore. But you *were* once, and I know what that's worth. Believe me."

But then a primordial curiosity seized the soldier, an elemental question began to burn inside his skull, and he slowly drew his sidearm from its sheath.

"I have to see what it looks like when a person has reached this point. I can't do you any more harm. You mustn't be angry at me if I take away a bit of you, just a little bit on the tip of my knife."

He thrust the weapon into the parchment paper covering the opening, tore a largish hole in it, and with trembling hand lifted out a little mound of ash. He smelled it; it smelled of nothing at all.

Could just as well have been wood, or tobacco, or paper.

Proska stood up cautiously and held the knife in front of the broken window. The airstream pounced on the ashes, scattering them all over.

"Forgive me if you can," the assistant growled.

He was angry that the girl hadn't come back. Again he squatted down beside the jug, slowly, and without really wanting to, he stuck his knife in a second time. But the weapon didn't go down very deep. The jug, it turned out, was at most one-third filled with ashes.

What can this be? It sounds almost metallic. Is there something else under the ashes? Maybe she was fooling me, the prophetess with the beautiful breasts. I've got to see what's underneath. Her brother could just as well have been a piece of wood. He picked up the jug in both hands and held it through the window. The wind blew away the ashes, and at the bottom of the container were four gleaming sticks of dynamite!

Proska's arms were shaking; he'd expected anything else, only not this. *What a dupe, what a fool! I helped her transport these things!* Four dynamite sticks: enough for two trains and two weeks' conversation fodder in the village. Four dynamite sticks meant twisted railroad tracks, shattered railroad cars, and shredded corpses—in other words, new unrest, new fear, new reprisals.

He shut his eyes, breathed deep, filled his lungs to bursting with evening air, and drew back his right hand a little. Then, exhaling hard and exerting his full strength, he flung the jug down the embankment. The container struck a spruce trunk and broke apart, but there was no explosion.

Exhausted, he retreated from the window and sat on one of the bench seats. He felt sweat running down from his armpits and wetting his shirt.

"Lying bitch," the soldier murmured.

Ly-ing-bitch, the train clattered.

Just you wait, he thought.

Just-you-wait, the wheels rumbled.

The marsh began. A sweetish smell wafted into the compartment, a full, round smell, a smell of joyous, exuberant life.

Proska thought, *That's what I get for being nice. She lay down right here on this seat and stretched out her legs. Lovely legs, I have to admit. If I had known dynamite was in that jug, not her brother! What a devious little thing! If I ever see you again, I'll . . . I'll thrash the living daylights out of you!*

Night strode over the marsh and drove off the heat. The air became cooler. The man in the compartment shivered a little. Conifers grew rarer. Now, on both sides of the track, only modest birches could be seen. How indifferently the wood awaits the ax! The human soul is a cuckoo; it flies to God when the sun shines. The willow shrubs, dozing like old beggars. You can never trust them . . . Sleep, Proska, sleep! Your father was a sheep! Your father yanked the tree around and dynamite came tumbling down! Sleep, for goodness' sake, sleep!

He stretched out on the seat. First he tried lying on his left side, but then he wrenched himself over onto his right and fell asleep at once.

And so he never actually beheld the marsh village of Tomashgrod. And in any case, the little train stopped there no longer than two minutes. The engine seemed to be longing for its sooty stable. In the supply car, the sentry didn't even get down from the train. He merely stuck his nose out into the night for a moment; but since he could detect nothing, or only things he found irrelevant—for him the moon was irrelevant, and for him the silence over the marsh was irrelevant, as was a bird's solitary, peculiar cry—and therefore could discover nothing that appeared important to him, he sat back down on his crate, lit a cigarette, turned it in his fingers, and observed the small, glowing tip.

Had Proska been awake, perhaps he would have tossed the girl's forgotten raincoat out the window.

With that raincoat, he would have flung his last memory of her far down the embankment. But he was asleep, asleep with his mouth open, his hard skull on the hard bench.

The train got moving again faster than it had in Prowursk. The locomotive was certainly small, but it probably already knew that there were finer things than work. Tomashgrod, the shaky, shoddy backwater, did not stir.

Pfee-pfee-pfeeee, the locomotive cried.

Proska heard the cry in his sleep and threw himself over onto his left side. What a miracle! At that very moment, Proska's brother-in-law Kurt Rogalski, asleep in his goose-feather bed in Sybba, near Lyck, also turned onto his left side. Coincidence had tweaked them both in the loins at the same time, pure coincidence. But Herr Rogalski, of course, couldn't know that Herr Proska was lying in a narrow-gauge railroad car. Nor could he dream about his brother-in-law, for whenever he dreamed, he saw only wheat, turnips, and potatoes. After all, those things occupied his mind more than Walter Proska, his wife Maria's brother.

The assault rifle, its safety catch off, was leaning in a corner. In the compartment's luggage rack, right above the sleeper's head, lay the package with the earmuffs and wrist warmers for Captain Kilian. A falling star streaked across the sky. God's missile.

He let it go from His hand as a mysterious sign to the few who looked heavenward, searching for Him, that they might persevere in their search with attentive patience, a sign that He was indeed there and thoroughly understood their yearning toward Him but could not present Himself to their sight. However, by way of soothing and cooling the fervid pain their searching caused them, He gathered the strength of His hand, lobbed His missile, and let them go on hoping.

Shortly after midnight, the train ran over a mine. The little locomotive was blown frighteningly high in the air, its hot steel body blasted open. The imprisoned steam hissed out into freedom. Four civilians, who by chance happened to be carrying submachine guns, and who by chance happened to be sitting in a tree that overlooked the curve where the misfortune occurred, actually thought at first that the engine would only make a giant leap over the bent, twisted, and burst tracks, land on the sound tracks as though nothing had happened, and travel on. But the four men then had to admit that they'd given the diminutive locomotive too much credit. A jet of fire shot out of its forehead, and then it did a somersault, crashed down onto the edge of the embankment, could hold itself upright no longer, and rolled—like a heavy, mortally wounded animal—down the slope. Into the ditch with it, the engine dragged the two cars it had been assigned to pull. When engine and cars came to rest, two rear wheels kept spinning helplessly, like the movements of a turtle thrown onto its back. The rest of the water the locomotive had taken on in Prowursk flowed out of a burst pipe and seeped into the earth.

Medical corpsmen often came upon fresh corpses with wet pants.

· THREE ·

Proska thought, *I don't care what happens next, I can't hold out in this overturned railroad car any longer. Maybe they even watched the wreck. If they did, I'll bet they don't feel any need to verify that everyone who got blown up with the train is dead. They probably withdrew from the scene a long time ago. But who knows with these guys? My spine hurts, it's trembling as if someone strummed it. If I could only stand up straight and stretch. My rifle seems unharmed—it lets me chamber a round. Now I just have to get out of this repulsive crate. If they shoot at me, at least I have good cover. Besides, the sun must be about to come up. Who knows what would have happened if I hadn't fallen asleep. While they nod off, the Lord protects his own. Or am I fooling myself? When you get right down to it, am I just imagining I'm here? What a laugh, really. I dare to doubt my survival even though my spinal column hurts and my bladder's about to burst. Shall I act like the people who scatter earth on their heads when they feel themselves doubting their existence? I've got to get out of here!*

The assistant tilted his head back and gazed at the broken compartment window, which was immediately above him. He stretched out both hands, grasped the metal frame, and pulled himself up. To begin with, he could see nothing but the sky, and its boundless respectability encouraged him to thrust his head through the opening and venture a look at his immediate surroundings. First he became aware of some treetops, spruces, then of their trunks, and finally, as his eyes slid lower and lower, the army of birches, shivering in the early morning fog, and the tenacious, eccentric undergrowth of wild blackberry tendrils. The railroad tracks, blown off the crossties by the upward force of the exploding dynamite, lay bent and twisted like thin wax candles.

Suddenly, Proska heard someone say, "*Pjerunje!* There one still alive."

He turned around at once and spotted, behind a willow shrub, a tall, thin soldier. He stepped out and slowly approached Proska with his rifle braced against his hip.

"Where did *you* come from?" asked Proska, amazed.

"Gleiwitz," said the lanky soldier, grinning.

"I mean, what are you doing here? Is your outfit posted nearby?"

"You really alive? You mighty lucky! Guy sitting at front got squished like bug between tin cans. And engine driver grew wings and flew into tree, head first. What have happen? Well, one thing sure: great big boom."

"Are they all dead?" Proska asked. His question sounded as though he still didn't believe he was alive.

The tall soldier nodded. He had big, somewhat protruding ears, a cocked nose (so to speak), and brown eyes. It was obviously not easy for him to see out from under his steel helmet, which was at least two sizes too big. He stopped in front of the overturned railroad car and said, "Now we must hurry up. Run away, fast as possible. Everything else *schwistko jedno*. Get out quick! You have rifle?"

"Yes."

"Then bring with and come."

While Proska was squeezing himself through the window, the other peered up at the treetops and whistled through his teeth.

"You see something?"

"There," the tall soldier said, pointing his rifle barrel at two spruces. "They sit up there and watch while train blows up."

"How do you know that?"

"Hurry up, *pjerunje!*"

"But where can we go? Wouldn't it be safer to stay here?"

"Yes, but only afternoon. From two to eight."

"So what are you doing here now?"

"Guard detail for railroad track."

"By yourself?"

"Five other man and corporal in charge. Not of railroad track, of us."

Proska braced his weapon against his hip and took two steps on the soft ground. Then he said, "Actually, I should stay here. I have to go on, I have to rejoin my unit."

The soldier from Upper Silesia got angry. He replied, "Well, you stay or you come! Next train pass in maybe three hour. By then, you could already have hundred—" With his index finger he poked his helmet and his chest alternately several times.

"Where are you bringing me?"

"Come now."

Proska clambered back into the car and returned after two minutes with his haversack and the package for Captain Kilian.

"Should we just leave all this the way it is?"

"Mobile railroad patrol come and put everything in order. We telephone right away. Is enough."

The tall soldier went ahead. He dragged his left leg a little, as though his boot were too tight. Proska looked at the seat of the man's pants and thought, *This guy has no ass at all. I'd like to know how he keeps his pants up. People with no ass look best in suits. And they're not to be trusted.*

They silently cleared themselves a way through the thick underbrush and soon reached a narrow, well-trodden path. Proska couldn't help noticing, on both sides of the path, gigantic, uprooted trees, dependable hazelnut switches, and thick weeds. Pure, unsullied wilderness, a patch of earth no human hand had ever altered. It was hard even for death to slip through here; if it scorched one life, a thousand new lives rose up against it. No doubt it was high time to lend death some assistance in this prideful district, for everything that breathes is great only insofar as it yearns for the abyss. Here, however, there seemed to be no abysses.

Without warning, the Silesian stopped short; Proska, walking behind him, trod on his heel.

"You see something?" Proska asked.

"Airplane. We must to walk faster. There, there!"

The tall soldier stretched out one arm and pointed to a scrap of sky visible through the treetops. "You see?"

"What of it?"

"Pay attention, soon they drop dandelions."

"Dandelions?"

Two black dots fell free of the airplane and plunged toward the earth. Parachutes suddenly sprang up over the dots and slowed their hurtling descent. Two longish jerricans dangled from the parachutes.

"Supplies," said Proska.

"But not for us," the tall man replied. He pushed his helmet back on his forehead, touched his companion's shoulder, and said, "Come. We have only little time."

They went on, quickening their pace.

"What's in the canisters?"

"Tinder," the tall soldier said without turning around. "Munition. Dynamite." He was taking big steps. With his free hand, the one not holding the rifle, he pushed aside branches that then sprang back and struck Proska's face and upper body.

"Do we have a lot farther to go?"

"No, no."

"By the way, what's your name?"

"Zwiczosbirski."

"What?"

"So: Zwiczos like *tsvitch-oss* and birski like *beer-ski*."

"Is that Polish?"

"Upper Silesian."

"And what's your first name?"

"Jan."

"You have a limp. Were you wounded?"

"Yes, that too, got wounded. Machine gun, *rat-tat-tat*."

"Where were you? Here in the marshes?"

"Not far. By Tomashgrod. Had to storm barn. Machine gun in front of barn, hiding behind bush."

"In daytime?"

"Morning. Around six. I run, jump over ditch. And when I in air, I see machine gun. See also three men and little black hole of machine gun." The tall soldier stopped walking, looked at Proska, and went on: "I think, I hope nothing come out of little black hole until I face down on ground again. But something come out, and three bullets bite thigh."

"Did it hurt a lot?"

"Nah! Now I limp, only good for guard duty."

"What did you say your name was?"

"Zwiczosbirski. But nobody can say this name. It breaks their tongue, they say. So all call me 'Thighbone.'"

"Because of your wounds?"

"Come now, is time."

They went farther and came to a less wooded slope. The path abruptly stopped.

The soldier from Upper Silesia looked cautiously in all directions.

"Do you see anything?"

"They pass often here."

"Who?"

"Good friends. You must speak more soft. What's your name?"

"Proska. Walter Proska."

"Must be very quiet, Proska. They have good ears and good eyes and good aim."

"Why don't you and your buddies take care of them?"

"Watch out!" Thighbone cried in a stifled voice. "On ground, damn it, don't move. Go on, face down. Flat, flat."

Proska instinctively dropped to the ground behind an alder shrub and looked up at his tall companion. "What is it?" he hissed.

"There!"

A group of men in civilian clothes, each armed with a submachine gun, was coming up the slope. Among them were some older men and some younger ones too, and the one leading them was a handsome youngster with green-blue eyes and a small, thin nose.

Proska carefully pushed his assault rifle through the alder shrub and set his sights on the young leader. He brought his rifle up from below and aimed at the place where he thought the youth's heart must be. Unsuspecting but not heedless, the men came closer. The assistant took up the initial slack on his trigger.

I'll give him ten more meters, he thought. *Eight more meters, six, four—*

He received a blow in the ribs. Suddenly the tall soldier was lying beside him and gasping out, "No shooting, you idiot. For God sake, don't squeeze trigger. They make kindling of us. Put gun away." The tall soldier pressed the rifle barrel down.

The airplane was circling above them. As the partisans moved along, they glanced up briefly. Halfway up the incline, they came to a stop, had a conversation, and then split into two groups. One group turned back the way they had come; the others marched past Proska and Thighbone toward the railroad. Proska stood up first and asked, "Why didn't we shoot?"

"Why?" the man from Upper Silesia repeated, grinning slyly.

"He would've gone down like—"

"No need. You already on ground."

"They would have run away."

"No. Would have shot, would have shot good. They know how. But we don't shoot much."

"Why?" asked Proska, slapping his muscular neck with the flat of his hand.

"You want shoot 'squitoes with shotgun? They maybe hundred and fifty, we six plus corporal in charge. What is point? They shoot not much, we shoot not much. See, what is point of making elephant mad? He whack you with trunk and you through."

"So what are you and your outfit doing out here?"

"Guarding railroad. I say that already. Can we walk more fast?"

"You all sure have a funny war going on in these parts."

"War always funny," the tall soldier said. "Nobody knows if life good luck or bad luck. One looks for bullet and doesn't find, another never looks for bullet and gets hole in hide. War always surprise."

"I know about that, I was at the front myself. I saw a lot."

"Different here. Can you compare sauerkraut with Führer-bust? I say no. At front, you can't go to sleep, and when death come, it there. You feel it when it come. Here you don't feel it. When I wake in morning, I bend big toe. If hurts, death not come. So far, always hurts."

"Do we still have far to go? Where's your unit located, actually?"

"Have built little wood Fortress. Corporal supervised. You can say him good morning soon, if he still alive."

"Why? Is it so dangerous where you are?"

The Upper Silesian didn't reply. They were moving through tall, wet grass. The ground squelched under their feet. A dragonfly whirred past Proska's ear. There was a smell of stagnant water. The wind stroked the reeds with its invisible hand, and they ducked obediently. The surface of a pond glinted behind birch trunks.

"It's beautiful here," Proska said softly.

"Maybe, maybe not," murmured Zwiczosbirski. He stopped a few meters from the pond, adjusted his rifle sight to the shortest distance, signaled to his companion to stay and wait for him, and proceeded—as cautiously as possible—to the edge of the pond. But Proska followed him.

The pond water was clear; you could see all the way to the bottom. Among the plants were swarms of beetles and water fleas. Little crucian carp snapped after the insects, and if the fish bumped against the bottom or touched it with their tail fins, then mushroom-shaped clouds of sludge swirled up to the surface, and it looked as though down below, in the teeming, oppressive silence, grenades were exploding.

All of a sudden, the tall soldier raised his rifle and took aim, but before he could squeeze the trigger, the water in one part of the pond became disturbed, and in a flash Proska recognized the duck-bill-like snout of a giant pike. The fish threw itself halfway into the air and with a powerful snap of its tail disappeared among the water plants.

"Satan," groaned the Silesian, lowering his weapon.

"Did you want to shoot him?"

"Tickle him," said the tall man fiercely. Beads of sweat stood on his forehead.

"That was a pike," Proska said ingenuously.

"Well, what else? Butt with ears? I know him well, we old enemies. He escape me fifteen times already: break four rods, ruin one basket. But one day I get him."

"Old pikes are smart."

"I more smart."

"He must be twenty years old."

"I forty-four," said Zwiczosbirski in a superior tone. "Frying pan wait for him, eight months now."

"You think you're going to catch him?"

"Think? No, I know. In four weeks I have him."

"The water's very clear here."

"No wonder. Little ditch keep everything clean. Little ditch child of big river. Sometime pike in big river, sometime in ditch, and when he want digest meal, he swim here. Big fish need big house, big man need many servants. When you come to world and want know how people live, then just lie down by water and wait. You hear not much, no, no, but see. Fish—"

Very close to them, the nervous chattering of a submachine gun broke out. A fearful cry assaulted both men's ears: a human cry. The tall soldier raised his head, narrowed his eyes, murmured, "Stani," and sprinted over to a little stand of mixed trees, hardwoods and conifers. Proska could barely follow him.

"What's going on?" Proska panted when they were both in the shelter of the trees.

"Stanislaw scream."

"And so?"

"Come," said the tall soldier. "Quick, he need help."

They found Stanislaw lying facedown in a blackberry bush, his shoulders twitching, his fingers dug into the soft earth. Another soldier had already reached him and was trying to turn him over.

"He dead, Helmut?" asked Zwiczosbirski.

Helmut, a younger soldier with a long face and apathetic lips, said, "I don't think so. They shaved his nose off for him, and his eyes are probably damaged too."

The tall soldier threw his rifle on the ground, fell on both knees, and shouted, "Stani! *Zo ti tem srobjis! Ti nge bidsches sdäch! Pozekai lo!* Stani! *O moi bosä, moi Schwintuletzki. O moi Jesus!*"

Helmut stood up and went over to Proska. Both watched as the tall soldier caressed his fallen comrade's body, shouting and sobbing all the while.

"Is that Polish?" Proska asked softly.

"Something like it. Stani's his best friend. They're both from Gleiwitz. When they get excited, that's all they speak . . . Were you on the train?"

"Yes."

"The only one?"

"No, there were also—"

"I mean, the only lucky one?"

"Yes, it seems so . . . Was it Stani who screamed a little while ago?"

"Yes, he wanted to hunt for lapwing eggs and—"

"So early in the year?"

"They must have surprised him while he was at it . . . By the way my name is Poppek, Helmut."

"Proska, Walter."

"We have to get Stani home. Keep your eyes on the treetops. The second you see something, shoot!

A few of them must still be lurking around here somewhere."

Helmut clapped the tall soldier on the shoulder. He grasped the signal, and the two of them lifted their fallen comrade.

"You must go careful, Helmut," said Zwiczosbirski.

"Yes."

They set off slowly. One of the wounded man's hands hung down and was scratched by blackberry branches. He felt no pain; he'd lost consciousness.

"Halt," Helmut said suddenly. "Put him down."

They laid Stani on his back and saw, for the first time, that the upper half of his face was completely shredded. His nose was missing; of his eyes, nothing could be seen. The bullets must have been fired down on him diagonally from above.

"My pants and my shoes are already full of blood, Thighbone. Do you have a first-aid pack? We've absolutely got to bandage him."

"Have left pack in Fortress."

"How about you, Proska?"

"I don't have any."

Helmut said, "Well, then, we'll just have to go on like this."

The tall soldier threw himself on the ground next to Stani again and began to wail.

"Stand up, Thighbone, no point doing that. If we don't get him back to the Fortress fast, he'll die."

Stanislaw's shoulders weren't twitching anymore. His fingers had relaxed too. None of the three, neither Proska nor Helmut nor the tall soldier, was sure that the wounded man was still alive. They were all suffering unspeakably from the muggy heat and the mosquito bites, and if it had been up to Poppek alone, he would simply have left Stani lying where he was and seen to it that he himself, Poppek, made it back to the Fortress. He dared to think that, but he feared to do it.

And so he only murmured impatiently, "Take hold of him, Thighbone, we have to hurry. But let me take his legs. You won't mind getting Stani's blood on your pants as much as I do. One, two, three!"

They lurched forward again, staggering over the yielding terrain, with Helmut in front, the tall soldier in the middle, and Proska last, trying hard to keep a close watch on the treetops, but only seldom able to tear his eyes away from Stani.

As they were wading across a ditch, the wounded man groaned.

"He alive!" Zwiczosbirski shouted joyously. "He not dead!"

"Yell like that again and you'll be gargling mud," Helmut said.

"Let them shoot," the tall soldier said, gnashing his teeth. "I show them my magic rifle."

"Shut up," said Helmut, "or I'll toss your Stani into the water."

They stopped talking. The back of one of Proska's hands swelled up and turned red. The insect bites burned horribly. He drew his hand through the water, barely soothing the pain.

Their sweat liners were stuck to their necks. The men were finding it hard to breathe.

After they were out of the ditch, Proska asked, "So where is your Fortress?"

"Soon," said the tall soldier. "We must make small detour."

They panted up a slope, pulling and dragging Stani with them. The sky grew cloudy overhead.

Helmut groaned, "Put him down, I can't go anymore."

They stood up and straightened their spines, which made them feel like kings. When a man thrusts his head out from between shoulders crushed under the heel of destiny, he becomes as God originally conceived him: upright, fearless, and good, a tree in his stride and pure water in his thought.

Rat-tat-tat, a sudden hammering. The men flung themselves on the ground, locked and loaded their weapons. *Rat-tat-tat*, the shots rang out again and then again, and the men heard the rounds sizzling away above them, and sometimes, when a bullet struck the ground ahead, they could also see the earth ripped up and sprayed about.

The tall soldier rolled on his side, pulled his helmet down on his forehead, and raised his head. His gaze fell on three alders, and he immediately suspected they were where the shots were coming from. The trees' foliage was too thick for him to tell whether the shooter was sitting on a branch. But Thighbone was a patient man, and he waited for the next burst of fire—which was obviously meant for him—and aimed his weapon.

"Watch this," he said in a strangled voice.

Proska and Poppek stared at the group of trees.

Zwiczosbirski fired, and in the same moment, all three of them saw a man come crashing down from the tree in the middle.

"Little bird up in tree make such pretty sound, now no singing up in tree, little bird on ground," sang the tall soldier, and then he got to his feet.

When the other two saw that no more shots were being fired, they too stood up.

"Now bear goes wild. Why they make him mad? Angry animal bite faster than contented one. We can go on."

"There's no point," said Helmut.

"What?" asked Proska in consternation.

"I think Stani's dead."

"But he groaned," cried the tall soldier, horrified. "What you want?"

"It's best for us to leave him here."

Proska said, "I think you're crazy. We can't just leave a man lying here like this."

Poppek spat to one side. He said, "And if all three of us croak on account of him? No thanks, I'd rather not." He raised his right foot and kicked Stani's hand with the toe of his boot. "Look, he doesn't even move. He's better off than we are in this goddamned wilderness. We can put him in a coffin later."

Without a word, Proska slung his rifle around his neck, elbowed Poppek out of the way, and said to the tall soldier, "Take his legs. You and I will carry Stani back."

They tramped farther, lugging the wounded man between them: first Zwiczos, hanging his head, and behind him Proska, open-mouthed. Helmut followed, covering them. All of a sudden, Proska felt an insect on his tongue, a raft spider, a fly, maybe a beetle. He himself had no idea what kind of little beast it was. He tried to spit it out, aiming over and across the man they were carrying, but he didn't succeed right away. Before he knew it, the thing was between his teeth, and he instinctively bit down. When he realized what he'd bitten, a heavy wave of nausea surged up in him; he could taste the stomach acid slowly flooding his mouth. But Proska got a mighty grip on himself, suppressed his urge to vomit, and so avoided the necessity of putting Stani down again. Had they laid the man with the shattered face on the marshy ground, on the ground that now smelled like a morgue attendant's moldy clothing, then all three of them would have seen that Stani was dead. But they needed their eyes for the task of finding the best way through the tonguelike creepers hanging down from the spidery, bony trees. The trees oddly resembled old men with beards that reached the ground, and when the wind blew through their hair, they seemed to shiver. The wilderness, innocent and sensuous, gazed at the men, whom—had you observed them from a decent distance—you wouldn't have described as wheezing, groaning, all but desperate creatures, because seen from afar, they looked like the figures in certain old copper engravings one sometimes finds, engravings that depict people moving about market squares merrily, aimlessly, randomly, free of all gravity.

· FOUR ·

They called the Fortress *Waldesruh,* "Forest
Peace," the name given it by a certain Hoffmann, a soldier who had disappeared without
trace more than six months previously. Hoffmann had
carried around with him (God knows where he got
it) a piece of chalk, a dry, four-sided piece of teacher's
chalk, and when the so-called Fortress—a house con-
structed of thick planks, against whose walls so many
big clumps of turf had been piled that a hand grenade
exploding outside would not have particularly en-
dangered the skat players within—when, that is, the
people building the Fortress had finished their work,
Gottlieb Hoffmann, a bookbinder from Leipzig, had
taken a piece of chalk from his pocket, stood on the
long-limbed Zwiczosbirski's shoulders, and written
over the entrance, in exaggeratedly ornate capital letters, *WALDESRUH.* One day, Goofy Gottlieb, as his

fellows called him, had failed to return from a patrol, and nobody could say whether he'd been shot, met with an accident, or simply—out of the blue—skedaddled. The men hardly spoke of him anymore, but when they looked up before entering the Fortress, they could still see the remains of Gottlieb's baptism. Rain and time had of course had their way with his chalk, and it wasn't very easy anymore to make out the name. Even initiates could hardly read more than *ESRUH*. But at least they knew that once upon a time, the word *WALDESRUH* had stood there.

The tree trunks the walls had been made from were impervious to any infantry fire. On the day when the sweating men stood before the finished structure, the corporal had taken the matter of the security assessment into his own hands by bracing a submachine gun against his hip and firing an entire magazine at the wooden structure. Next, the others were ordered to determine how deeply the bullets had penetrated into the wood. Then the corporal, a hoarse, boozy fellow with a dried-up face, called his unit together and bellowed that the construction of the Fortress had taken them four hours more than he had reckoned, and that they could be grateful to him for relieving them of the most important duty of all, namely the security assessment. This noncommissioned officer was called Willi Stehauf. He had the responsibility for his people, distributed the mail, which turned up about once every three weeks, gave out as many cigarettes and as much schnapps and RIF soap, and no more, as could be reconciled with his conscience, and also determined who would go on railroad patrol and where, so it was no wonder that Willi Stehauf deemed himself the busiest and most harassed of men, and his facial features reflected so much sullenness that everyone—maybe with the exception of Thighbone and Stani, because they could lighten their hearts in Willi's presence by cursing him in Polish—preferred to be outdoors in the marshy landscape rather than enveloped in the miasma of sweat and schnapps that emanated from their corporal.

The Fortress stood on a little height, from which you had a view, on the left, of a less overgrown but also unwalkable marshy meadow; behind the block-house, two birch trees, slender, white, innocent; on the right side, a luxuriant, mixed-growth forest that could comfortably be reached in ten bounds. A few steps from the entrance, a ditch two meters wide held putrescent water. This ditch connected the pond to the big river. A resilient alder trunk that a painter and varnisher from Kappeln an der Schlei named Paul Zacharias had laid across the ditch served as a bridge.

In addition to Thighbone, Poppek, Stani, Willi, and Zacharias, two other men—one and a half, in the corporal's estimation—had been assigned to this out-post. One was Ferdinand Ellerbrok, a slovenly former circus artist with a Levantine face, and the other was Wolfgang Kürschner. Ellerbrok had glued to his bunk an old, well-worn visiting card on which was written, in discreet lettering, FERN ELLO, ARTISTE, and on the next line, slightly smaller, PRESIDENT OF THE GERMAN FIRE-EATERS' ASSOCIATION. When his comrades saw the card for the first time, they bombarded him with requests to eat flames before their eyes. And Stani had even been prepared to sacrifice his cigarette lighter fluid for the proposed special performance. But "Melon"—as the artiste, on account of his large head, was called, first by Willi and then also by the others—explained repeatedly that in order to "lay the fire" properly, he had to have a bottle of schnapps. And since with the exception of Wolfgang Kürschner none of the others could declare themselves prepared to contribute their schnapps ration to him, Melon shrugged his shoulders regretfully and waddled outside to his hen, Alma. He'd known her since she was a chick, as he was wont to say, and now he wanted to tame her.

Wolfgang Kürschner was the so-called Half-Portion, the Milk Roll, a young, long-haired, dreamy-eyed soldier who suffered from a weak stomach. He sent and received the most mail. His father, a regimental commander, had fallen in battle at Warsaw; to his mother, who worried about her only son in Podejuch, a suburb of Stettin, he wrote long letters in which he earnestly and ponderously meditated on consolation and death.

Tall Zwiczos was very fond of him, and the Upper Silesian had once come very close to punching out the corporal, who found Wolfgang even more unbearable than all the others. Willi hated the frail kid and made sure the young man could feel his antipathy.

When they reached the alder trunk bridge, Thighbone stopped and said, panting, "Put Stani down. On ground. We arrive now."

They set down their burden; Proska used his handkerchief to wipe the sweat off his neck and forehead and looked over to the Fortress. The wooden building had the air of a workplace after closing time. Two soldiers were sitting on a bench. One of them was whittling a branch; the other, a chubby little man with a fat head, was balancing a chicken on one hand and trying to train the fowl to jump first onto his right shoulder, then onto his head, then back down to his left shoulder, and finally to his left hand.

"Hey!" Thighbone called over to the two men. "Come here! Come fast! Something terrible happen Stani!"

Both soldiers looked up. The shouting scared the hen, which fluttered to the ground.

"But we can carry Stani over the bridge ourselves," Proska said.

"You right," the tall soldier said. "Lift up!"

Cautiously, they carried the wounded man over the ditch and brought him up to the building. Taking great care, they laid him on the bench. The fat little man forgot his chicken and stared at Stani, who wasn't moving, with frightened eyes.

"But he's dead," said the fat-headed soldier.

"Not dead," Thighbone retorted decisively. "He make groan, and if can groan, cannot be dead, no? Have I right, Walter?"

Proska nodded, although he knew no trace of life remained in Stani. He pulled out his no longer clean handkerchief, unfolded it, or actually tugged it apart, and covered the shredded face with it.

Suddenly, the corporal appeared in the Fortress entrance, sullenness and infinite self-assurance in the desert of his face. His first look fell on Walter Proska, and he bawled at him in a hoarse, drunken voice: "What does that guy want? Where did you scare him up? He won't present himself? What kind of swamp scum is he?"

The assistant went up to him, saluted, and said, "Private First Class Proska, Ninety-sixth Grenadier Regiment, Sixth Battalion, First Company."

"And what are you doing here?" the corporal yelled.

Tall Zwiczos chimed in, saying, "Train fly in air with him inside. I pick him up. We must make phone call."

"We don't get any supplies here, including cigarettes and schnapps," Willi said to Proska. "We have to procure everything we need ourselves. You got that?"

"Yes, Corporal."

"Good. In that case, you can march back to the railroad and wait for the next train."

Thighbone said, "They bust up Stani's face. But he not dead. He make groan, word of honor. When we pull him through the water."

"Have you brought him back with you?" asked the corporal.

"Yes. Walter give help."

"Who's Walter?"

"This one here," said Zwiczos, laying his arm on Proska's shoulder.

"Where's Stani?"

"Here on bench, Corporal. He alive, he make groan, word of honor."

The corporal stepped close to Stani, snatched the now blood-soaked handkerchief from his face, bent down, and performed an attentive examination, so that all those watching him thought he looked like a meat inspector. Then he clenched his teeth and said laconically to the fat artiste and Zacharias, "You two haven't done anything yet. Go dig a grave. Stani's dead. Take his pay book, his dog tags, his wallet, and his rings. If you plant them with him, you're in big trouble!" Then he said to Thighbone, who was standing there as though turned to stone, "You're just as stupid as you are tall. Dragging around a useless piece of dead flesh, what a guy. You ought to be punished for being so dumb. Just be glad I'm good-natured. Suppose they had caught you out there! Before you had time to lay that"—he jerked his head in Stani's direction—"on the grass, none of you would have been good for anything but coffee strainers. Am I right?"

The tall soldier stood there like an old, solitary pine tree, making a desperate effort to draw up nourishment out of the stingy ground. He looked as though he might topple over any second, and his frightened eyes, which were darting around in all directions, appeared to bring him only the melancholy certainty that it basically made no difference which way he fell, for now that Stani was dead, there was no one standing close enough to break his fall, no one to support his continued existence, however askew it might be. Thighbone's arms dangled at his sides like branches someone had tried to break off but then abandoned, because the bark was too unyielding. His gaze seemed to come to rest on the place over the entrance where the remains of Goofy Gottlieb's chalk letters could still be seen.

Everyone, including the corporal, looked up at him, and no one dared to say a word.

Then, unexpectedly, he turned round in a circle once, and just when the men were thinking he would fall headlong to the ground, he got hold of himself, walked slowly and perpendicularly down the slope, crossed over the ditch like a sleepwalker, and then turned to the right.

After Zwiczosbirski had disappeared into the woods, the corporal said, "It's going to take our tall friend some more time to get over this. His thoughts have a longer way to go." He—and nobody else—grinned at his remark.

"Melon and Zacharias, I've already told you what you're supposed to do. And you, come see me. But first I have to telephone. What's your name again?"

"Proska, Walter."

"Good. Wait here. Or—just come on inside now."

They entered the Fortress. Along one wall stood three double-decker bunks, in front of them a small, dusty potbelly stove. A crude table board fashioned by the men themselves lay atop the stove, and around it were six stools, arranged in a semicircle. In one corner there was a single, more comfortable bed, and in front of it, on a box that had once contained canned goods, a field telephone.

Willi lifted the receiver and quickly started turning the little crank. He said, half turned toward Proska, "I hope they haven't cut our line . . . Hello! Tomashgrod! Please respond . . . Post twenty-five here . . . Tomashgrod, yes, sir, Corpo— . . . Please? Ah. Yes, sir, Sergea— . . . Corporal Stehauf of Post twenty-five speaking . . . Yessir . . . That's the reason for my call . . . The train attack took place in our sector . . . Survivors? Yes, one, as far as I know . . . Of course I do, his name is Proska . . . I didn't understand . . . Private First Class Proska . . . His unit will be notified . . . And another thing . . . I didn't understand . . . Yessir . . . To report the loss of one man . . . The fellow's name was Paputka . . . Stanislaw . . . Yessir . . . a half-Polack . . . Yessir . . . As you say, Sergea— . . . I agree completely . . . his place . . . I believe so . . . Sauerkraut . . . Many thanks . . . Over and out."

The corporal hung up the receiver, turned around, and said, "You're going to remain here, understand?"

"But I have to—"

"Shut your trap or you'll catch a cold in the guts. You'll remain here; your unit will be notified. Don't give it any thought; I do the thinking here, for you and everyone else. Understand?"

"Yessir."

"You can throw your things on Stani's bunk right now. The timing's perfect. One goes, another comes. Look, it's there on the far end, your new stinkpit. And just so you know: in this unit, duty is strict, and free time is fun. If you don't sweat before you laugh, you're not allowed to laugh. Can you laugh?"

"If I have to," said Proska, trying to remove the blanket from Stani's bunk.

"What are you doing?" asked Willi.

"I want my own blanket . . ."

"Stani's blanket stays where it is. I'll confiscate yours. It's Wehrmacht property, right?"

"Yessir."

"Sleeping under his blanket will get you used to things here faster." Willi coughed, a hard, dry cough, and struck himself in the chest with his fist. "This damned lung fungus," he said. "Do you have any matches?"

"Yessir."

"Then give me some. You have cigarettes as well?"

"Yessir."

"So much the better, I'll take one of those too."

Proska handed the corporal a cigarette, lit it along with one for himself, and took a few steps around the room.

"By the way," said Willi, "you do your washing up in the ditch, and the latrine is behind the two birches. The fat guy's our cook—we call him Melon. He's a circus artiste, you know. Just don't step on his Alma's feet. That's his hen, heh-heh-heh. As for cigarettes and schnapps, you get those from me—when there's some to be had, naturally. Have you ever been at the front?"

"Yessir, Corporal."

"How long?"

"Three years."

"Well, so you have experience lying in shit. Good. I'm going out to see how Stani's gravediggers are doing. When the one with the bad stomach's back, you and Thighbone will go out on patrol, down to the railroad. He'll tell you what you need to know. You haven't met the stomach sufferer yet, but he's a young know-it-all—you'll see what I mean. All the rest you'll learn in time. And then you'll see whether you're still alive or already dead. Sometimes out here, I'm not sure myself."

Before the corporal went out, he asked Proska his name again, and when Proska repeated it, Willi considered for a moment and whistled through a gap in his teeth. "Are you a half-Polack too, like Switch-switch or whatever his name is? Or like his pal Paputka? Can you speak that zhchystzki too? Come to think of it, where are you from, actually?"

"I'm from Lyck."

"And where might that be?"

"In Masuria. Seventeen kilometers from the former border."

"In that case, you're lucky," said the corporal, and went out.

Proska threw his things on the bed, pulled a stool over with his foot, and sat down.

The Fortress had only one window, an unmoving eye fifty centimeters across set in the front wall.

The man peered through the window and saw a thin black cloud cleaving the sky, and on its heels a white cloud—feather-light, gossamer-textured, kicked and trampled by the wind and its thousand boots into all sorts of shapes—pursuing its erratic course. He felt as though his low forehead were pressing on his eyebrow ridges; Walter Proska thought something or other, an inspiration, a notion, an idea, was trying to break out of him. Following an imperious urge to disperse some stored-up energy, he stood up and struck the table board atop the potbelly stove with one big, ruddy hand.

"Don't destroy our furniture," said someone behind him. Turning, he recognized the fat soldier.

"My name's Proska. I'm supposed to stay here with your unit."

"Heartfelt congratulations. You can read my name here, on this visiting card. And should you chance to be illiterate—oh, do you know the joke about the rookie who reports to his NCO? Nah, you can't possibly know it. I'll tell it to you later. When we're finished with the grave . . . I'm sorry about Stani. He was a wonderful guy, and above all a hearty, grateful eater. You could cook sweat liners for him, and the sweetheart would eat them like smoked bacon. Ah, well. Incidentally, do you know where Dover is? On the English coast, right you are. It's always being fired on, over and over again. You always hear about it:

'Dover under fire.' You know what that looks like? No? Well, pay attention!"

The fat soldier pulled a matchbox from his pocket, took out a match, struck it, and slowly raised it above his head. Then he made such a face that Proska had to laugh.

"A 'Dover' under fire, *capito*?[1] Now I've really got to go. Where can the other spade be? I brought that joke back with me from my last leave. All right, see you soon."

Melon grabbed a field spade and waddled outdoors. Proska thought, *He seems pleasant enough . . . if only the others are like that . . . the tall one's great too . . . wonder where he's gone . . . surely he'll be back in time for the patrol.*

He heard the corporal yelling outside: "Faster, faster! This area's not a refrigerator for old meat. If you two keep going at this rate, we'll have to wear gas masks for the next few months. Come on, Melon, when you're digging you have to move your hams. The earth won't bite you! And you, Zacharias, you're acting like you need to lie down in that hole yourself! Your wife's expecting a baby, right? You don't want to miss that, do you?"

Proska stood up and went over to the little window. At brief intervals, he pursed his lips and exhaled

---

1 Translator's note: "Dover," pronounced in German, has the same sound as *Doofer*, a colloquial word for "fool."

cigarette smoke against the glass. The smoke rebounded and brought tears to his eyes. He slipped a hand into his pocket, feeling around for his handkerchief, and then he recalled that Willi had snatched it off Stani's face and dropped it on the ground. He slowly moved away from the window and stood in the doorway. The blood-soaked cloth lay under the bench. Poppek was sitting there, holding his rifle between his knees as he smoked a cigarette.

"You see, Proska?" he said. "What did I tell you? We carried him here just so we could put him in the ground."

"So what?"

"Suppose they had caught us on the way?"

"Wouldn't have mattered. Stani groaned when we were carrying him over that ditch. It was our duty to bring him in. Besides, even if he'd been already dead, I still would have dragged him here."

"Funny way of looking at it . . . So when are you leaving?"

"I'm staying here with you all."

"Does Willi know that?"

"He's the one who told me."

"Then here's to good neighbors."

Proska stepped out of the Fortress and sat on the bench next to Poppek. "They sure seem to be in a hurry," Proska said, leaning down to pick up his handkerchief.

"It's best for him and for us. Here the mosquitoes and the flies wage war against us too. Have you heard about Goofy Gottlieb yet?"

"No."

"He was also here, and then one day he vanished without a trace. I personally think the muggy air and the mosquitoes and the partisans drove him crazy. He most probably just ran away."

"And nobody's heard anything more about him?"

"Nothing," said Poppek. "When somebody disappears from here, there's nothing left of him. He's barely even a memory. Have you been at the front?"

"Yes."

"Where?"

"Near Kiev."

"I guess things are clearer over there, right?"

"They were clearer before. When Captain Kilian was still alive."

"And now?"

"Now I don't know. I was home on leave. His wife gave me wrist warmers and earmuffs to take to him— see, my captain and I lived on the same street back home. On the way back, an MP told me he'd been killed."

"That's the way it goes," said Poppek. "Do you think we're going to get out of here alive? They'll drill holes in all of us somewhere. A little hole in the head for one, a big hole in the chest for another, and so on. We won't make it, not one of us."

Proska raised his head and looked curiously at Poppek's face, at his sullen, indifferent-cynical features.

"So why are you here?"

"What do you mean?"

"If you believe there's no chance you'll get out of here alive, you can still just take off. That's what I'd do in your place. Why don't you?"

"Because it would be absurd. It would be exactly as absurd and idiotic as our being here. Everything's absurd, everything. Except maybe foraging for firewood. That *does* give you a wonderful feeling. Almost like being in bed with your wife. You know what I'm talking about? Are you married?"

"No. But what exactly is your idea of foraging for firewood?"

"I'll give you a precise explanation. Pay attention. You climb up a tree, but not an old tree—you pick a young thing instead. You climb up high, as high as you can, and then you try to tame the tree. It will sway and shake, but you wrap your legs around its trunk and tie a rope around its neck. Then you holler, 'Ready!' and the man on the ground below starts pulling on the rope, and he pulls you and the treetop way over to one side, he pulls and pulls, and suddenly you're hanging in midair, a weight around a birch's neck, or an alder's.

In those seconds, you feel like you do in bed with your wife. Above you is the sky, and under you, well, you know what's under you. You're wrapped around the tree, you're holding on to it tight, the way you'd hold on to your wife, and then all of a sudden you feel it give way, you feel it get weaker and bend down farther and farther. But just at the moment when you decide you're going to hold on to that feeling, you're not going to let it go, you're going to lock that feeling up inside you, at that very moment, there's a loud crack, a jolt, you hear the boughs rustling, and maybe it even sounds to you as though the tree is groaning. Of course, you don't know for certain. Young trees always act so mysterious, don't you think? As though they had something to hide from us. I think nature sometimes wants to hide from all of us, from you, from Thighbone, from Willi, and from me too . . . What do you actually do, Proska? What kind of work?"

Proska was about to answer, but Poppek went on with his monologue. "Can you understand why I always volunteer when Melon says he needs a man for firewood duty? Tell me, were you with a woman while you were on leave? How was it? Tell me! But slowly, and in great detail."

"They're finished with the pit for Stani," said Proska tonelessly, rising to his feet.

Zacharias and Melon came back, sweating profusely and carrying their short field spades.

"Get yourselves ready," called Willi, who was still standing beside the pit.

The two soldiers walked over to the little mixed-growth forest. Stani was lying facedown in the moist black earth.

"Shall I get his tarp?" Zacharias asked.

"That's Wehrmacht property. It could still come in handy," said Willi.

The men fell silent. They all looked into the hole, where the shiny ends of roots sliced through by the sharp-edged spades glittered in the walls, and they could hear the voice of the wind in the leaves and the distant, breathless *pee-wit, pee-wit* of a lapwing. And then the fat fire-swallower took off his garrison cap, and the others also reached for their head coverings and removed them. Five men stood there bareheaded and sensed that the silence they were submitting to couldn't last much longer.

Then Willi, standing at the head of the grave, began to speak in his hoarse voice: "Comrades. Flesh will return to flesh, and earth to earth. Stani, our Stanislaw Paputka, is made of earth. No need for me to prove that at any length. If I say it, you can believe me. Understand? Do you understand my meaning?"

Poppek and Zacharias said, "Yessir"; Melon and Proska nodded.

"Good," said Willi. "So we must mourn the loss of a good comrade. Stani was a good friend. Damn these blasted mosquitoes! What I wanted to say was, Stani has fallen, for his Führer and for the Great German Reich. The inhabitants of Königsberg must thank him, and so must the citizens of Hamburg and Upper Silesia and all the rest. Stani will live on. Damn, one of these savage little beasts just bit me on the neck. The man who lies before us here is made of earth. Earth is so organized that it gets back everything it has given. It dropped Stani off in Upper Silesia, and now it wants him back. Is that clear? Has anyone failed to grasp that? I also wanted to say, to Melon and Proska: You two are now going to put him in there. But carefully. Try to be less clumsy than usual."

The two took hold of the dead man and lowered him into the grave.

"But you can't lay a man to rest facedown. Are you both crazy? Obviously, you've never done this before in your lives." Willi shoved the men aside and turned Stani over. "So," he said, "now he can see the sky again."

Proska knelt down and placed his handkerchief over the shattered face.

"Is that Wehrmacht property?" asked Willi.

"No. It belongs to my sister, Maria."

"Well, that's different . . . Stani, farewell. We'll meet again somewhere. Old comrades always stay in touch, understand? All right, now you can bury him."

The fat soldier and Zacharias got their spades out of the Fortress again and started filling the dead man's grave. When they were finished, they formed a mound over him, broke some branches off the nearest trees, and thrust the branches into the earth.

"So," said Willi, who had supervised the work until the very end, "that's done. The night patrol can now get some sleep. Especially you, Proska. Take a few hours' nap, don't miss your chance. Sleep isn't something you can swallow like a pill. Or do you have a different opinion?"

"No sir, Corporal."

"In that case, good night."

Proska exchanged introductions with Zacharias and climbed up onto Stani's bunk. He took off his belt, unbuttoned his uniform jacket, ran his tongue over some swollen mosquito bites on his hand, and stretched out. He thought, *This Willi person is a pig . . . God willing, my unit will send for me soon . . . Staying in this place could cause brain rot . . . Wherever can the tall guy be? Hope he makes it back . . . there's nobody I'd rather go on patrol with . . .*

He turned onto one side, laid his head on an arm, and closed his eyes. Sleep came to him more quickly than he'd expected. The last thing he heard was Willi's voice saying, "When the mail comes, remind me that we have to send off Paputka's things. I'll also have to write a letter. Doesn't matter, duty's duty. I hope his mother can read German. With people like that, you never know where you stand."

Proska was awakened by a lot of noise. Day had already broken outside the Fortress, and Willi, Poppek, Melon, and Zacharias were sitting around the table board that lay on top of the iron stove, bellowing and laughing.

"Melon," bawled Poppek, "we've waited long enough. Eat some fire for us now, or I'll slaughter your Alma."

"We'll seduce her," the corporal roared.

"Even better," Poppek yelled. "So come over here. Here's some gasoline."

"I already told you: there has to be a good store of fire already in the stomach. Give me a bottle of booze."

"A whole bottle, just for you?" asked Willi.

"You all could let me have Stani's ration."

"How about the new guy?" Zacharias asked.

"He's going to be on guard duty until his kneecaps stick out of his chest," said Willi. "Before he gets any schnapps, he has to earn it. So, to all present: Cheers. Cheers, I said!"

"Cheers," said the others, bringing their canteen cups to their lips.

"And now," Poppek yelled, "Fatso here is going to eat fire. Zacharias, watch out you don't get too close to him, or your wife will have a premature baby. Actually, you'll have to tell us how you did it. Quiet!"

"Zip it," Willi commanded in a boozy voice. "*I* give the orders for quiet around here, you got that? I want to know if that's clear!"

"Yessir."

"There you go, that's better. So, now we're going to give Melon a whole bottle. If we had more fuel, maybe we could send him into action against the partisans as a flamethrower. I'll put in a request to that effect from the head whatchamacallit. If the boys on the other side get too cheeky, we'll give Melon something to drink, and then he'll spit fire in their faces . . . What do you think this idea's worth? Huh, Zacharias?"

"Ten bottles."

"Don't talk nonsense. At least twenty, plus the War Merit Cross, with swords and citations and all the trimmings. Good. Poppek!"

"Yessir."

"Here's the key to the chest. Stand up, sonny, when I talk to you. Take this damn key and get two full bottles. You'll give one of them to this fathead here. Got that? Bring some cigarettes too."

Proska remained on his upper bunk, pretending to be asleep. The smell of liquor and clouds of tobacco smoke reached him where he lay. Now and then, he opened his eyes and looked at the men.

Poppek put two bottles filled with white liquid on the table, and the artiste immediately snatched one up, tore off the leaden cap with his fingers, and tried to pull out the cork with his teeth. When that attempt failed, he said, "Does anyone have a corkscrew?"

"Behead it!" Willi shouted.

"With a corkscrew—"

"I said, 'Behead it,'" the corporal repeated furiously.

The fat soldier looked around helplessly and then struck the neck of the bottle against the stove. A third of the bottle's liquid contents sloshed onto the floor.

"That's show business," Zacharias said with a grin.

Melon looked at the wet spots on the floor.

"Do you want to lick it up?" cried the corporal. "Now we'll drink, and then we'll have full-scale fire eating. Fire stimulates the appetite. I'd rather quench inner flames than outer ones. Hurry up! Or I'll start sniffing red-hot horseshoes myself. If you don't—"

Suddenly a man holding his hands in the air, a civilian, came into the room. On his feet he wore light canvas boots; his trousers were dark blue, and a heavy jacket covered his naked torso.

The corporal's words died on his pinched lips; had Stani suddenly walked in among them, their surprise could not have been greater.

The man who stood before them with imploring hands was about sixty years old. His forehead was both broad and high, his ears unnaturally large and thin, his chin weak, and his eyes softly glowing.

The drinkers sprang up from their seats. Zacharias took his submachine gun down from a nail, flicked off the safety catch, and aimed the barrel at the stranger.

"What are you doing here?" asked Willi mistrustfully.

The civilian turned around; behind him stood Wolfgang "Milk Roll" Kürschner.

"I picked him up along the way," he said excitedly.

"He was alone?"

"Yes."

"Was he carrying any weapons?" the corporal asked.

"No. But he might have tossed them away at the last minute."

"So, no reason to get worked up?"

"The man speaks good German," said Wolfgang.

"Where did you find him?"

"Under the railroad bridge. I watched him slowly coming our way."

"And then?"

"When he was in front of me, at first I wanted to shoot him."

"And why didn't you, you big baby?"

"He was standing only four meters from my hiding place. I would have had to shoot him in the back of the head. I couldn't . . ."

"And suppose he would have put a couple of new holes in your lily-white ass? You would have said, 'Thanks,' right? You must have peat for brains. Wait outside until I call you in again. Got that?"

"Yessir."

"Then beat it . . . As for you, my friend," Willi said inscrutably to the civilian, "you'll have a seat here with us. And now you'll tell us a story. But for God's sake, not a fairy tale. Fairy tales are only good for grownups. And we're children . . . Melon!"

"Yes."

"Give him some strong drink."

"From *my* bottle?"

"You are obliged to offer our guest some refreshment. That's an order! Who taught you manners? Did you grow up inside a gasoline can, or what?"

"All right, all right, I'll give him a drink . . ."

"Come on, Gramps," said Willi, "sit down with us. We honor the elderly. We have a high opinion of the Stone Age, that's what you used to call it, I think. Here, take the stool in the middle. Right, that's it. Old bones need to rest. So what's your name?"

The civilian spoke seriously and with dignity: "My name is Jan Kowolski, and I'm the parish priest in Tomashgrod."

"You don't say. Your name's Jan, and you're a priest. A soul-catcher, right?"

The corporal took the cup the fat soldier had filled and pushed it over to the old man. "Drink, little brother," Willi said. "Down the hatch, to the health of our souls. We sure need it. Don't you want to?"

"I don't drink," the priest said.

"Oh, you don't drink," Willi repeated cynically.

Poppek, looking at the stranger through glassy eyes, called out triumphantly, "Your Jesus was a boozer too. Don't you remember Cana, Bible-thumper? If you don't drink, I'm going to beat your—"

"Quiet!" Willi screamed, laying his hand on the priest's shoulder. "Anyone who assaults this man will have to deal with me. Listen, Switch-switch, or whatever your name is: Did the kid who brought you here do anything to you? Did he hit you or abuse you in any way? Don't worry, you can tell us. If he did anything like that, he'll be punished for it."

"He treated me decently," said the civilian. "He asked me to come along with him, and that's what I did."

"Of course you came along with him. Otherwise you wouldn't be here. So you're saying he didn't hit you?"

"No. At first he pressed the barrel of his rifle against my back, but when he saw I wasn't making any move to run away, he stopped."

"Hmm," said Willi. A coughing fit forced him to stand up. His spine formed a curve and his mouth filled

with saliva as he hurried to the entrance, leaned—
still bending forward—against one of the doorposts,
gestured over to the table for someone to help him
breathe by pounding on his back, and finally stood up
straight while Zacharias's fists cautiously pummeled
him from behind.

"Rust in the lungs," he said, spat, and went slowly
back to his stool.

"So where were we?" Willi asked. "Ah, right:
Milk Roll treated you well."

"Yes."

"Glad to hear it. Do you think he would have shot
you if you had tried to escape?"

"Yes."

"Well. Thank God. And you were caught by the
big bridge?"

"I was passing near it."

"You were passing near it. Are you sure you don't
want just a sip?"

"No, thank you." The priest sat there rigid, his
hands flat on his thighs; he seemed like a machine,
mechanically answering questions.

Willi said, "Did the kid knock you down?"

"No. He jumped out suddenly from behind a but-
tress and ordered me to put my hands up."

"And that's what you did. You were surprised,
weren't you?"

"I was surprised."

"And your pistol, did you throw it away?"

"I never carry weapons."

"I know," said Willi. "Only sticks of dynamite. God works in mysterious ways."

"I don't understand," the priest said softly.

"Don't worry, I don't understand it either. But say, would you like a cigarette?"

"I thank you, but I don't smoke or drink."

"You take long walks instead, I know. Tomashgrod is far away, isn't it? You must have started out before noon today. Is that your priest's suit?"

"I was called to minister to a peat farmer. When I have to go to the country, I always wear old clothes."

"Which allows you to save on shirts, as we see. Aren't you cold?"

"It's warm in the daytime, and when you're walking—"

"But it's so easy to stray from the path," Willi said, interrupting him. "Did your way take you past the bridge?"

"I wanted to avoid a detour."

"You speak good German. Where did you learn it?"

"I was in Germany thirty-two years ago. I studied there. In Königsberg and Jena."

"Just listen to this. You probably studied how to make long ways short and short ways long. What do you think about Germany? Tell the truth!"

"I liked it a lot. Königsberg meatballs."

Poppek cried out, "He was really there! Whoever eats those meatballs—"

"Quiet!" Willi commanded. "What did you like about Germany besides *Königsberger Klops*?"

"Tilsit cheese."

"And what else?"

"Kant."

"What's that?" Willi asked before draining his cup in one swig.

"A philosopher."

"So," said the corporal when the priest fell silent, "that's what you liked the best. What else do you know about Germany?"

The civilian stayed quiet.

"You probably don't know there's a war going on at the moment, do you? The whole world's trembling before us, even before me, Prussian Corporal Stehauf! And you don't know that! And I'm sure no one has told you that every now and then one of our trains gets blown up in these parts!"

"I have heard about that," said the priest.

"Do you have your papers?"

"I'm sorry, I don't have them on me."

"Jesus is your identity card. Was that what you were about to say? Say his name, and you get through every checkpoint. That's what you thought inside your little head, right? But your head was mistaken!

A complimentary ticket, you thought, a free ride! Where's your pistol?"

"I don't carry a weapon."

"You want me to make him talk?" asked Poppek.

"You stay in your seat," said Willi. "This man has told the truth, and those who stand up for the truth have nothing to fear. Do you all understand that? If you're up to your neck in lies, they're going to drown you one day. Nothing can be done about that." Willi turned to the priest and went on: "On your feet, old boy, stand up. You can go wherever you want. You've earned your freedom, because you didn't abuse the truth. So why are you still sitting on your stool? Are you stuck there? Hit the road, my friend, quick quick quick! Before I change my mind."

The priest rose timidly, staring at the corporal with incredulous eyes.

"Do you want to spend the night here?"

"No, no, sir. I'm going. Many thanks, sir. Good evening."

Stepping hesitantly, the civilian left.

Willi went to the window and pushed it wide open. He signaled to Zacharias to hand him his submachine gun. Proska sat up in his bed; the other men crowded around the doorway.

The priest was stiffly descending the slope; at the alder bridge, he stopped and with one foot tested the stability of the tree trunk. Apparently satisfied, he drew up his other foot, transferring his weight forward, and started to pick his unsteady way across.

Then the clattering roar of the submachine gun burst the silence; the priest threw up one arm, lost his footing, spun in a circle on one leg—a movement that struck Melon as practically balletic—and plunged into the ditch.

Zacharias and Poppek wanted to run to him, but Willi called out, "Stay here! You can pull him out tomorrow morning. I just wanted to make sure the dynamite got soaked."

"He's got dynamite?" the fire-eater asked excitedly.

"In his inner jacket pocket. You'll see for yourselves tomorrow."

· FIVE ·

S uddenly they could all feel a thick, unyielding
fatigue in their bones, and none of them was as
enthusiastic as before about seeing the fat soldier swallow fire. That he had received a considerable
portion of schnapps for nothing, with no performance
in return, was a matter of indifference to them, even
though ordinarily they would have attached great im-
portance to it. They became quiet, almost pensive;
their gestures lost all pugnaciousness. They made faces
as though they were suffering from a shared, invisible,
but nonetheless painful disease, an indefinable disease
that made them rise above themselves and brought
them to the realization that every loud complaint,
every superfluous word, every blasted cliché was
a sign of their extreme absurdity, and that they did
well, and possibly even best, when they kept silent, sa-
vored their weariness, and unhesitatingly conformed

to the boundless equanimity of the landscape they were living in. This disease was a kind of nostalgia for nothingness, a macabre longing to plunge into remote pools of oblivion, to be no longer there; the men felt heavy and surfeited, a feeling reflected in a cool-headed disdain for death.

Willi walked over to Proska's bed and said in a neutral voice, "Get ready to go on patrol. Do you have a carbine?"

"An assault rifle," Proska said, and he swung himself down from his lofty bed.

"Very good," the corporal opined. "Automatic weapons are more useful here. You'll go out with little Milk Roll. The kid's waiting outside. If you fall asleep, you'll be court-martialed. But I don't have to explain that to you. Get going."

Proska got going. He wound the footwraps around his ankles, put on boots and jacket, seized his weapon, and left the Fortress.

Little Milk Roll was sitting on the bench outside.

"There you are," said the PFC.

"My name is Wolfgang Kürschner."

"And I'm Proska, Walter . . . You know the paths we're supposed to take, right?"

"Paths is an exaggeration. I know how to get there and how to get back. We won't lose our way."

"If you're so confident, I'm sure we won't. As far as I'm concerned, we may as well leave now."

The two men entered the mixed-growth forest, entered a boisterously fermenting, matted, and interwoven paradise of fecundity. The alders struck at them and the birches struck at them, and the underbrush grabbed at their legs with ghostly hands. A lush darkness surrounded them, a darkness sated like an Arab after the banquet that ends his fasting; a darkness that could have belched at any moment; a completely different darkness from what one imagines under a nun's cruel skirts: this darkness was oily and warm, it was the darkness of the marsh forest, and you could have banged your head or your shin against it.

Milk Roll, tired and silent, led the way. Actually, he already had one watch behind him, but he found it pointless to wonder how he came to be on patrol again already.

It occurred to Proska that he hadn't eaten anything, and while he was considering whether he should go back and grab at least a slice of bread, he collided with the young soldier.

"Is something wrong?" he hissed.

"I don't know," the other said. "We have to keep right if we want to reach the railroad. It's always red hot here."

"What does that mean?"

"You can't see, and you're being seen."

"Let's go right then."

The two soldiers fought their way through the darkness; they stumbled, cursed, and ran into tree trunks, but they made forward progress. They were unobserved, and no one could have prevented them from lying down on the ground to sleep, and in sleep to forget and to overcome fear, which both of them, even though they wouldn't have admitted it, had in their hearts. But they pressed on, pushed by habit, pulled by Willi's orders.

Bathed in sweat, they reached the edge of the forest. They were standing on a knoll. Before them lay a marshy meadow, and beyond it they recognized the artificial embankment of the railroad. The rails gleamed like dead metallic worms. Proska sat on a fallen trunk and said, "Don't you want to rest for a bit?"

Milk Roll sat down next to him. They held their weapons across their laps like children.

"It's not so dark here," said Proska. "Do I dare light a cigarette?"

"I wouldn't. The second they see a spark, they shoot."

"They're apparently very enterprising, the folks around here."

"And unpredictable. I sometimes think they keep us alive just to torment us."

"What makes you think that?" asked Proska. He tried to make out Milk Roll's face.

"There are seven of us. There are probably more than a hundred of them. They shouldn't have any problem smoking us out of the Fortress. They'll probably do it one of these days. I'd just like to know what's stopping them from doing it now."

Proska was silent for a while, and then he said, "You seem resigned to the idea that you'll never get out of here alive. So why do you stay in this godforsaken place?"

Milk Roll answered, "My father was killed in battle near Warsaw. My mother's worried about me, but if I were to desert, she'd die. Maybe I stay here for her sake. You've been at the front, and when you're there, you have little or no opportunity to think about running away. It's different here."

Proska said, "We have to stick it out. But the sight of this Willi person makes me want to do the opposite. There have been times before when I was on the point of going AWOL. But something always forced me to come back."

"It's this so-called duty," said Milk Roll contemptuously. "They've shot us up with the stuff, like dope. They use it to make us crazy and dependent. They give us a refined injection of duty serum to get us good and loaded. When someone around us plays a few notes on the fatherland flute, a hundred listeners get red, thirsty throats, all at the same time, and they cry out for some national consciousness schnapps!

That's the way things are. Then toasts are drunk and oaths are sworn, and you're in the trap."

"Are you a student?" asked Proska.

"Yes—and then there's this obedience. Consider Stehauf, who's just a stupid, nasty guy. He can do whatever he wants to you. I can't take it anymore, Walter. If he keeps tormenting me the way he's done in the last few weeks, I'm going to disappear."

"What did he do to you?"

"He got drunk while I was on patrol, and when I came back, he made me wade through the latrine, not once, no, but four times. Thank God Thighbone was close by. He got furious and grabbed his submachine gun and fired off a barrage over our heads. That put a scare into Willi, and he ran into the Fortress."

"He's a prick," Proska said. "If he tries that with me, I'll lay him out. Were you there when he shot the priest in the back?"

"I was outside. I saw the man fall into the ditch."

"Stehauf said he had some sticks of dynamite in his coat pocket."

"I don't know. Maybe he did."

Proska slowly stood up, plucked at the soaked seat of his pants, which was stuck to his skin, and said, "If I stay here another month, I'll stop being normal. Then we can make a break for it together. I don't know why I'm here anymore either. I'm waiting for the coup de grâce, but why? For who? For my sister, Maria? She's doing fine. Maybe right now, as we speak, she's lying in her goose-feather bed with my brother-in-law and letting him knead her thighs with his torn-up hands. For Rogalski? He's my brother-in-law. If I wasn't around anymore, everything would be going just as well for him as it is now. And Hilde? She's the woman I sometimes . . . well, you know what I mean. Who knows who she's undressing for tonight? For Germany? What is Germany, what can that be?"

"Right," said Milk Roll, almost panting with excitement. "What *is* this Germany they stuff our ears with? Danton declared you can't carry your fatherland away with you on the soles of your shoes. I can! Do you understand that? Germany isn't a cloud of incense, it's a thing you can taste, feel, cut. I can carry my fatherland away under my shirt, and if they shoot the life out of my head, then there just won't be any Germany for me anymore. Don't misunderstand me: of course there's a country where I was born, a country I especially love. I love it because I know its highways and byways, because it's locked up in my heart. But I wouldn't let myself get gunned down for some highway or byway, like my father. He actually spoke of 'Duty' and 'Willingness' and spouted all the rest of that rhetorical poison they drip into you. You understand me, Walter? We're Germany too, it's not just those others, and since we're Germany, it would be complete idiocy for us to sacrifice ourselves for

Germany, that is, for ourselves. That would be just like a bear cutting a slice off his own haunch and starting to eat it, even though he's in great pain, and all the while he keeps persuading himself that he must make sacrifices."

"You're right, Wolfgang. Where did you figure all that out?"

"Not in our garden at home, and not in the lecture hall, but here. You can't figure it out unless you're here. I've always been a lonesome dog, but always glad to be self-sufficient. I've never had a girlfriend with a well-cared-for, perfumed body, waiting at home for me. I had myself, and nothing else. But anybody who puts himself under the knife and makes a few good incisions will realize he can never lay that knife aside. He'll have to keep operating on himself for the rest of his life. And do you know which people are their own best surgeons? The ones who give themselves a silent diagnosis and crawl into their inner solitude and take their own pulse there, with brutal honesty."

"I don't entirely understand you, Wolfgang. Have you studied medicine?"

"Look, Walter. In the world where we live, we have to orient ourselves toward the good. That sounds banal, I know. But since evil presents itself in many different guises, it's necessary to reconsider contaminated intentions, identify the damaged areas, seal up the holes in our findings, and revise the results.

And that requires a huge amount of analytical ability and radical frankness about oneself. If you perceive that something you've run after for twenty years is not only wrong but base, underhanded, dangerous, and murderous, you must have the strength to kick it away. Maybe you know what I mean. We must beware of the national Pied Pipers. Stick our fingers in our ears, run water into them, plug them with wax! I cherish freedom, and skepticism too. We should spread the dung of freedom in our hearts and plant skepticism in it. Do you understand me? I guess I'm a little excited. And no wonder. You're the first person I've ever confided in, Walter. You have to remember that—I'm bursting with things to say . . . I send my mother letters about consolation. She needs those letters, but every word of solace I write makes me ill; it strikes me as a betrayal. You wouldn't think I'd feel that way, would you?"

Proska struck himself on the nape of the neck with one big hand. Behind his low forehead, the wheels of his thoughts were turning hard, and it seemed as though their rotation loosened something in him that until then had existed as a timorous cramping. He felt himself set free, ready for an undertaking; he saw a way. Slowly and a little apprehensively, he stretched out an arm and laid it across Milk Roll's shoulders. Then he said, "I can't express myself the way you can, Wolfgang. But I'd like to tell you that you can always count on me. If anyone tries to torment you, come to me. In the place we're in, we have to rely on each other."

"No," Wolfgang said dramatically. "This isn't the only place where we have to rely on each other. Men who think the way we do must come together everywhere. The fellowship of the reasonable is small. Because we all—"

Rat-tat-tat: a sudden hammering. They heard bullets whistling in their direction and impacting the trees around them. Some rounds whirred away over their heads like evil insects.

"Get down," Proska cried. "Behind the trunk." Milk Roll flung himself on the ground beside him. "Did you see the flashes from their guns?"

"Yes. Over there, behind the embankment. How did they . . . ah, you lit a cigarette! Put it out, Walter, quick. There's no point provoking these guys."

Proska flung the glowing cigarette away. It struck a tree trunk and sent out a shower of sparks. At the same moment, there came another fusillade of automatic fire, and the two men pressed their faces into the damp ground. They smelled the harsh odor of the grass and felt the dew wet their hands.

"Shall we answer them?" the assistant asked.

"There's no point," said Wolfgang.

"So what are we supposed to do? If we lie here all night, we'll have pneumonia tomorrow."

"Maybe they have something planned for the bridge today."

"We ought to go there."

"Ought to? That's pretty rash, Walter. If they surprise us, it's all over. Usually they have people standing guard."

"And if they blow up the bridge?"

"We'll notice it soon enough."

"Aren't you going to come with me?" Proska asked.

"Of course I am. Let's go. We'll skirt the edge of the woods. Hopefully the moon won't be too curious about us while we're crawling over the meadow. At some point, we'll have to crawl, Walter. If you walk upright, you'll draw their fire right away."

They both stood up and walked with long strides along the margin of the mixed-growth forest. There was nothing hasty, nothing anxious about their movements. They felt well protected in the austere shadow of the foliage; one might have thought that for them, the difference between life and death had ceased to exist. They continued on to a place where the woods suddenly stopped and the meadow formed a kind of bay, as if it had surged into the forest in that spot. And there the moon pounced on the two soldiers. It attacked them with its light, exposing their approach. But Proska and Milk Roll had no doubt reckoned on that, because now they were moving more circumspectly, no longer so heedlessly that someone watching them might have thought no more dangers threatened mankind. Although neither of them had spoken a word of explanation or warning, not so much as a tiny syllable, they both fell on the ground, laid their rifle barrels across their left arms—a reflex that had been etched into their brains—and waited.

Milk Roll hissed, "Ready," and then both started crawling over the meadow grass: knee, toe-tip, elbow, knee, toe-tip, elbow. Their sweat glands went to work. Onward, you sons of hope, drag yourselves through the marsh! So what if your pants get wet and your nipples bathe in stinking, putrefying water. Your nostrils tremble. Let them tremble: they won't capture such sublime scents for you again anytime soon, the scents of fatal lethargy, the fumes of the earth that death and life are fighting over. Such a little patch of marsh possesses a double sublimity, a double dignity, namely that of another, departed world and that of your own. Don't forget that, breathe, breathe. Unlock your lungs; whoever has the privilege of getting so close to the earth should savor it. Every now and then there was a slight squelching sound, as when a mother leans over a barrel of fermenting sauerkraut and presses it down with her soft fist. But in the end, so what? And if a frog that's taking a break from vocal sac training should get caught under your knee, the accident will neither stop nor change your course. What a shame, how regrettable it is, though, that you can't take the time to listen to earth's primordial babbling.

"We're close," Milk Roll panted. "We must be close."

Bushes suddenly seemed to spring up in front of them, offering them cover. Both men got to their feet.

"There's the bridge. Can you see anyone?"

"Nobody ever sees them."

"Shall we go on?" Proska asked.

"And then?"

"Then maybe we'll catch them."

"Or they'll catch us."

"What should we do?"

"Wait."

"For what?"

"Wait for something to happen."

"And what's going to happen?"

"That question can't be answered in advance."

"Are you afraid?"

"Nonsense. How about you?"

"I'll go on," said Proska.

"You stay here, Walter, I'll go."

"Then let's both go."

They crouched down and drew near the bridge, availing themselves of the cover the bushes provided. The bridge rested on the strong shoulders of four concrete pillars, in front of which the river created little whirlpools. In addition, the abutments on the banks were secured by struts as broad as a man's chest. All in all, this bridge appeared to be a remarkable bastion against time.

The soldiers pricked up their ears in vain. They heard not a sound. They noticed no one trying to get too close to the bridge.

"Looks dead and deserted," Proska said dryly.

"Lots of flowers bloom in graveyards."

"You mean you see one of these—"

"*Ssst!*" Wolfgang hissed.

"I think you're too tense. If there were anyone here, we'd have spotted him already."

"At the front, it's different."

"It's exactly the same. And to make you understand, I'm going to light a cigarette now."

Proska stuck a cigarette in his mouth, lit it, and smoked it greedily.

"There, you see?" he said. "No one has any objection. They probably think we've reinforced the guard in this area. Remember, this is where you all grabbed the old guy. Surely that must have instilled some respect in them."

"These people know nothing of respect—and they're not acquainted with fear either. You can lay their hand on a block of wood and raise your ax: they won't tell you any secrets. You can bring the ax down: they'll turn pale and look at you in excruciating pain and remain silent. You can hack off the other hand:

the pain will drive them mad, they'll jump and scream and groan—but you won't learn what you want to know. You can even bring them to where their wives and children are and make them watch while their families are shot: they won't speak . . . Someone who has no respect for death has no need to fear us. Because killing is already the worst thing we can come up with."

"Are we going to stay close to the bridge until morning?"

"No. We'll stay on the riverbank. There are some well-protected places a little farther upriver. Shall we go there?"

"All right with me."

Hesitantly, they moved out of the shadow of the bridge and waded into the bright yellow swath of light shed by the moon. No shot, no scream, no fall, no gasping, no blood.

The river gnawed at the bank, as skulking and wary as a rat. And its patience was paying off. It chuckled as the men crept along the low, sloping ground.

"Come on," said Proska, "we can sit here. Our pants are soaked in any case. Here, between these bushes. We can still see the bridge."

And they sat on the ground and snatched their steel helmets off their heads. The night wind landed on their foreheads and brought cooling. They both stared at the river.

Damn, I'm hungry, thought Proska.

She had hair like a gypsy, thought Milk Roll.

"What are you thinking about?" asked Proska.

"Eve."

"The one with the apple?"

"No. She had blue-black hair."

Proska said, "Like a gypsy girl?"

"Yes, exactly. And her skin was as brown as a May bug's wings."

"Does she think about you?"

"No."

"Are you sure about that?"

"Yes . . . We used to play tag together when we were eight, and we went out for ice cream when we were fourteen. We'd stand on the docks when the fishermen unloaded their big baskets, and we'd look at each other when a ship's horn blew. She and I were the same age; we were always holding hands; and when we went to the dairywoman's, she'd say, 'You two are going to make a pretty couple,' and when we went to the greengrocer's, each of us got an apple, and he too said, 'You two are going to make a pretty couple'; and when my mother was standing at the window and saw us coming down the street hand in hand, she'd say, 'You look like a pretty couple.' On my seventeenth birthday, I got a kiss from her—the first. We simply abandoned our friends and met secretly in the garden. I put my arm around her shoulders, and all at once we stopped walking, and she looked at me. I felt how hot her skin was, and then she moved closer to me and we closed our eyes."

"And couldn't find each other," Proska chuckled.

"Her mouth was like a little red magnet, it was like a burning lens, you know? And afterward—it took us a pretty good while before we could find words again— we talked about getting married. Slowly, we went back to the house, slowly, slowly. Not slowly enough. Now and then we stopped and embraced and kissed. The last kiss came at her front door, and I felt her body pressing against mine: strong, determined, and full of longing. I understood that longing. I kissed her on the neck. Then she gave me a complicit look and ran inside."

Milk Roll stopped talking and drummed his fingers on his rifle stock. His long hair had fallen down and covered one ear.

"Was her skin as brown as a May bug's wings all over? I figure you found out the answer to that pretty soon."

"Two days after my birthday, I invited her to go swimming. I had laid a plan, a beautiful, promising, reliable plan. We'd travel out to a branch of the Oder, to a spot where there were hardly ever any people. Some bushes were growing there, right at the edge of the water—big, sympathetic bushes that hid anyone who didn't want to be seen. You understand me, Walter?"

Proska nodded.

"Good. So I decided not to give Eve any long explanations about where we were going—I just told her to meet me at the train station at three o'clock. If you can, I said, don't make me wait too long . . . I was right on time; she didn't come. When it got to be four o'clock and she still hadn't shown up, I boarded the train by myself. At first I was angry at her. But later, when I was lying in the isolated spot where I'd planned to take her, I forgave her. I assumed she'd been prevented from coming by some unforeseen problem. And so, not unhappy but a little disappointed, I enjoyed the afternoon. When evening came and it got dark—about as dark as it is now—I sat down among the bushes. It was a delightful evening, and I wasn't thinking about leaving yet. I saw the lights of the ships sailing down the Oder, I heard the miniature music of the crickets, and I was satisfied. I conversed with myself; I wanted to pat myself on the back, I congratulated myself on what I hadn't yet experienced, what was still to come. The longer you postpone great pleasure, the more painful and avid . . . Ah, you know what I mean."

"I know," said Proska.

"But as I was sitting there, lost in my little private dreams, I suddenly heard two voices, one male and one female. I resolved to keep quiet so I wouldn't be discovered. But all at once, curiosity seized me by the collar and turned my head in the direction the voices were coming from. There stood a man lighting a cigarette and a girl rearranging her clothing. I recognized her profile against the night sky. It was her, her! She was laughing softly, and happily. The man, a guy as big as a gorilla, took her in his arms and pressed his lips against the down on the nape of her neck. I heard her sigh—my ears didn't let me down. Well, so what else can I tell you? I couldn't move, I couldn't shout; it was her! They said goodbye. He, the gorilla, went off in the other direction; she passed right next to the bush I was lying behind. I didn't call to her, I didn't budge. Now I knew who she was."

"Did you see her again?"

"No."

"Hmm," said Walter.

The soldiers were silent. Proska's belly became impatient. "How long do we have to stay out here?" he asked.

"Until dawn," said Milk Roll.

A waterfowl with swiftly beating wings whirred across the river.

"He's in a hurry," said Proska.

"Quiet!"

"What is it?"

"I think someone's there."

"By the bridge?"

"*Sst!*"

They lay down and gripped their rifle stocks and curled their index fingers around the triggers.

"There, Walter, there!"

They held their breath; each could hear the other's heartbeat. A person was slowly coming toward them on the gently sloping riverbank; this person was a girl. Both of them could tell immediately from the silhouette of her head. Like them, the girl must have been lying low among the bushes along the river.

Milk Roll took aim at her as well as he could, determined to squeeze the trigger at his next opportunity. But then Proska's big hard hand came down on his rifle barrel and pressed it to the ground. The girl came closer, calm as could be. Now she was two paces from the men, now even with them, and now past them already. When she was almost out of sight, Wolfgang asked, "Why didn't you let me shoot? The girls around here are often more dangerous than the men."

Proska answered haltingly: "It was her, her. She double-crossed me on the train and spoiled my plan. I recognized her profile against the night sky. Her name is Wanda, and her hair is red like squirrel fur."

· SIX ·

"Quiet! Let those two sleep!"

"I just wanted to say—"

"I decide what gets said here. Is that clear?"

"Yessir. But we have a visitor. I believe—"

"No believing here. A visitor?"

"Yes."

"Where is he? Tell me he's not another Dynamite Jesus."

"No, he's not."

"What is he, then? Speak up."

"I believe he's the mail officer."

"Ah, the mail officer. Why isn't he in here right now? It's about time he shows his face again. Bring him to me."

Melon waddled out the door; Willi counted the cigarettes he kept in his chest.

A promising morning had made its way to the Fortress and awakened the soldiers. The dew hung twinkling on the grass, the sky looked on, hopelessly cheerful, and the sun shuffled over the treetops without a sound, like a weightless old woman. Proska was asleep and Milk Roll was asleep. They had eaten, hung up their uniforms to dry, and then thrown themselves onto their bunks. Thighbone hadn't returned yet. But that fazed no one; they all knew they couldn't lose a man like him so easily. He was too careful, too alert, and too cunning.

Before Poppek and Zacharias went out on patrol, they had fished the old man out of the ditch and searched his coat pockets. When they couldn't find anything, they'd gone to Willi and told him so.

"Then I made a mistake," the corporal had answered, and when the others asked what they should do now, he'd shouted, "Maybe he gulped those sticks down as fast as he could. Move him far away from the Fortress, just in case he explodes later on today."

Melon pushed the mail officer into the Fortress. He was a man with sloping shoulders, and he was carrying a bundle of parcels on one side and a leather bag filled with letters on the other. A submachine gun hung diagonally across his chest. It wasn't easy to make out the expression in his eyes, for they were screened by the thick, highly polished lenses of his spectacles.

Sighing loudly, he approached the stove table, threw the parcels and letters on it, and leaned his gun against a stool. Then he went to Willi and said, "The mail, the mail, the mail is here!"

The corporal growled, "Are you always so witty?"

That rendered the mail officer speechless; he swallowed the saliva of embarrassment and waited until the corporal turned toward him. Willi closed the lid of his treasure chest and said, "Why has it been so long since we've seen you?"

"When I come isn't up to me," the mailman said.

"You're still based in Tomashgrod?"

"A little outside of it."

"Ah. And otherwise, you have no complaints?"

"How do you mean?"

"Just a thought. Do you think too? We do a lot of thinking here. Every night, two sacks, filled with thoughts. We immediately tie up the sacks and throw them in the ditch. What would you think if we sent all that stuff, all those thoughts, home in the mail? You'd have to commit a whole battalion of mail officers just to handle the post for me and my men here. And the people at home would have to spend all their time reading mail . . . Have you brought a lot?"

"In four weeks all sorts of things start to pile up, heh–heh–heh."

"Why are you laughing like an imbecile?"

"I'm laughing like an imbecile, Corporal?"

"You're laughing like a tickled gelding."

"There's probably a total of forty letters."

"I'm not surprised. Twenty of them are surely for our dyspeptic."

"Your dyspeptic?"

"Our stomach-sufferer. Kürschner."

"Yeah, pretty many of them are addressed to him."

"Anything for me?"

"Two letters, as far as I know."

"Well, let's see these surprises . . . Have you got a light?"

"Yessir."

"Have you also got cigarettes?"

"Just two left."

"Hand them over, and a light too."

The corporal took three or four deep drags and then went over to the stove table. He rummaged in the mail pile until he spotted his name, picked up the envelope, and thrust it into his breast pocket.

"You don't want to read it right away?"

"For what?" Willi asked. "The words aren't going anywhere."

"You never know, sometimes you have to make a quick decision, heh-heh-heh."

"Stop that idiotic laughing, man, you're making my ears nervous. Did your father command the joke brigade, or what?"

"He was a locomotive driver, Corporal."

"There, you see, practically the same thing."

While Willi talked, he pushed the letters apart, read their addresses, perused the contents of cards that had no envelopes, removed the wrapper from a newspaper meant for Zacharias, and threw it on his bed. The mail officer, who was watching him, commented, "There's only one letter for you? That's not much in more than three weeks. I thought I saw your name on two letters, but I must have been mistaken . . ."

"Think away," the NCO said without looking up, "but not too much. You can rest your brain and leave the thinking to me and to your superior officers. After all, we're responsible for you. Is that clear?"

"Yessir."

"Good, I like to be clear."

All at once, the corporal gave a start; holding a card in his hand, he hurried to the window and read the card a second time in the brighter light. His thin lips parted, an uncharacteristic smile twitched the corners of his parsimonious mouth, and his Adam's apple rolled up and down his ruddy, leathery throat. He absentmindedly flicked his half-smoked cigarette onto the floor and crushed it out with his boot sole. Then he bared his teeth and began to laugh loudly; he laughed until a coughing fit seized him and bent his body in half. His eyes bulged out of their sockets, sprays of saliva flew through the air, his hands groped for a hold. He made a weary sign to the mailman, who immediately understood and delivered several heavy blows to the NCO's back.

"Lung remnants, fall in on the right and make way for oxygen," Willi croaked when he was feeling better. With the balls of his hands, he rubbed his eyes, pressing away the moisture that his tremendous efforts had brought welling up. He shook his head resignedly, held the card high again, and as he didn't want to take the chance of laughing aloud, contented himself with letting the hint of a benevolent grin appear on his drinker's face.

"That must be pretty amusing, no?"

"What?" Willi asked hoarsely.

"That card. It seems to be making the corporal laugh."

"So what? It really is laughable. Even you would laugh at it, you and your idiotic heh–heh–heh. Let me hear it again."

"You want me to laugh?"

"You can't laugh. I want you to go heh–heh–heh."

"At what?"

"At yourself. But why aren't you doing it? It's an order, carry it out."

The mailman was silent, as though secretly testing his vocal cords.

"Well? Let's go! Let's hear it!"

The slope-shouldered man didn't change expression, but looked at the corporal and went, "Heh-heh-heh, heh-heh-heh—"

"All right, stop, for God's sake. That's enough for me, you're torturing my eardrums. Furthermore, you can disappear now. But if you let another three weeks pass before you come back, you're going to have some bad luck. Understand?"

"Yessir."

"Here, don't forget your SMG. That's Wehrmacht property. You have to treat it like your own eyes. But I see that your eyes . . . well. I suppose you've laughed yourself to tears at your own jokes so much you can't see anything anymore. What's your view of the situation? I mean, through your double pupils. Everything's going according to plan, right? Good. You can clear out. But take this letter with you. We lost a man. With any luck, his mother can read German . . . Maybe you're from Upper Silesia too?"

"From Farther Pomerania," said the mailman.

"Ah, from Farther Pomerania," repeated Willi. "Does everybody there laugh that way?"

"Yessir."

"Then I can understand why you have so many wolves."

Willi watched the mail officer until he disappeared around the edge of the mixed-growth forest. Then the corporal read the contents of the postcard for the fourth time and shouted, "Melon!"

The circus artist with the fat head looked up from his cooking pot and waddled over to his corporal.

"Melon, listen to the card Zacharias got," said Willi, and then read it aloud:

Dear Pappi, I hope you won't be mad, but it's a boy. He weighs seven and a half pounds and screams a lot. Everybody says he looks like you. The birth was easy. In ten days, I can leave the hospital. You must be happy—now we've got what we wanted. Can you come home on leave? We're all waiting for you. Erna's husband wrote to her—he's been taken prisoner by the Americans. She thought he was dead, it had been so long since he wrote. You could write a little more often yourself. An army postcard would be enough. Shall we name the little one Willi or Lothar? Erna says Lothar. With all my heart, your wife Liesel.

"Thank God," the artiste said with relief. "Now he can stop describing his dream to us every morning. In his mind, he's always been at his wife's bedside."

"They should call their little offspring Willi," said the corporal, "like me. Maybe he'll choose a career as a noncommissioned officer too."

"I think we should surprise Zacharias," said the artiste.

"And how. Every morning the same thing: 'I dreamed my wife had a baby.' Just wait, my boy, we'll give you the news in bite-sized pieces."

"I have to go back to the fire, otherwise I'll burn the cabbage."

"Cabbage again?"

"Yes, but cooked with pork rinds."

"You should take off your Alma's dress and stick her in the pot instead. She's bound to taste better than those goddamned pork rinds."

"When she reaches retirement age," said the fat soldier, "when she reaches retirement age," and returned to his cooking pot. He lifted the lid, waited until the steam made its vertical escape, picked up a wooden spoon, and began to stir. As hc did so, he bent so far over the pot that his head was directly above it. When its contents were burbling again, when the fire had so overcome the water that it started jumping about like a whipped top, when the little bubbles were climbing up to the surface, where they lived their short, hot, seconds-long lives—hardly born and already burst—then Melon pressed the cabbage down with his wooden spoon, powerfully, energetically. The fire could return to the attack.

Without looking, the artiste stretched out a hand for a piece of the firewood that Poppek so happily supplied him with and tried to place it under the pot. It didn't go in all the way, however, and the effort made him turn his head to one side. Then he got a fright. Two meters away, a big rat was sitting and looking at him through calm black eyes. Its long tail was all too visible, lying across a stick of firewood. The animal moved only its nose, displaying as it did so some large yellow teeth. It ogled the cook with an expression that combined curiosity and expectation.

Melon carefully lifted the spoon, intending to hurl it at the rat as hard as he could. But even before his arm could reach the necessary throwing position, the animal spun around and with lightning speed disappeared into a hole in the ground next to the woodpile.

It'll come back, the fire-eater thought. He seized his carbine, which was lying on the bench in front of the Fortress, loaded the weapon, knelt down, and trained the barrel on the hole.

He didn't have to wait long. First he saw the yellow teeth, then the shining black eyes. The rat crept partly out of its hiding place. Its hindquarters and tail remained out of sight.

Melon didn't shake; his technique was nearly impeccable as he aimed at one of the rat's eyes and squeezed the trigger. At that instant, the rat sprang wildly out of its hidey-hole, did a flip in the air, clamped its teeth on a piece of wood that was sticking out of the pile, jerked and kicked its hind legs in mortal pain, and suddenly fell.

Then the man could see that he'd shot away only one of the animal's ears and a tiny piece of its head. He loaded another round and took aim. The rat reared up again, and clean red blood dripped on its fur. It started running around in wild circles and then burrowing through the grass. It was searching for its hole.

Mclon guessed the rat's intention and therefore gave up trying to hit it while it was still raging in the grass, mad with pain. He aimed instead at the nearly round, dark opening in the ground in front of the woodpile so that he couldn't miss the rat when it found its hiding place. Seconds passed, and he seethed with impatience for the moment when a little mass of brown fur, smirched with blood and dirt, would appear in front of his sights like a moving target in a shooting gallery. Then all he'd have to do was pull the trigger. He thought, *It should always be so easy . . . just aim and fire . . . the target ought to seek out the bullet, and not the bullet the target . . . that way things would be easier . . . someone should invent such a thing . . . and then Willi would just say, go out there and find some lead . . . but where in hell is this damn rodent?*

He squinted out of the corner of his left eye and saw the animal lying rather calmly in the grass, stretched out on one side and slightly moving its little feet. Its tail was vibrating, as if the tiny charge of electricity in a toy battery were flowing through it.

The fire-eater walked over to the rat, and when he was very close, he pointed his rifle barrel down, took meticulous aim, and pulled. The bullet tore the animal's body to shreds, splashed much of it high in the air, and left behind, on the spot where the creature had lain, a small, funnel-shaped hole trimmed with bits of fur and guts.

"What's going on, Fatso?" Willie suddenly shouted. "Are you shooting away the dirt under your toenails?"

"No. Did you know, Corporal, that rats sometimes have a human look in their eyes? I just exterminated one. A perfect shot. The little beast was looking at me as if it wanted to give me some tips on how to cook cabbage."

"It's not too late for you to learn, you should have let it talk. So where's the four-footed corpse?"

"There's hardly anything left of it. Bang, splat, gone. It blew up like a bottle bomb."

"Its intestine is still hanging on your collar. Go wipe yourself off. I hope we don't find more meat in the cabbage than you put there. Tell me the lid was on the pot."

"Yessir. The pot was tightly closed. You can see for yourself."

"I always do that at the end of the chapter, understand?"

The corporal was standing before the rat's remains with his legs wide apart and his hands in his pockets.

He slowly raised one foot and pressed clumps of grass and dirt over the little decorated hole. Then he said to Melon, "I have an idea for how we can surprise Zacharias. I'm going to wrap his news in greaseproof paper and tie it up tight. His fingers will be bloody before he can get to it."

"You want to wrap his card in paper?"

"What have you got inside that fat head? Who knows what he'll think is in the package. Maybe gasoline. The point is, we want to arouse his curiosity . . . We have to serve him this problem tastefully. You're an artiste, right? Haven't you ever been in high society?"

"Of course."

"There, you see? Fire guzzlers are half-aristocrats. That's what you call yourselves, no? And the noncommissioned officer is the spinal cord of society. Don't you agree?"

"Absolutely," said Melon.

The corporal turned around, walked over to the bench, and sat down. The cabbage slowly increased its pressure on the lid of its hot prison, which began— quietly at first—to make boiling sounds. The circus artist laid a piece of firewood on the lid, and the pot immediately grew silent.

"Hey," Willi said abruptly, "where's your Alma?"

"She went to the latrines."

"Isn't she well brought up."

"I think she's searching for gold."

"I wish her much success."

"When she's gathered enough, we'll melt it down and make ingots."

"When is she going to lay another egg?"

"The magazine has to be full first."

"That's a cute way of putting it. So can she learn some tricks?"

"Better than a dog."

"I thought chickens were supposed to be the dumbest creatures on the planet."

"The others, yes. But not my Alma."

"You ought to teach her how to preach too. Then she can cluck the Old Testament at us."

"That'll come eventually. Right now our training sessions are focused on climbing."

"Maybe we'll be able to use her for airmail service later. In ten years, I mean."

"Are we going to stay here that long?"

"We'll always be here, Melon. And if they come and get us out of here, we'll never be able to settle into any other nest. Once you've drunk from the Pripet Marshes, you can never spit them out again. Once you've breathed this air, it sticks inside your lungs. We'll never get free of this country, never again. It will follow us everywhere we go. You can believe your corporal—he's given this subject a lot of thought. And in the process, he's—"

Willi interrupted his discourse; all of a sudden, Zwiczosbirski was standing in front of the Fortress. Nobody had seen him coming, he'd just emerged, as if he'd climbed up out of a hidden well. The tall soldier perceived that his abrupt appearance had at the very least confused the two men, and he smiled good-naturedly. He looked exhausted; one trouser leg was ripped and the front of his field jacket was soaked through. He'd hung his carbine diagonally across his back. In one hand he carried his steel helmet, in the other a Russian machine gun. His hair was stuck to his scalp.

"Come here," Willi ordered.

Thighbone obeyed. He walked up close to the bench and laid the MG at his corporal's feet. The expression on his face combined humility with the expectation of being thanked, like a dog that fetches a stick flung by its master.

"Where were you?" asked Willi.

"Well, back now," said the tall soldier amicably.

"I want to know where you were. What you did is called unauthorized absence from duty. Do you know that?"

"But I bring back—"

"Close your trap or you'll get mosquitoes in your lungs. I know Stani's death hit you hard. But that's no reason to go missing from the Fortress for twelve hours or more. What do you suppose would happen if everyone did that? Just so you know, I'm going to report you to Tomashgrod. Then again, maybe not, I haven't decided yet. If you do better, this screwup might not turn out so bad. No firing squad for you this time . . . And now tell me what you've been up to, and where, all this time. That's a Russian MG. Did you find it?"

"Captred, sir, captred."

"You captured it?"

Melon waddled over inconspicuously so as to hear the interrogation better.

"Yessir. MG captred. When they bury poor Stani, I have feeling like they bury my own body."

"Ah," said Willi. "You had that feeling."

"Yessir. And right then I think everything for me *schwistko jedno*, undifferent, all same. Head not knowing where foots marching. Big circus in head, and I take gun and go to big river."

"And you took a nice, refreshing bath, or what?"

Thighbone made a dismissive gesture. "Nah," he said. "I listen water, and when listening finish, night already there. So what I do? I sneak down to railroad. Everything beautiful dark, nobody can see me. So I lying by railroad, and MG go *rat-tat-tat*. And little later again, *rat-tat-tat*. I wait and wait. Then two men with MG come by. Very quiet, but I see them. And when they close to me . . . well, yes, I go *rat-tat-tat* too, twice, and everything over. Here is MG."

The tall soldier looked over at Melon and said with a smile, "I have big hunger, could eat two loaves army bread. Knees shaking already. And bending, soft like sourdough."

"Give him something to eat," the corporal commanded, shaking his head.

Melon and Thighbone disappeared into the Fortress.

"Is mail come?" the tall soldier asked as he walked over to the stove table.

"There was something for you," said the artiste.

"Where? Give here. Must read right away."

"Wait a minute. Do you know the latest?"

"How can I know what happen in Gleiwitz when I not there?"

"Zacharias's wife had a baby!"

"Ah, *moi Jesus*, real happy news! No more so many dreams about it. He dream little baby into world. Very beautiful, yes? He already know big news?"

"No. Willi has thought up something good. He wants to surprise him."

"What his plan?"

"What his plan is, I don't know. But it must be good . . . I can't give you the cheese, it's for tomorrow evening."

"*Sst*, not so loud. You like trumpet. Milk Roll and new man sleeping."

"They don't hear us."

"How to know? . . . Where is mail for me?"

"Here, a little parcel and a letter."

"Letter from Father, and parcel . . . parcel from Father too."

As the tall soldier passed the two sleepers, he looked them in the face; then he sat on his bed and tried to open his parcel. He used his teeth to pull on the packing string; it didn't give. He tried to loosen the knots with his fingertips, but the knots wouldn't cooperate. Then, overcome with impatience, Thighbone reached into his watch pocket, drew out his cigarette lighter, flicked it on, and held it under the string. The flame licked the fibers, stretching and scorching them, and then spread along the twine, so that when the man gave it a single hard pull, it burst in half. He stripped off the rest of the packing string and tore the paper apart. Gradually there came into view a box that had once contained Osram lightbulbs, and when he opened it and shook its contents onto his blanket, he clicked his tongue for joy. Before him lay, still adorned with their price tags, two sturdy pike-fishing lines, along with two red-and-white floaters so big and ponderous that no living bait fish could have done much to disturb their calm; in addition, Thighbone found four leaden balls to weigh down the lines, a spoon lure whose hook was camouflaged with red feathers, and an artificial fly. For his purposes, however, the uselessness of the latter was immediately clear to him.

Pozekai lo, he thought. *Just wait. Now you can look forward to frying pan. These lines you won't know to break, not these lines. We'll see which of us stronger. I older than you, and cleverer. Just wait, Mister Pike! . . . Father understood me* dobschä. *Except artificial flies worth nothing, hooks too small. But spoon lure good. When is in your mouth, pan already warm.*

He put the fishing accessories back in the Osram box and shoved it under his pillow. Then he stood up, took off his pants, checked the damage, and resolved to sew up the tear before lunch.

P oppek said, "Stop! We've lugged him far enough. Put him down!"

"Let's carry him over there," Zacharias suggested. "Under the blackberry bushes."

"But then he'll be right beside the private road."

"That doesn't matter. We don't go to the river very often."

"All right, good. Then we won't lose our way anymore. A funny kilometer stone, huh?"

They dragged the dead dynamite priest over a clearing and laid him down next to some blackberry bushes. His facial features were contented, relaxed; he seemed satisfied with what had befallen him. The exit wound in his chest had stopped bleeding; his eyes were tightly closed; a thin trickle of ditch water flowed from one corner of his mouth to his weak chin. Nothing about the priest suggested that he was bearing his current situation, namely death, reluctantly—except, to tell the truth, his hands, which looked tense and cramped. His fingers were curved, as if attempting to grasp whatever he'd just been thinking about. And so his hands and his face were in an unusual contrast to one another; the former still remembered life, but the latter already showed the signs of a sublime equanimity, the consolations of a timeless state.

Zacharias noticed this as he and Poppek stood gazing down at the dead man and said, "His hands look like they were trying to grab hold of a branch. Look at them."

"He wanted to pull the dynamite sticks out of his pocket," said Poppek.

"But he wasn't carrying any dynamite sticks."

"Do you know that for sure?"

"Willi said he could have been mistaken."

"And so? You can't wish a man back to life. Bullets don't understand jokes . . . Do you feel sorry for him?"

Zacharias bent down and folded the priest's hands over his chest.

"Maybe he really wasn't to blame," he said.

"You mean, for his death?"

"Yes."

"Do you think he made any contribution to his birth? We can't defend ourselves from coming into the world, and we don't have enough influence to extend our lives for as long as we'd like. So I don't see why we should mourn for the dead more than for the unborn. If you want to feel pity for this man, you should also pity the child your wife's going to give you . . . Look at this fellow. You can step on his hand, he won't feel any pain; you can pull out all his teeth, no shot, no drugs, and he won't stir. This man isn't here anymore, theoretically, you understand that; he's gone, finished, blown up. You can't call every piece of rubber a balloon."

"No, of course not. I understand what you're saying, but nevertheless—"

"What does 'nevertheless' mean? We have to free ourselves from certain ideas. When you see a dead bird, you don't immediately think about the songs he might have sung. What you really see is nothing but a bag of useless matter. And when you look your dead father in the face—"

"No!" Zacharias cried. "Stop it! I have a different opinion. You talk like a block of ice. It's better you lend a hand and we'll lay this man a little farther under the bushes."

"You dream about your wife too much," Poppek said, bending down.

They pulled the corpse deeper into the undergrowth, laid him on his back, gathered branches, and covered him, so that no passerby could tell he was there—unless a strong wind pounced on him in his repose and blew his green hiding place apart.

Then the men stepped onto the narrow, so-called private road. And after they looked back one more time, they started walking one behind the other—their weapons braced against their hips, ready to fire—in the direction that would take them to the river.

The young forenoon lay innocently upon the marshes; blithe and foolish, it rubbed the landscape into good cheer.

> *Rise and shine now, silly man-child,*
> *Rub the morning off your eyelids;*
> *Soon the night will come and thrash you,*
> *And the water keeps on flowing.*

To be, just once, an element, water or earth, and moreover to know you're an element. To be water: to carry ships patiently, to bear your brother on your back; to have, as your home, a thousand homes; to be an element, not just to feel yourself as water, but to wash away the bridges of irreconcilability; to press onward, to become bigger and stiller; to carry stillness into the sea, into the world. Silence is good, and humility is good. Go, Brother, go to the water; look down. Make yourself become an element! Lose the language of money, the words of an agreed-upon deception, the pomaded gestures of vanity. Fling away prejudice like a too-tight shoe. We shall meet, Brother, when you are I and I am you; when we bear the burden on our shoulders, when you see with my eyes and I with yours, when you hear with my ears, when you and I have a single heart in common; we shall meet, Brother, when we become elements, water or earth, and when we know that's what we are.

Poppek stopped suddenly before a birch and said, "Here's a well-grown tree. I'd like to wrap my thighs around it."

"Now? Does Melon need more firewood already? He still has two big piles."

"We can leave it lying here."

"I feel sorry for the young trees," Zacharias said. "You always just break off their tops."

"They don't notice."

"Do you really believe that?"

"You can wrap your bandage pack around the wound."

"Leave the birch alone, Helmut."

"Why should I?"

There was something threatening in Zacharias's voice. He took a few steps backward and repeated, "Leave this birch alone, I said. If you lay a finger on it, you'll have to deal with me."

"Are you going to shoot me?"

"Keep your hands off the tree!"

"Do you know what that means to me?"

"I couldn't care less. If you kill this birch, I can't vouch for your safety," Zacharias said determinedly.

Poppek moved toward him, showed a faint grin, and declared, "I knew you were sentimental. But I didn't realize how sentimental you really are. That's probably because you dream about your wife and the baby so much. The marriage bed is where sentimentality grows best. Your bed must be particularly soft, no?"

"One more word—"

"Oh, are we about to get mad now? Come on, I'll spare the tree's life. We have to go down to the river. Maybe we can take a quick dip, it's going to be awfully hot today."

Helmut gave the older man a somewhat awkward clap on the shoulder, nodded to him, and walked resolutely on. Zacharias followed him at some distance.

They came to the river and stood side by side, unspeaking. Unless they changed direction, they could go no farther. They stared silently at the water, each of them contemplating the other's reflection.

He looks pretty distorted, thought Zacharias.

What a fluid physiognomy, thought Poppek.

Sighing, they sat down and removed their helmets. Zacharias used his handkerchief to wipe the sweat off his bald spot and then ran his fingers through his remaining hair.

"Shall we be friends?"

"Why, was there a problem?"

"You want a cigarette?" Poppek asked.

"Yes, I forgot mine . . . It's pretty damn hot."

"It'll get even hotter. Do you happen to know whether a man with a large bald patch is more susceptible to sunstroke than one who has a full head of hair?"

"Are you alluding to my chrome dome?"

"God forbid! The subject really interests me. I have a weakness for bald heads in general. Do you know where that comes from?"

"Nah."

"Well, how could you? Once I read about someone who had the idea of renting bald heads for advertising space."

"And?"

"And it's something I think about. When the war's over—it has to end sometime—then maybe entrepreneurs will find opportunities. We two, for example, could do some fantastic business. I'll be your advertising director."

"And what am I supposed to do?"

"Listen! After the war, people are going to start advertising again, they'll have to: for first-class scrap metal, for RIF soap—the stockpiles are enormous— and, of course, for another war. What would you say, for example, to having 'Correspondence Courses for Blood Donors' written on your bald head? Or maybe

'How to Treat Young Girls on the Sofa,' or 'Your conscience will shine like this if you use Hempel hand grenades. Samples and brochures upon request.' Of course, we'll have to get some business interested in this plan. If everything goes right, we could make a bundle. All you'd have to do would be to hang around places where there's a lot of foot traffic."

"And you'd collect the money."

"I'd eliminate the competition."

Zacharias smiled and stroked his gleaming pate with patriarchal delight. "Not bad, not bad," he said. "The most important thing is to get this apparatus home in one piece . . . At the moment, though, I could go for a quick bath. We'll stay refreshed for the rest of the day. Are you coming with me?"

"Of course. But don't you think one of us ought to stand guard on dry land while the other one goes in? Better safe than sorry."

"We don't have much time. Who's going to be hanging around here at this time of day? Come on, strip. One dive will do."

One dive!

The two men quickly took off their clothes. Naked, they craned their necks to see whether there was anyone around after all, looked at each other appraisingly, and quick-stepped to the water.

One dive!

Splat said the ancient river when they stamped into it. The sun was still promising a little too much; the water was colder than they'd assumed it would be. The next step: knee deep. Air bubbles detached themselves from the bottom, climbed shakily up the soldiers' lower legs, reached the surface, and died.

Poppek said, *"Brrr,"* snapping his fingers for good measure.

"The bottom's muddy," said Zacharias. "But it's sandier a little farther on."

He grimaced and wrinkled his scalp. He found the water cold too. Cautiously, he dipped his hands below the surface and then struck and stirred it. He sank into a slow crouch, and when he stood upright again, all trembling, he thought he was sufficiently cooled off to leave his feet and dive. With force and grim determination, he squatted down hard and then shot into the air for half a second; during his flight, or rather fall, he clapped his hands together above his head before disappearing into the river. When he resurfaced, he threw himself onto his back and began to kick, so that it seemed a feeble motor was driving him over the surface. When this method had brought him a third of the way across the river, he trod water and looked back to Poppek, who was holding on to a willow shrub with one hand and carefully wetting his chest with the other.

"You coming or not?" Zacharias yelled. "When you're all the way in, it gets warmer."

Poppek didn't answer.

"Shall I come and get you?" Zacharias called again, but then he turned around and swam toward the middle of the river.

Suddenly, on the other side, a submachine gun raised its dry, metallic voice. The shots whizzed over the river like swift water birds and chirped as they penetrated the surface and sent nasty little fountains spurting up. *Rat-a-tat-tat, plish-plish, sss-plish.*

One dive!

Helmut immediately jumped onto the bank and threw himself down in the grass, next to his clothes. He lifted his face and shouted, "Dive! Get underwater!"

Rat-a-tat, said the echo.

"Head down, Zacharias!" Helmut grabbed his rifle, jammed the butt against his shoulder. How oily, hard, and stubborn the stock felt! *The shots came from there, from that stand of reeds.* He lowered his weapon again and filled his lungs: "Stay un-der! Za-cha-ri-as!"

There, in the reeds. So shoot. Twenty-eight rounds still in the magazine. Automatic fire. Come on, shoot! Send twenty-eight rounds on a little journey. Looking for their target. Rifle butt tight against naked shoulder; pressure point; squeeze. There, it's coming from the reeds. Send all twenty-eight. Faster, the trigger's impatient, feverish for death. Poppek pulled the trigger, and the bullets swept over the water and shaved the reeds on the opposite bank.

One more burst. All twenty-eight. What are you waiting for? And the bullets left the barrel and mowed down the reeds.

"Za-cha-ri-as!"

Helmut jumped up—he could do so with impunity, as he was standing behind a bush.

Of Zacharias, nothing to be seen; he had gone under without a trace, and with the exception of his abandoned clothes, there was no indication that he had ever been there.

He'll swim underwater, he'll follow my advice . . . he understood me exactly . . . he should be back here soon . . . covering fire . . . I have to shove in a new magazine . . . over there, in the reeds . . . a cartridge case between my toes . . . kick it away . . . why doesn't he come? . . . He should be here by now . . . hope the current doesn't carry him too far downriver . . .

Poppek's eyes followed the river current, and then for a moment he saw—already a good distance away—a hand emerge and immediately go under again. And after a while, he also spotted something shiny, but again, just for a flashing instant; and then he clenched his teeth in terrible pain, because the shiny thing he'd seen in the distance had reminded him of Zacharias's substantial advertising pate. He lowered his head and heard his own shots, whose echoes had long since died away, chirping over the water.

One dive!

On the opposite bank, nothing moved. The river, that hypocrite, was silently carrying its contents to the sea, past low meadows and upright forests, past the granitic breasts of the bridges, past cities big and small, past, past and gone.

A man used to dream about his wife.

Past, past and gone.

He'd dream of a child whose shock of soft hair he could clasp in one big hand, whose toy fists pummeled his nose and his cheeks.

Past, past and gone.

A man had stood up for a birch, speaking earnest, threatening words.

Everything passes: fire from the lips, wishes from the eyes; tenderness, unwavering fidelity, and heart's anguish. Only the conscience remains unblasted, that proud, bitter landscape of justice, that fortress against remorse.

Helmut hastily pulled on his clothes, haphazardly buttoned his pants and coat, stood there for a while uncertainly, as if he didn't yet know what decision to make, and then stooped and gathered up Zacharias's clothes and gun and ran back to the Fortress as fast as he could.

The effort turned his face red. The marshy ground grumbled under his soles.

Run, run back to them, tell them what you've heard and seen. Past the birch your thighs are waiting for, whose neck you'd like to hang on, and which is supposed to replace for you the fathomless adventure of the flesh. The priest, the dead Dynamite Jesus, must be lying over there. You see, he makes an excellent kilometer stone, an infallible direction marker.

To Death by way of Lust for Life, 2.4 kilometers.

No one can get lost, there are no detours or deviations or byways. Everybody gets there; some striding powerfully, some hesitantly.

As Poppek was balancing over the alder bridge downhill from the Fortress, the corporal caught sight of him and called out, "What happened to you? Hey, Poppek! You're running like you have a burning fuse stuck in your butt. If you want to explode, please do it on the far side of the ditch. Don't put my men in danger. God, the guy looks like agitation on horseback. What's going on?"

Helmut charged up the hill, stopped panting in front of Willi, and looked at Zacharias's uniform.

"What is this? Has your comrade joined a nudist colony? He couldn't wait for his baby any longer, is that it? What's become of Zacharias? That's his uniform. And his weapon too!"

Helmut wanted to say something. He parted his lips, took a deep breath, looked again at the bundle of clothes under his arm, and remained silent.

"Have they cut out your tongue? I want to know where Zacharias is. He can't just have shriveled up."

"Corporal, sir," said Helmut with difficulty.

"Right, that's what I've been for seven years. You're not telling me any news."

"Zacharias—is—dead."

"You must have swamp fever!"

"Zacharias is dead, shot, drowned."

"What, what, what? Shot, drowned, dead? Melon!"

"Yessir."

"Come here, there's a mystery to solve."

"Just a minute, I just have to stir the—"

"Let your stupid cabbage turn into buttermilk. I said come here!"

"Here I am, here I am."

"All right, Poppek: now talk like a rational person. Remember, I'm your corporal. What happened to Zacharias?"

"Zacharias is dead."

Willi pointed an index finger at Poppek's chest and said, "Wait. Everyone has to hear this."

Then he stepped to the Fortress and called in through the open doorway: "Milk Roll and Prostate, or whatever your name is! Outside! Get moving! Dreaming's over! Leave those women alone!"

After a short while, the two soldiers thus summoned appeared in front of the bench, on which Helmut had meanwhile laid Zacharias's carbine and his uniform. A little later, Thighbone joined the group.

"Listen up!" the corporal ordered, and then, to Poppek: "Tell your story."

"It was so damn hot," said Poppek.

"That's no reason to die," said Willi.

"It was hot, and we wanted to cool off in the water. But Zacharias started swimming right away, straight out into the river."

"That sounds like him."

"He wasn't quite halfway across when they shot at him from the other side with a submachine gun. Zacharias disappeared immediately, and I thought he'd swim back to land underwater. But a little while later, I saw him. The current was carrying him away. He was dead."

"You couldn't be mistaken?"

"No. I saw his hand and his bald head."

The corporal said, "I don't know how you can be so quick to tell the difference between a bald head on a living man and one on a corpse. What do you say, Melon?"

"I've never had occasion to make a comparison."

"What are the eyes in your head for?"

At this point, tall Zwiczosbirski, who had been following the interrogation open-mouthed, intervened and said, "*O moi Jesus!* He always dream about little child, and now little child here and Zacharias not. Never even got to read surprise. *O moi bosä!* We should grab gun and—"

"Shut your mouth," the corporal ordered. "I'm the one who decides what should be done here. Everybody got that? Now I'm going to make a telephone call to Tomashgrod. This can't go on. If these marsh hens don't get their skulls cracked, in seven days not one of us will be left alive. Yesterday Stani, today Zacharias. Melon!"

"Yessir!"

"The world was created in how many days?"

Proska and Milk Roll exchanged glances.

"As far as I know," said the artiste, "in seven days."

"You're an educated man, as I've always said . . . And in seven days, there won't be any more world for us. Work proceeds at a good pace down here. Seven days for construction, seven days for demolition. What we're being put through is demolition. Do you all understand me? Good, then. Now I'll make that phone call."

Willi stepped into the Fortress, and all the others watched mutely as he picked up the handset, turned the crank, and listened hard, his attitude attentive, his posture rigid. No sound came over the line. He cranked the radio again and pressed the handset against his ear, but with no more success.

Melon said, "The sergeant major . . . seems to be having a snooze!"

The corporal flung the handset away, turned around, and said furiously, "Are you crazy, or what? Your superiors don't snooze, they rest. You're the ones who snooze, goddamn it, the whole drowsy bunch of you! I'm going to have to give you more to do, don't you think? You, Ello, on Saturday you'll maintain the latrines. You think you can get away with mocking your superiors just because you know how to swallow fire? You must have taken some bad advice . . . The field telephone line has been cut. There's not even a crackle coming through the wire. These damned marsh dwellers are doing what they want with us. So now we're cut off. Opekta! Yes, I mean you."

"My name is Proska."

"Ah, I thought it was Opekta. Do you know what Opekta is? Well, no matter. So, Proska: can you splice a telephone cable?"

"Yessir."

"Good. Get ready and go repair the damage, on the double. First have Melon give you some cabbage. And you three, Kürschner, Poppek, Thighbone, you'll go out on a reinforced patrol . . . But don't even think about going swimming or getting yourselves shot! Whoever gets shot will be punished. Getting yourself shot is stupid, and stupidity doesn't protect you from punishment. Understand? You too, Switch-switch? I want to know if you understood me."

Thighbone gave his corporal a hostile look, unexpectedly moved very close to him—so close that the others thought he was going to strike him down—and said, his expression unchanged, "I understand real good. If I get little bullet hole, then I come give you greetings from Death. Maybe he give me little package for you. Must wait and see. Nobody knows what will happen . . ."

The corporal grinned and replied, "You're becoming quite a wit, my boy. While you were out, did you happen to meet the mail officer?"

"Meet, no," said Thighbone. "But smell with nose."

"Well, that's a relief. But if you start smelling with your teeth and biting with your nose, report to me at once. And now you can all go and eat. I have another letter to write—to Zacharias's wife."

The soldiers got out their mess kits, let the artiste with the fat head serve them cabbage, looked for a place—Poppek sat on the bench, Thighbone went down to the ditch, Proska and Milk Roll stayed close to the fire—and began, after an extended search for a bit of meat, to slurp up the broth and the shreds of overcooked cabbage.

Proska had to search for four hours until he found the place where the telephone line had been cut. The two ends lay twenty meters apart; in all probability, the missing piece had been simply removed.

As a precaution, however, he'd dragged a spool of cable along, and now he rolled it out, inserted the missing section, spliced the ends together, insulated the splices, and then smoked a cigarette while resting on a tree trunk amputated by a storm. A green, moist silence surrounded him, a silence that at length tired him and invited him to take his ease. He imagined this silence as a slow-working anesthetic; he didn't want to think about anything, and his muscular neck felt weak, so flabby it could scarcely hold up his head. His veins swelled up, his big, ruddy hands softened and grew even bigger. Whenever he wiped his low forehead with his handkerchief, new sweat broke out at once. The soles of his feet were burning, his knees gently trembling; his underpants stuck unpleasantly to his behind.

Apathetic, he looked at his rifle butt, whose weight was pressing it into the soft earth and causing an inconspicuous water ring to form around the metal buttplate. The innocently gazing eye of the rifle barrel was pointed at the sky.

In front of him was a largish stand of reeds, flanked on both sides by bushes and trees; behind him stood blackberry bushes and some old and already rather unstable alders. While Proska was sitting there, immobilized by weariness and the unrelenting heat, his brother-in-law Kurt Rogalski in Sybba bei Lyck adjusted his repaired eyeglasses on his nose (which was fleshy and liberally planted with little blond hairs), pushed a cube of lean bacon between his lips, took a last swallow from his coffee cup, and disappeared behind his newspaper, the *Masuria Messenger*. He read meticulously, laboriously, word by word. Nothing escaped him; there was plenty of room in his voluminous skull. After all, he paid good money for the *Masuria Messenger*, and you don't just throw away money, you want something for it, even if it's only news and not calves and piglets.

The door opened.

"Maria," he grunted from behind his newspaper.

"Yes?"

"I don't think things are looking very good."

"You mean it's going to rain tomorrow? But the cows are still making solid pats."

"No," he said, without looking over the paper. "I mean things aren't looking very good in the war. They're coming closer and closer. I'm already feeling sorry for all the geese and the horses."

"Which geese? Ours?"

"Well, obviously. What did you think, Schlie-bukat's geese? If they come any closer, shooting up everything, we'll have to slaughter some stock."

"Oh," she said, picking up his cup, "don't worry about that. We still have time before that happens. And besides, Walter isn't back yet. When he comes, we'll have time enough. And then he can help us."

"With the slaughtering, but not with the eating."

"I'll can the meat. That way we'll have it longer."

He threw the newspaper on an old-fashioned corner table, stood up, and said, "I'd really like to cancel my subscription. You spend so much money on a newspaper in these parts, and what you get in exchange is nothing but bad news . . . I'm going to water the horses now."

"Yes, go ahead . . . Who knows if Walter will ever come back at all."

Walter Proska, reclining on his amputated tree trunk, had a sudden feeling that his head was being cut off, and cut off in a very protracted, agonizing way. Something warm and slim encircled his neck, gradually clasping it tighter and tighter, though not so tight as to cause him difficulty breathing. At first he didn't dare move, because he feared the clamp around his throat would become so strong he wouldn't even have time to register it. He was afraid that the slightest movement could be the end of him.

Then the present reasserted itself in his consciousness, his muscles contracted, and he forgot his burning feet. At the same time, he realized that the clamp he'd so feared in his half-waking state was nothing but a human hand. He carefully squinted down at his rifle. It was still standing next to him. With a tremendous effort, he jumped up, simultaneously snatching his weapon, turned 180 degrees around while still in the air, and leveled the barrel at—

"I told you we'd meet again, Walter. Don't you recognize me? From the train, you remember. Your comrade, the sentry, wanted to shoot me. He wasn't friendly at all. How's he doing?"

"Squirrel," he said, looking at her uncomprehendingly.

"Did I surprise you that much?"

He lowered his assault rifle.

"You should always reckon on surprises, Walter."

"You lying bitch," he said in a strained voice.

"What's a bitch?" she asked, smiling. She was wearing the same little leaf-green dress she'd had on in the train, and her breasts were just as provocative as before, her waist as narrow as the middle of an hourglass.

"You wanted to blow up the train. Your brother's teeth hadn't turned to ashes—they looked a lot like dynamite sticks."

"You must have made a mistake."

He didn't budge, looked at her immovably, and said, "I should comb your fur with bullets, my little squirrel!"

"You want to shoot me too?" she asked, looking up at him.

"No. What would I get out of doing that?"

She took a step closer to him. "Stay where you are," he ordered her. "Why didn't you come back that time? The policeman left right away. I waited for you."

"I was too scared."

"You knew there was dynamite in the jug?"

"Did anything happen to the train?"

"I don't think so," he said ironically. "Otherwise I wouldn't be here. Did the people in your village talk about a derailed train?"

"Yes."

"I suppose you're looking for your brother."

"No."

"Who, then?"

"You!"

"How did you know I was here?"

"A lapwing told me. He saw you."

"Can that be true?"

"May I read your forehead again?"

"I don't trust this peace we're at. Are you alone?"

"No."

Proska looked around hastily, in all directions. "Who else is here?"

"You," said she. She sat on the tree trunk he'd been sitting on, crossed her knees, looked at him, and smiled.

He thought, *Maybe she really is harmless . . . someone else might have hidden those sticks in her jug . . . it's possible she knew nothing about them . . . I don't believe she would be capable of anything like that . . . too bad Wolfgang isn't here . . . then again, it's a good thing he's not . . .*

His eyes pierced her like two shots. He asked, "Did you wait for me here?"

"Yes."

"You knew I'd come?"

"No."

"Did you cut the wire?"

"Yes."

"Why?"

"I thought, maybe they'll send Walter out to repair it."

"Did you really think that?"

"Yes—but you didn't need to fix the cable. The soldiers have left Tomashgrod."

"Heading in which direction?"

"West."

"All of them?"

"All of them."

She stretched out her suntanned legs and straightened her upper body and threw her hair back with a toss of her head.

"That's funny," said Proska.

She shrugged her shoulders and waved him over to her. He obeyed. He stepped to her with downcast eyes and sat down next to her on the fallen tree.

"You don't need to worry," she said.

"I don't worry. All this will be over soon."

"All what?" she asked, and curved her fingers around his powerful neck.

"This whole swindle; all this nastiness, this fear, these disappointments."

"Are you glad I'm here with you, Walter? I am."

He nodded absentmindedly, pulled out a cigarette, and lit it.

"You were nice to me." She ran her index finger back and forth over the nape of his neck. He stared straight ahead; worried, she gazed at him from the side.

"What are you thinking about?" she asked.

"Milk Roll."

"What's that?"

"My friend."

"Is he here too?"

"Yes . . . Were your brother's ashes really in the jug?"

"I think so, yes. Are you sad?"

"No, no."

All at once, his face relaxed. He turned to her and kissed her on the cheek and laid his heavy hand on her round shoulder; he could feel her skin under the thin fabric.

He said, "I saw you around here once before."

"I know," she said. "By the river."

"How do you know that? You really seem like a clairvoyant, Wanda."

"I heard your voice. Who shot the priest from Tomashgrod?"

"Willi."

"Who's Willi?"

"Our corporal . . . Are you glad you've found me?"

"Yes, I already told you I was."

"Can we meet again later? I mean tomorrow or the day after . . . You see, now everything's going to turn out the way I told you it would: you'll wake up, and the sun will be shining, and the blackbird will be singing, and everything, all the things that tormented us so much yesterday, will be gone, blown away like feathers. The face of the earth will be healed again, and the marsh, which I think of as a weeping scab on this big face, the marsh will look friendlier too . . . When will we meet again, Squirrel? Tonight?"

"But I'm here now," she said. It sounded like an affectionate reproach.

"Do you by chance have a dead grandfather with you this time?" he asked abruptly. He looked her in the eye, hard and sharp. She said nothing.

"How many more times are you going to surprise me?" he asked. "Do you want to lure me into another trap?" He gazed searchingly at the margins of the reed stand.

"Why don't you trust me?" she asked softly.

"Because I've had a certain amount of experience with you."

"I'm twenty-seven," she said.

"A fine age," he growled, and then he flicked away the end of his cigarette.

"Come," she said. "It's time for us to go."

"Where? Do you have to go back already?"

"The day's getting tired. Come on, stand up, give me your hand. Don't forget your rifle. Come with me."

"Do you want to stick me in a jug and take me for a train ride?"

"Don't talk that way, I can't bear it. Don't remind me of what happened, and don't ask me about it either."

She held his swollen, hot hand in hers and pulled him behind her.

"Where are you taking me?"

"Wanda's taking you where it's quiet and where nobody ever goes."

He smiled.

She stopped before the stand of reeds, closed her eyes, breathed deep, and then, parting the stalks, kept moving forward. Proska raised his free arm in front of his face to block the reeds as they sprang back. A weary wind blew over them as they crackled and rustled. A marsh bird gave its warning call, *kehreh-kehreh-keekeekee*, right beside them. The air between the plants was sultry, thick, and dangerous for the blood.

"Halt," the man suddenly commanded.

She paid no attention to his order and penetrated deeper into the reeds.

"Please stop, Squirrel, I can hardly breathe anymore."

"Come on," she said. "We're practically there."

And after a few more steps, they reached a small, peaceful pond. The evening clouds, which were slowly and laboriously beginning to gather, stared into it thoughtfully.

"I could live here," Proska said. He pulled off his uniform jacket, laid it on the ground, and sat down. "Do you want to keep standing up, Wanda? There's enough room here for both of us."

Proska rolled up his shirtsleeves and wiped the perspiration from his muscular forearms. She huddled next to him. He laid his hand on her suntanned knee and was astonished when she let him.

"You," she said.

"Yes," he said.

In the distance, there was a rumbling like thunder.

"I like you a lot, Squirrel." He pressed her upper body backward so that she lay stretched out before him, and his eyes glided up and down her and finally stopped on her mouth.

"You're so beautiful," he said. "I noticed that on the train. Are there more girls like you in these parts?"

"I don't know," she said. "I'm not enough?"

"Almost too much," said he, and he bent over her and kissed her on the chin.

She stared at the thick, bulging vein that was becoming visible on his forehead and shivered.

Then he wrapped his strong arms around her,

lifted her up to him, and when he felt her returning his kiss, he bit her on the throat—on her throat, which smelled like fresh hay—and panted, "Why do you make me wait, Squirrel?"

They both got to their feet and took off their clothes, and then he moved close to her and clasped her hourglass waist with his fingers, squeezing so hard he thought she would break.

In the sparse birch forest, between the sighs
of red insects, the girl tends
her hot distress. When it rains,
she feels good.
When it rains, then all her wishes
shoot up high like chanterelles, and
hope's a Ferris wheel whose tickets
sell for half the normal price, and
sunlight's awkward, out of place then
when it rains.
Freedom dwells in moss, and on its
tender back the ashes gather
after every strike of lightning.
Girl, my girl, this rain will only
break your heart in little pieces;
flower that cannot be named, O
flower with the thirsty stem, you
will not drown before your time is
up! The tongue of night, as rough as

any ancient cat's, will lick your
fingers, lick your thighs. My girl, you
ought to listen, hear the storm! In
every war's vermilion claws, a
clock there is of monstrous size, and
from its hands come dripping down the
soldiers' final hours. The pride of
life collapses, fades away then
without echo, without voice; the
wind abducts the names and sets them
on the seesaw of forgetting.

Proska fastened the cable spool to his leather uniform belt, played with the safety catch on his assault rifle, and said to the girl without looking at her, "The day after tomorrow? I'll wait for you here."

She nodded.

"Are you sad, Squirrel?"

"No, Walter."

"Maybe the war will be over by then. I'll stay here with you. No one will have anything to say against that. We'll live in a little house, and I'll go to work, and when I come home, you'll be in the garden, waiting for me . . . My greetings to your brother. I'll talk to him soon. Go on, Wanda, in an hour it's going to be dark, and it's a good long way to Tomashgrod. Goodbye! But just until the day after tomorrow, in this very spot."

"The day after tomorrow," she said softly, and then she turned and went away.

He watched her go for a while, and seeing her walk away like that, so young and carefree, made him feel like calling her back again. But he didn't do it, for his thoughts were already in the Fortress with his young accomplice Milk Roll. Once Wanda had disappeared behind the reeds, he lit a cigarette and, a little worn out but with a heavy, satisfying feeling in his chest, began to trudge unhurriedly toward his lodgings. The evening was silent and beautiful, something like a discreet, honest citizen who gives no one pause. Citizen Night offered—or at least so it seemed to Proska—nothing suspicious. In the sky, the innocent clouds were grazing; the mute herd made one forget the war. War, yes: the wine-pressing time, when the blood is trampled out. War: the time of iron and its mighty rage, when tanks with indifferent jaws chew the landscape to death. War: the gruesome/absurd adventure that men go on when madness stings them, the days when forbearance and patience grow rare, when a stopwatch is running for everyone and nobody knows the sepulchral timekeeper. War, war, war: the shattered glass of the heart, the springtide of the red sap, the short-circuit of desire. War! Who are you, and what? You, sleep's blotting paper! You, who breathe on us the sharp breath of misery!

Proska fell to the ground like a block of wood

and didn't move. He was lying on a hill, behind an alder trunk, and he watched a young man coming up the slope, peaceful and unsuspecting, with a submachine gun slung diagonally across his back. He was a civilian. He stopped in front of a blackberry bush, bent down a branch, and examined the as yet unripe fruit at length and from all sides. He looked so utterly unwarlike, and he corresponded so little to Proska's conception of war, that Proska, who already had the stranger in his sights, became impatient, even angry.

The young civilian released the branch and looked up at the sky. He seemed to find this evening ravishing.

He's not normal, the soldier thought. *As far as he's concerned, the war is probably a sentimental walk in the country! Better be on your guard, my young friend! How can such behavior be possible? A man at war must pay attention; he has to kill or get himself killed, and if he isn't capable of that, he ought to go home. That's just the way things are. It's not my fault that I'm here, or that my rifle's pointed at your chest. But I* am *here, there's a war on, and both of us, you and I, have to act accordingly. We have to obey the war, even if we hate it like the plague. After all, we'd both like to live, you and I, and whoever wants to stay alive in a war must think about nothing other than his blood. You should go away, walk in a different direction, do an about-face, or lie down and go to sleep. But don't dare come any closer to me.*

Because then I'll . . . then I'll have to shoot. That's what you would do, that's what you'd have to do, I know, I'm sure of it. Go away, young friend, I can't take it anymore. Why are you staring at the grass like that! This is war, friend, at least for now. I can't help it if I pull the trigger right away. You must see that; now we belong together; you, the man my rifle's aimed at, you must be the first to forgive me, you alone; for you're the only one who can understand me. Why don't you give me some thought? Do you think this is easy for me? No, don't come any closer. A secret binds both of us. Why don't you turn around! I don't love you, but I don't hate you either. I don't dare call out to you, for then I might well lose everything. Who knows what you've done.

Slowly, his eyes on the ground, the partisan came nearer. His face was relaxed; Proska noticed, sticking out of the young man's left breast pocket, a marsh flower's yellow, weary head.

Ha! What did I tell you! Why are you torturing me like this? Go in another direction, you still have time. I'll give you ten steps; I cannot, I may not be more generous than that. You've furloughed your vigilance, and that's your fault. You'll realize it when it's too late. Stand still, young man, or beat it. That way, I won't need to wait so long. For ten more steps, I'm the lord of your life; ten steps. Can't you sense how tormented I am, how furious I'm becoming? If you only knew what I'm thinking about right now. I see women standing in front of the entrances to their houses. They're staring incredulously at the men coming home from the war.

They look at them with big, oddly calm eyes and speak not a word. And the men wave to them and crack jokes. But all to no avail, all in vain, because none of the women laughs. Listen, young man: I see your mother standing there too, and your wife—I don't know if you have a wife yet, but I spot her all the same—and both of them have their eyes on the soldiers. Maybe you won't believe me, young friend, but none of the women is looking for her man or her son. They don't call out for Walter or Jan or Günter or Stani; they don't shriek or wail or cry; for their eyes don't see one particular man, they see them all, all those who return home. The men are surprised to find the women aren't glad to see them back; they're surprised and can't understand why that's the way it is. But you know the reason, don't you? The women never leave us alone; they're always there, wherever we are; when we eat cabbage, when we wash ourselves, when we load our weapons, and when we're on the march. And when one of us falls, when he goes down, never to rise again, then a woman goes down too. You see? And yet some men are surprised when they come back and the women don't laugh and rejoice.

Three more steps. Now it's already too late. I'm aiming at the weary little flower in your shirt pocket, see? If anyone forgives me, it will have to be you. You must defend me, because you know how cruelly you vexed me.

Proska curled his finger and pulled the trigger, pulled it with his eyes closed. All the bullets sped away, and then the magazine was empty. He hadn't seen how the young man clutched the left side of his chest with a slightly amazed, slightly bewildered expression on his face, and how his knees then buckled and he doubled up and fell backward in the grass, rolled over once, and lay still. Proska's index finger released the trigger only when his magazine could no longer provide death with firepower. Then he stood up and listened for a while, and when he was convinced that the coast was clear, he walked in a crouch to the dead partisan. Proska took away his submachine gun and rolled him onto his back.

· SEVEN ·

H e knew that fish don't bite as well in the early afternoon as they do in the evening, say, or at sunrise, and he also knew from hard experience that when the weather's hot and the water's clear, you can have the best lure in the world and you'll still get barely a nibble. He knew all that very well; and if he had nevertheless gone down to the languid, lazy river, it was only because he couldn't wait to try out the new fishing gear his father had sent him from Upper Silesia.

When Zwiczosbirski was leaving the Fortress area for the river, he'd run into the fat, fire-eating artiste, who'd addressed him with theatrical contempt: "Look, Thighbone, if that pike bites this time and you don't pull him in, I'm going to lose all confidence in you. I'll be convinced that a fish is smarter than Zwiczosbirski."

And the tall soldier had replied with a friendly grin, "You can slice off chunk of fat from back of neck and melt in pan, *pjerunje*! If pike bites, all over for him, or I go crazy. This line pike line, he can't break. This line hold better than Stalingrad front."

The fat soldier had clapped him on the shoulder and then, hoarsely calling "Alma, Alma," had disappeared in the direction of the latrines.

Ten meters from the river, precisely far enough to keep his shadow from falling on the water, Thighbone stopped, pulled the Osram box from his pocket, and took out the fishing line and the spoon lure. The lure was a good ten centimeters long; just beyond the triple hook, which was hidden by little red feathers, there were two notches in which glass eyes were mounted, and the whole, when dragged through the water, must certainly have whetted both the curiosity and the appetite of every large fish that saw it. Thighbone didn't own a spinning reel, and in order to prevent the fish from escaping far away with both lure and line should the fishing pole break, he secured his gear by methodically wrapping the line around the whole length of the pole. When he was finished, he could hold the end of the line and the fishing pole in one hand. His preparations now complete, he scrutinized the river, took a small length of line, the one from which the artificial bait was hanging, between two fingers, twirled the shiny metal lure around his head several times, and then released the line. The lure whirred through the air and flew a good distance before diving into the water, whereupon Thighbone started pulling the line slowly backward, against the current. Now and then he could see the little decoy flashing on the surface; the game of fatal seduction had begun. The tall soldier's first catch was a bream, a broad, goggle-eyed, somewhat naive fish that the lure must have grazed, allowing its camouflaged hook to catch on the creature's belly. The bream put up but little resistance; once it was out of the water, it hung motionless on the line; and two short blows to the head from Zwiczos's fishing pole sufficed to stun it. Before throwing out his lure again, the Silesian opened a knife with a lockable blade and slit the bream so wide open that it would never awaken from its daze.

Again and again, the camouflaged hook whirred through the air; the man on the riverbank constantly changed his position, moving ever closer to the bridge. He pulled in a few perch, a smallish pike, two tench, and even a zander, and he put all the fish in a retired flour sack and hauled them along as he went. But the one he wanted to catch, the one that seemed to know him, the one his heart was set on, the wise old pike— that fish he had not seen. He was annoyed, but he consoled himself with the thought that the fish he was after might at that very moment be in the little pond or the ditch, that there would be other days, and that his would come.

He wanted to make one last and rather difficult try from under the bridge. It was difficult because he could hold the pole only horizontally and so couldn't cast with it forcefully enough. He was standing right next to a strut, and as he paused to decide where he should throw his lure and his eyes were gliding over the submerged portion of the farthest concrete pedestal, he gave a sudden start. Very close to the artificial stone, a long shadow hovered, still, waiting, in unmoving readiness.

Very carefully, Zwiczosbirski tried to put himself in a position favorable to casting; actually, he did nothing more than shift his body weight from one leg to the other and place his free hand on the strut. However, the old pike noticed the slight movement immediately and shot like a silent torpedo into deeper water.

Thighbone cursed but didn't concede the match. The lure circled and whirred through the air in the direction the big fish had swum away in. Trembling, the angler pulled back on his line: nothing. And so he threw out the lure again, and then again, and yet again; in the end, Mister Pike would get irritated and angry, and . . .

There was a mighty tug on the line, which instantly grew taut, and the fishing pole bent in a deep curve. A large shadow appeared on the surface for a few seconds, churned up water, and vanished. The man on the riverbank recognized his wet, powerful foe—Satan, as he called it—and he groaned with pleasure and happiness while sweat ran down his body. *He weighs thirty pounds*, Thighbone thought. *Just keep cool. Give him line—let him fight like crazy until tired—then we see who older and smarter—you have four lines broken, one basket ruined—now you must bite.*

The pike pulled on the line, but as soon as it threatened to break, Thighbone paid out more, and when he felt the beast relax for a moment, he cautiously drew it in again.

The struggle lasted a good half hour; then the fish's snout emerged from the water right next to the bank. The tall soldier gazed into his adversary's exposed maw with a feeling of immense satisfaction and triumph: one of the lure's hooks was fixed deep in the pike's lower jaw. Thighbone looked his rival in the eye, a calm fish eye, undistorted by fear, gazing indifferently, an eye that reflected neither pain nor death nor danger, seemed at once sinister and friendly, and rested on the man with eerie composure. He was afraid the line wouldn't withstand the pike's weight, and so he avoided lifting the fish out of the water. Instead he drew the beast so close to the bank that although its belly still rested on the river bottom, its dorsal fin was already visible above the surface. While the tall soldier opened his knife with one hand, he stepped into the river himself, holding the line short so that the pike had little possibility of movement. Then he bent down, keeping an eye on his prey's snout and tail, took a high step like a stork, and having thus caught the pike between his legs, he slowly lowered his knife to a point a little above the nape. His intention—if he didn't immediately kill the heavy, dark-green-striped Satan, which surely weighed no less than twenty-five pounds—was at least to pin his victim to the river bottom, to (as it were) nail him to the earth. Then something happened that Zwiczosbirski hadn't expected: with a desperate effort, the big, calm-eyed animal shot up into the air and turned over, and as it did so, its snout grazed the fisherman's pants. The pike fell back into the water, and when the man struck at the mass of whirling rage, his knife missed the flesh. With horror, he realized that the fish was free, and that the lure was now hooked onto his pants. He lifted one foot, aiming to stamp hard on the animal's thrashing tail while simultaneously sticking his knife in its back, but then it made another leap, an energetic, long, supple leap the man wouldn't have thought it capable of, plunged into safer, deeper water, shot up above the surface again, this time already near the middle of the river, and disappeared forever.

The line was intact; on one of the lure's hooks hung a piece of the pike's hornlike snout.

Zwiczosbirski stood there as if someone had driven a ten-inch nail into his forehead. He was trembling in every limb, but jerkily and intermittently; an observer might have thought that what remained of the electricity of life was leaving the man's body in that way. He threw his fishing pole aside, paid no attention to the lure that was still hooked to his pants, clapped his hands to his face, and started weeping and cursing in Silesian Polish. The tall soldier had a dismal feeling, like a man who has saved up money his whole life, finally takes the money, which he keeps in a cigar box, to a real estate agent to buy a house, and is informed at the agency that all his cash is counterfeit.

It was late afternoon.

Zwiczos stopped crying all at once, and when he took his hands from his eyes, his face was changed. It bore the signs of a strange, alarming exhilaration, the features of a lunatic recklessness, and what he now undertook happened spontaneously, with exactly the same assertive fearlessness with which Nature sets off on its adventures. With his open knife in his hand, he ran to the railroad embankment and without looking around or pausing for breath headed down the track. Swamp fever was rumbling in the tall, thin fellow's brain. Limping, sweating, and groaning, he ran between the rails in the direction of Tomashgrod. His mouth was as dry as a linden leaf one comes across while paging through old books.

At the Tomashgrod train station, there was no one to be seen. Nobody dashed out of the little station house to stop the two-legged locomotive, which passed by with whistling breath and drawn knife. And in any case, no stationmaster could have halted him so easily.

His steps, which had become much slower after his long run, sounded muffled and solitary on the village street. Children and chickens scattered out of his way, women watched him through windows, and several men came out of their houses, gazed stunned and incredulous at the soldier as he lumbered past, nodded to one another across the street, and then went back to observing the wild man in uniform, waiting to see what he would do. And each time he passed a house, the women who lived in it appeared as well, accompanied by a pack of serious, apprehensive children, and all of them stared and stared. Everyone in Tomashgrod wondered where this soldier had come from so unexpectedly, at a time when his comrades in arms had long since gone away and he had every reason to fear the worst, particularly since he was all on his own.

Without lifting his head, Thighbone turned off the village street, climbed over a fence made of dry brushwood, and entered a dirty, wretched straw hut. Its owner, an old fellow with weather-beaten skin, crossed himself at the sight of his visitor and asked, "*Zo Pan chzän?*" What do you want?

Thighbone gave the old man no answer. He pushed him aside and stepped farther into the hut, whose interior smelled of sweat, the coarse-cut Russian tobacco called *machorka*, and goat cheese. Thighbone kicked a pot out of his way; its contents, goat's milk, poured out over the floor.

The old man started whimpering: "*Moiä mlika,*" he murmured, "*o moiä mlika.*"

"*Tschicho,*" the tall soldier suddenly shouted, his voice shrill, "*bunsch lo tschicho ti diablä.*" Laughing hysterically, he sat down on the floor, in the spilled milk, pulled the pot closer to him, grabbed it by its handles, and brought it to his lips. While he was slurping up what milk remained, some of it trickled out of the corners of his mouth and down onto his uniform jacket.

"*O moi Jesus,*" the old man whimpered.

The soldier stood up and limped out again, knife in hand. Near the brushwood fence, the men who had followed Zwiczos were waiting; they stepped back when he came out of the hut. He didn't even look at them; it didn't bother him that some of them were holding cudgels in their fists.

Then one of the men yelled, "Hey! What did you do in there?! What are you looking for in Tomashgrod?!"

Thighbone stopped and turned to the man who'd yelled at him.

"We want to know what you're doing here. And we want to know now."

The tall soldier called back, "Oh, I have here lost my Jesus. He is fallen out my pocket." Then he laughed furiously and turned his back on the men and ran away, as fast as his limping gait would allow. For his questioners, this was the signal to go into action. They who so far had only followed the soldier in suspicious, leaden silence now started running after him, shouting and gesticulating and occasionally brandishing their cudgels in his direction. One of them even fired his revolver—which he, who knows how, had held on to despite the surveillance and the house searches—at Zwiczos in his headlong flight, but the shot missed him. When the bullet hummed past him overhead, he took a quick look back at his pursuers and realized that the distance between them and him was getting not greater but instead smaller and smaller; he looked for a good hiding place that he could escape to as a first resort and then, if he had to, defend. In wild haste, his searching eyes fell on a fairly big wooden building with two small towers and long, narrow windows.

They don't find me so fast in there . . . can hide for whole while . . . just don't turn around . . . if I run into little house, they surround me right away . . . ha ha ha! You men with fishing line . . . come and get me . . . just try to catch old pike . . .

A giant key was sticking in the door under the handle. Thighbone reached out a hand for the key, grasped it, opened the door, and locked it again from inside. Panting, he leaned against the wall and waited. It wasn't long before the men were banging on the door and calling, "Come on out, you toad, we'll puff you up good! Just wait!"

And Zwiczos laughed at them, shrilly, deafeningly.

"*Chotsch lo!*" he howled. "Come on! What you wait for?"

They understood him, they grasped what he meant, and they shook their heads in wonderment.

"Who are you?" one of them called through the wood.

"Old pike," Thighbone howled in fearsome joy. He waited for more knocking, but there was none. After a while, he bounced his back off the wall with a jerk and thrust aside the simple gray curtain that blocked his view inside the house. Before him appeared the stuffy interior of a village church. A few people were there, sitting on uncomfortable, hard wooden benches—six or seven women, and in the midst of them, looking comically out of place, a robust young man. In the narrow pulpit stood the priest, his heart laden with God and his tongue well schooled. He spoke down to his congregation in an undertone, sometimes spreading his fingers and stretching them out to the little group of listening faithful. Zwiczos, however, couldn't understand what he said; the man up there was speaking too softly.

The priest raised an arm, looked at his little marzipan fingers, and filled his lungs with air so that the word he planned to say might be given the necessary weight. Then he discovered the soldier. He forgot to lower his arm; as though held up by a taut, invisible cord, it pointed heavenward.

The soldier limped past the wooden benches to the pulpit, in one hand the knife, and in the other the key. The women and the robust lad turned around toward him, their heads moving so uniformly they appeared to be attracted by a magnetic force. Nobody stood up, nobody said a word. An old woman dressed in black—in a dress that looked as if she'd been wearing it for more than ten years, like many old women, who give the impression they're mourning their own death in advance—surreptitiously crossed herself. There was a moment when Zwiczos disappeared from their sight, when he was mounting the clean, narrow steps to the pulpit. They heard the sound of his hobnailed shoes and noticed that their priest turned his back on them and looked down at the man who was climbing up to him. And then the man's head appeared over the railing, and his throat, and his chest.

"*Rub, zo sgingest*," he said abruptly. The priest immediately disappeared from the pulpit.

Then the soldier began to laugh and curse in a bawling voice. He thrust the knife into the railing in front of him and laid the key beside the knife. His face was twitching. The priest appeared below him and went to the first bench and sat down.

Zwiczos cried, "Jesus is big pike. You catch him with fishing rod, better watch out . . . if not, he break line . . . but what do I say? No one can pull pike to riverbank . . . we all too weak. Who has enough strength is not enough smart, and who is smart has not enough strength . . . What we supposed to do, *pjerunje!*" He jerked the knife out—it flashed through the air—and buried it deeper in the railing.

Then he was howling again: "Jesus has teeth, he can bite . . . everyone must tremble for him. What we supposed to do with Jesus who cannot bite, eh? What we supposed to do with him? My Jesus has teeth, pointy and sharp . . . and so should! That is right . . . World bad, rotten . . . World like locomotive: shiny brass, dirty boiler . . . Jesus must know how to bite . . . if he give nothing but love, nothing worth much . . . nothing worth nothing. Man who doesn't get bited doesn't know pain . . . and man who never his whole life has pain cannot know what is great love . . . My Jesus is big pike and has teeth, eh . . . Ha ha ha! Cannot preach love with false teeth . . . love not pure! Love like water . . . everything swims in it . . . ha ha ha! You do not know what swims in it:

in water of love swims fear and pain and hope and sweetness and everything else, ha ha ha! And even more, you old pikes! Death swims in there too, eh, death is big big love . . . Jesus is love too, is cholera. Out one eye comes life, sweet and wonderful . . . out other eye comes death . . . soft and good-natured. Just wait. Now I show you big preachment. I can sing too, if you want hear how I can sing! Here it is, like this."

He opened his mouth and constrained his chest to utter a monstrous, bloodcurdling chant. As he sang, he fidgeted with his knife. Zwiczos's voice took a powerful running start and pounced savagely on the ears of the assembly, who sat there as though frozen in place.

The robust young man looked at the priest, and the priest looked at the youth, who rose from the gray-painted wooden bench. He walked through the sound of the soldier's thunderous singing, reached the pulpit, and climbed up the steps. The singing broke off, it splintered the way hard dry branches splinter.

With hostility in his eyes, Zwiczos scrutinized the young man as he came closer, his face calm but resolute. The knife blade thirsted for his throat.

"Come," said the soldier. "Come on. Don't be afraid. I over, you under. *Chotsch lo, moi Schwintuletzki,* I the king, *ja jestem Krul.*"

The women watched the young man's hair appear over the railing and were already wondering why the soldier was making no attempt to stop the person intent on displacing him when the tall intruder slightly lifted one foot and drove his hobnailed boot into the pit of the young man's stomach, once, twice. The youth's face contorted, he gasped for air, and his fingers released their grip on the banister. He slumped and slid down the pulpit stairs in what was not a particularly dangerous fall. And into the lamentations and wailing, into the cries of fear and the prayers for swift help from above, Thighbone howled, "Jesus must bite! Amen! Jesus must have teeth! Amen. Amen, amen, amen!"

He took up knife and key in one hand and left the pulpit. The little group of frightened faithful cowered as he passed the wooden benches, striding upright with an expression of serene joy on his face. Something had fallen from him, he was free, the foam had been skimmed off his blood.

He opened the door all unsuspectingly, without bothering to verify whether the villagers were still waiting for him outside. That wasn't important to him. He left the church and seemed not at all surprised when, cudgels in hand, they intercepted him on the street. And then he did something he certainly wouldn't have done a short time previously: he smiled, blithely, trustingly, casually. He smiled at the silent men, and some of them smiled back. No cudgel was raised against him.

Zwiczos walked by them as one walks by statues. But when he was already a good way past them, they closed ranks and followed him at a distance they apparently had no intention of narrowing. His footsteps on the village street sounded decisive and self-assured in the evening air. It always makes a powerful impression when a man walks through a village alone.

He went back the exact same way he'd come. A man came charging out of the little station house and asked, "Where are you going? What's happening?"

By way of reply, the tall soldier gave him a smile.

"The train . . . there are no trains," the stationmaster stammered.

"*Schwistko jedno*," said the soldier.

As soon as he was on the railroad embankment, he broke into a ponderous run. He ran between the rails, which led—out there, in the far distance, where no eye could reach—to the sky. His followers stood on the embankment and watched him go. They stared at his retreating figure as one would look, simultaneously bewildered and sorrowful, at a departing miracle. He became smaller and smaller, his shape seemed to dwindle as he got farther away, the setting sun struck his back, and for an instant, his knife flashed as he held it in his hard fingers. It was like a last goodbye.

· EIGHT ·

It will be dark soon, Walter. I have to read faster.
Do you still want to listen?"

"Yes," said Proska. He clapped his hand to his
forehead and killed a mosquito.

Milk Roll read in a soft monotone:

> . . . *and you can always console yourself with the
> thought that death is nothing but the last and
> probably most mysterious form of sleep. Bourgeois
> sleep—and in this, of course, it differs from death—is
> a holiday of limited duration, an operation with a
> functional purpose. But don't say that death therefore
> accompanies us for no particular reason. It well knows
> why it remains our neighbor. We, naturally, don't
> know this, and not one of us will ever learn it. Death
> doesn't condescend to speak with us, it's conceited, and*

for cause. Many a one who took up with it in order to solve its riddle has realized that the knowledge thus gained contains a new riddle. You shouldn't think that I look up to it only in fear, or that I suffer torment when it gazes at me, its neighbor, longer than usual. For then I always tell myself that its look could be meant for someone standing near me just as easily as it could be meant for me; and there are so many men standing near me. There wouldn't be any point in trying to deceive it, it would in fact be foolish to try, that is, to withdraw oneself from its sight. Death must be a man, he's proud and strong. He overthrew Father, who certainly possessed great strength, with no more effort than I would need to knock down a two-year-old child. Unusual as it may sound, I'd gladly suffer defeat at the hands of such a man as death is. It would be, it must be, a splendid, manly defeat. You defend yourself and you're grabbed hold of and you feel you're tangling with something a thousand times mightier than you. Who would be capable, in such a moment, of thinking about some guileful subterfuge, some insidious counterhold that would allow him to delay the inevitable by a few absurd seconds? No, I'm telling you, whoever wants to be a man must go down with his head high. And no one can hold up his head if he lacks capacity.

Death is a man, Mother. He may be vain, he may be unjust, he may even be petty; but you will

admit that he's proud in his solitude, severe, vigorous,
dependable, and intrepid. Just consider how hard he
has it, and how easily we would despair in his place:
before him this immense, determined mass of life, this
bunker of blood, this mountain of flesh and breath—
and he? Alone, obedient, and male. He remains
undaunted, where every one of us would necessarily be
daunted, because none of us would have the courage to
endure. Mother, I don't think anything is harder than
enduring life. If people nevertheless resist, endure, let
them not think they've subjugated it. For resisting and
subjugating are two different things.

Death, as I said before, is the most mysterious
kind of sleep. I'd like to think it's also the most
innocuous. Father will know, even though he can't
confirm it to you. Sleep is not rest in itself; true rest,
definitive, purposeless rest, can be found only in death.

"Things . . . in . . . themselves"—Milk Roll was
having trouble deciphering his own words—"are
innocuous . . . But . . . with . . . the . . . It's no use,
Walter, it's just too dark. Did you understand what I
meant?"

"And how," said Proska. "But the mosquitoes are
really bad. I could barely listen. How long does a letter
take to reach your mother?"

"Twelve days. How about yours?"

"Sometimes four, sometimes fifteen."

"How can that be?"

"No idea."

"I hope this letter doesn't take any longer to get home than usual. The day after tomorrow, I have to go to Tomashgrod. I'll mail the letter from there. Do you have anything you'd like me to—"

"I think you can forget that."

"What?"

"Going to Tomashgrod. You can't."

"Why not? I want to mail the letter from headquarters."

"It'll take you a long time to find headquarters. It's not there anymore, it's gone."

"Did Willi tell you that?"

"No. He doesn't know it yet. If he knew, he'd be easier to deal with."

"So who told you?"

"A squirrel."

"Are you making fun of me?"

"No, Wolfgang. Wanda told me. You know who she is. Not so long ago she came walking along here, in this same exact place. You wanted to shoot her, don't you remember? If you'd shot her, we wouldn't know what was going on."

"You met her and talked to her?"

"Yes."

"And she said the battalion headquarters had been transferred?"

"They pulled out. Didn't lose a man. We have no more soldiers in Tomashgrod."

"Then we're done for, Walter. Then I can take this letter and—"

"Don't tear it up," Proska said, interrupting Milk Roll. "Give it to me, I'll hold on to it . . . We've been done for from the start, Wolfgang. As long as we hang around in this marsh, we're done for."

"I'm curious to see the last act."

"You shouldn't be, kid. You'll get knocked down and you'll stay down and you'll never be able to get up again. The final act is the simplest in the world."

"At least I still have my rifle."

"So what? What does that mean? Come on, give me the letter."

Wolfgang handed him the letter and heard Proska's fingers fold it a couple of times and stick it in a pocket.

"It won't be so easy for them to get me, Walter. My father took a bullet in the head. That's his business. Me, I'd rather take a shot in the back."

"You're thinking about running away?"

"Yes, and as soon as possible."

"But that wouldn't do you any good."

"People always say that at first."

"Believe me, Wolfgang, running away makes no sense whatsoever. Where would you go? There's the river. Marsh on both sides, and them behind you. You wouldn't get far."

"I don't care. But before I go, I'll introduce a few of them to some lead."

Proska laid his heavy hand on Milk Roll's shoulder and pressed down on his collarbone. They heard the river licking at the bridge's concrete pillars and stretched their necks to listen to the weary rustling of the reeds, whose sound reached them from the other bank.

Milk Roll wanted to stand up.

"Stay down," said Proska. "If you weren't so excited, you'd know you're talking nonsense."

"Do you have a cigarette, Walter?"

"I thought you didn't smoke."

"I'd like to try it."

They each lit a cigarette.

Proska said, "Things won't get as bad as all that. I believe we'll receive some help."

"Who are 'we'?"

"You and me."

"And who's going to help us?"

"Wanda."

"The girl you met?"

"Yes. I know she's got good connections."

"With death?" asked Wolfgang ironically.

"Now that's enough," said Proska. "You know, we were together in the reeds. She took off her clothes without saying a word."

"Well, well. But what's she supposed to tell us about?"

"Do you like the cigarette?"

"Ugh. No, damn it. I'm going to put it out. But what do you get out of it? Here, you can finish it later. That stuff's awfully hard on your throat. Doesn't it bother you?"

"Absolutely not."

"Your trachea must be made of lead."

"Of steel, like a tank."

"Bulletproof?"

"Bulletproof."

"Really, Walter, what do you want with my letter? Why shouldn't I just tear it up? There's no point in keeping it. I don't think we'll be passing any mailboxes."

"Are you absolutely sure about that?"

"Pretty sure."

"Let me tell you something, Wolfgang. I'm still here. You can count on me in every way. I've already told you that. Just don't worry, we'll get out of here. Leave it to me."

"Do you have a plan?"

"Not yet. Up to now, we had no idea how things were going to go."

"When the war's over, Walter, I—"

"It's not over yet. For us personally, for you and me, maybe it'll be over soon."

"Are you thinking about being taken prisoner?"

"Among other things."

"The only other possibility is death."

"There's a third one."

"And that is?"

"Quiet," Proska ordered suddenly. He pushed himself off the ground and remained in a squatting position. "Do you hear anything?" he asked.

"No. Is there someone by the bridge? Shall I take a look?"

"Stay down . . . There, there it is again. Sounds like someone's running between the rails."

"I'll teach him how to do a somersault," Wolfgang murmured, caressing the bolt of his rifle.

"What's wrong with you? You weren't like this before. Are you scared? There, look over there! That's a man. Now he's about to jump down the embankment."

"I'll help him with that," snarled Wolfgang, aiming his weapon.

"Are you crazy? Don't shoot! If you—"

Blam-blam-blam went Milk Roll's rifle. The man the bullets were meant for tumbled down the embankment and vanished from sight.

"One less," said Wolfgang, and Proska's heavy hand slammed against his face. He dropped his rifle, started whimpering, and touched his jaw.

The assistant went into a crouch and crept to the embankment with his finger on the trigger of his weapon. He found a tall man in uniform, lying facedown and not moving.

"It's Thighbone!" Proska called out in bewilderment. "For God's sake . . ."

The tall soldier drew up one leg, stood up, and grinned. Massaging his right arm, he said, "Wish you good evening, Proska."

"Are you wounded?"

"Ah, have turned ankle. Why you shoot at comrades?"

"Did he hit you?"

"*Pjerunje*, if you make me kaput, I jump for joy . . . Was you that shot?"

"No . . . My God, you were lucky."

"Luck not involved. Was smart, that's all. If I don't lie still, you shoot some more."

"I didn't shoot at you, Thighbone."

"Who shoot, then? Pikes don't know to use complicated rifle."

"Milk Roll fired at you. The boy's nerves got the best of him."

"Ah, so not bad. If he don't miss me, then bad."

They slowly went back to the river.

"Where are you coming from?" asked Proska.

"From Tomashgrod," said Thighbone.

"What did you do there?"

"What I did there? Oh, I play priest. I go in church and preach."

"Preach what?"

"I preach this and that . . . Where is Milk Roll?"

"We'll join him in a minute or two. Say, did you see soldiers in Tomashgrod?"

"Soldiers? No. Only dust, and women and big sticks."

"That's all? How about at army headquarters?"

"*Pjerunje,* I go to Tomashgrod as private citizen, not on army duty. Who you two wait for here?"

"The moon."

"He go for swim already? You want to watch him take off undershirt and pants?"

Proska said, "Can you hear him whimpering?"

"The moon?"

"Milk Roll. He got a bite of my fist."

"You hit him?"

"Yes. He can tell you why . . . Hey, Wolfgang, you know who you shot at?"

No answer.

Proska yanked on the tall soldier's sleeve and whispered softly to him: "He's probably sulking . . . I can understand, at his age."

The tall soldier stood still and considered. Then he moved his lips close to the assistant's ear and said, "I disappear now, fast. Wolfgang must not say me hello. When he see who he shot at, he will be sad, maybe even despaired. You understand? He will blame himself."

"Suppose he asks me?"

"Then you say him, he make big marsh bear kaput."

"Where are you going now, Thighbone?"

"To Fortress! Where else? Corporal will be very mad. Ah, *schwistko jedno.*"

"Aren't you carrying a rifle?"

"Rifle? Ah, cholera, screwup by numbers. Must be on ground around here, close to river. Will make big show tomorrow. Maybe can find gun before. I search morning early. Sun will help."

He left Proska standing there and limped back to the bridge, where the deep shadows swallowed him.

Wolfgang was sitting on the ground and didn't raise his head when two fingers pulled some strands of his long hair out from behind his ear and threw them in his face. He asked hesitantly, "Walter . . . did I . . . did I shoot him?"

"Yes."

"A grown man?"

"Yes."

"Is he dead? Or . . . "

"He is grazing in the heavenly pastures. But calm down, he doesn't hold it against you."

"I'm not angry at you for hitting me, Walter. You shouldn't assume I am. You know, sometimes I wonder about myself."

"I wonder about you too."

"Won't you sit down? Morning won't be here for a while yet."

"We hope."

"Is he lying on the embankment? I'd like to go over there. But it's incredibly hard. It's awful. The trigger's so easy to pull, Walter, you don't expect much to come of it; at least, when I pull a trigger, I never think I could bring a man down. The trigger deceives us by making itself seem tamer than it is. This trigger is a Lucifer, a seducer. As long as the prey is alive and inaccessible, you have an idiotic ambition to see it lying at your feet. But when it's on the ground in front of you and no longer able to move, then you get furious. So maybe I could give the prey a kick and bring it back to life . . . I'm not going to the railroad track, Walter. And you?"

With a sigh, Proska sat down and said, "You don't need to go there, nobody's asking you to do that. Your nerves deserted you. You can never let it happen again. If twenty partisans had been in the vicinity, we'd be lounging around with death right now. You were lucky. What was running between the rails was a bear."

"There are bears around here?"

"Probably not that many."

"Is one of them lying on the embankment?"

"No."

"So how do you know I shot a bear?"

"There was a strong odor of bear sweat."

Proska smiled to himself and was on the point of telling Wolfgang the truth. He changed his mind, though, because he decided Thighbone's reservations were well founded.

Milk Roll thought: *I fired and missed, thank God. Father would have hit me too. He was like Walter in many ways. Justice doesn't reside in the fist, it resides in the head. The sense of justice doesn't depend on the spirit of any individual. Spirit is immortal . . . So what does death mean to a man who has lived the life of the spirit? At best, nothing. And in any case, a liberation from the profane cares of this world . . . Which should preoccupy us more, what's moral, or what's useful to us? What's moral isn't always useful. What's useful isn't always moral. Evidence: the theory of the State. Malice, duplicity, and cruelty are unabashedly applied. And many States in that category have a baffling answer ready, an explanation pulled so to speak out of their coat sleeves. They answer: if all people were angels, the State could renounce the use of harsh measures. Diabolical irony. The despots' dialectic. Can passions be shut up in the chambers of reason? What are laws, really? Structured, controlled brutality . . . What am I doing here? How did I let myself wind up here without resisting? And why? Because they would have shot me? Duty to the State is a kind of dried exaltation, enthusiasm in tin cans, long-lasting, shippable, absolutely suitable for storage. Two little holes and it starts dripping out already. A State should be as moral as Nature. Its only subjects should be those who are defective in morality or knowledge. Humility as its Constitution. Article One: mercy. The wind as one member of parliament, the earth as another. Who's really lying out there on the embankment? I saw him fall over. Now I know who I'll shoot at.*

Proska thought: *Who knows what her role is . . . Good connections, that's what she has. Good breasts too . . . I took no precautions. Suppose she's pregnant? . . . I could live with her. Would Rogalski be amazed, or what? And Maria! I wonder what they'd say if I should arrive there one day with my Squirrel. My good brother-in-law Rogalski . . . that thick-headed Masurian. He knows what he wants, you have to give him that. All the other farmers in Sybba had to hand over five or six horses, but he, of course, only two. It wasn't his fault that Lene got away from him. A wonderful mare, though she sure was a little wild. The farmhand, Schlimkat or something like that, has her on his conscience. God knows how many whiplashes on the head she took from that awful creep. My God, the farmhand really tormented the poor horse. Especially when he harnessed her for plowing. I was glad about Rogalski's bad temper back then . . . that time by the lake, the Tatarensee . . . he watched Schlimkat banging his boot against the horse's head. My brother-in-law Rogalski is, after all, a pretty decent guy. He went over there and snatched the whip out of the fellow's hand and beat him half to death with it. But Lene was already ailing, already too far gone. She bit Schlimkat twice. She should have bitten the fingers off the hand he used to beat her with. Lene had plenty enough opportunities to do that. Too bad that animals don't usually know how to take advantage of opportunities. We're much better at that sort of thing . . . If only we could find an opportunity to get the hell out of here . . . Anyone who makes war his profession is a criminal. The top brass ruling over us from on high, for example. While we're sitting here in the marsh. We should knock them off, 'cause then we'd have some peace. Then we could all go home. But the Gang that rules us—they're very hard to get to. They're dug in, entrenched behind their sentries. The sentries are comrades, true. And if you want to get to the Gang, you have to go through the sentry posts, but they send everyone away. The Gang must be suppressed! Even though some of the sentries must believe in it. I'd be ready to take on that task. With a good conscience, too . . . If a man goes to bed with freedom, he must defend it by all possible means. Everything's permitted to him. I wonder how all this is going to turn out . . . Damn it, what keeps biting me behind that knee . . ."*

Suddenly Wolfgang asked, "Are you asleep?"

"No, not all the way."

"I thought—"

"Mistake."

"I hit him, didn't I, Walter? I'm sure he's lying dead on the embankment."

"Go over there and see for yourself. Not a corpse in sight."

"You got rid of it, right? You hid it!"

"Go have a look, kid."

"I'll be right back, Walter. Five minutes."

Milk Roll crept along the riverbank, beside the old, ironically gurgling water, strained his eyes, looked under the bridge: darkness. Looked over at the reeds: darkness. Looked at the bushes, looked east and west: darkness. Night reigned everywhere, night and its speechless ally darkness. High over the marsh twinkled the steadfastly melancholy, shimmering faces of the stars. Wolfgang looked up at them.

"Children," he murmured.

He bent down and put two fingers in the river water. It was warm. Far beyond Tomashgrod, a shooting star streaked across the sky. A second soon followed, this one with a gleaming trail. Feigned wealth. Ashes. The mosquito air force soared and dove and produced a dull, monotonous music. Close to the ear, the mosquitoes' hum sounded evil, malicious, like the voice of a tiny, indignant Siren.

Proska fell asleep. He'd stretched out full length among the bushes, and that was his error. Had he remained sitting, it couldn't have happened, but while he was wandering in fabulous weightlessness through the grottoes and quarries of sleep, he didn't notice that five minutes had passed some time ago, that in fact his pocket watch had recorded the passage of four hours, and that Milk Roll was still not beside him. He became aware of that, however, after the river began to breathe and the cool fog of early morning rose up over the marsh. Proska's hands and back were cold. Nevertheless, he blinked insouciantly into the dawning light, scratched the hollow of his knee, yawned, reached for his steel helmet and his assault rifle—and recalled that there had been two of them on patrol. He sprang up at once and looked around.

Of Milk Roll there was nothing to be seen. He wasn't under the bridge, and not by the railroad track either.

Where's this boy off to now? You can't close your eyes for a minute without something happening. He just wanted to go over to the track . . . so where the hell is he?

Proska called softly, "Wolfgang?"

There was no reply.

"Wolfgang, I know you're around here somewhere. What are you doing? Hey! Why don't you speak? Wake up, wake up, now!"

A wild duck flew over his head with loudly flapping wings.

"We have to go!" Proska called. "Don't you hear me? Hey!"

Increasingly uneasy, he scoured all the shrubs and bushes in his vicinity, then went over to the railroad embankment, investigated the pillars supporting the bridge, searched, called out softly and searched, but discovered never a trace of Milk Roll.

The assistant clamped his rifle between his knees, took out what remained of Wolfgang's partly smoked cigarette, and lit it. He yawned and cursed.

Did he run back to the Fortress? But why would he do that? Willi would just chase him out again. As he well knows.

"Wolfgang! Hey, Woolf-gaang!"

Well, that's pretty upsetting, Proska, isn't it? Consternation turns you into a top, you spin round and round so fast you don't know what to do next. Crying out is useless, as you've noticed—Milk Roll doesn't report when you call his name. The marsh has swallowed up the boy for an early breakfast. How many possibilities of becoming invisible does the world offer? The marsh has lots of ways of making a man disappear, yet it doesn't have any more teeth than a chicken. How two-faced Nature is, and how indifferent. Just turn and look around! Milk Roll has gone missing here, and the marsh is silent, as it's silent about everything, all the same, about the countless births and the countless deaths that take place here every instant. How paltry we are; we still can't even tell whether the marsh is angry at us or totally uninterested in our presence. Milk Roll didn't reappear.

After Proska finally acknowledged that all his searching and calling were futile, he slowly made his way back to the Fortress, hoping that nothing bad had happened to his young comrade. From time to time, he halted—before the bend in the mixed-growth forest, in the middle of the blackberry bushes, and lastly as he was about to cross the ditch—always in the expectation that Wolfgang would show himself. Proska hoped in vain.

Shivering with cold, he precariously picked his way over the alder trunk and with weary steps trudged up the hill to the Fortress. In the entrance, he ran into the long-limbed Zwiczosbirski, who with a wink gave him to understand that he wished to speak to him outside.

"What do you want, Thighbone? I'm dead tired. Besides, I have to talk to Stehauf right away."

"He just this minute creep under warm blanket again," the tall soldier said.

"What's going on?"

"Ah, he wants to report me."

"For what?"

"For I stay away so long."

"And so?"

"When he hears I lose rifle, he makes double report. Then they do me like this: *pfft*." Thighbone put his index finger to his forehead. "This time he make phone call, I know it. House belong not just to people but to bugs too. And Zwiczosbirski's life belong not just to him alone, but also to his corporal. Stupid me, I rent away my life. And get what for it?"

"That's nonsense," Proska interrupted him. "Why are you babbling such foolishness? Who's guarding the Fortress?"

"Poppek."

"Where is he?"

"How can I know where is he? Must be around somewhere. Maybe latrines."

"So you left your rifle somewhere?"

"Left or lost. Nobody know for sure."

"*You* don't know."

"Yeah, I don't know."

"Don't you want to look for it? If you find it, then everything will be okay."

"I about to ask could you help me look for gun. You or Milk Roll? You tell him who he shot at?"

"No."

Thighbone stretched his neck and inspected the edge of the woods. While the tall soldier stood gazing, Proska considered his Adam's apple, which rolled up and down quickly twice, and the not very regular line of his pinched, frayed-looking mouth. Little veins showed through his thin-walled ears.

"Where is Milk Roll?" Zwiczosbirski asked.

"Disappeared."

"Dead? *Pfft?*"

"He disappeared. I have no idea where he could be."

"*O moi Jesus.* They shoot him?"

"No. I would have heard shooting. If I had told him who he shot at, he'd be here now. He thought he'd killed somebody, so he went over to the railroad tracks to see. He couldn't rest without knowing, even though I told him he wouldn't find anyone. He didn't come back."

"Is my fault, Walter?" Thighbone turned his head and looked at Proska with tired, worried eyes. He rubbed his thin fingers together, and then he said, "Is hiding. Can be he just go for walk. Maybe will come back soon. What you think? Is possible?"

"No. Wolfgang wouldn't stay gone for so long. Something must have happened to him."

"Accident?"

"Could be. I'm going to wake Stehauf up now and tell him."

"Ooh, and my rifle? What do I do, Walter? Let corporal sleep some more, yes? He get even more angry, and when he wake up, he crank telephone and speak with Tomashgrod."

"All right, Thighbone."

"You help me look for damn gun?"

"Yes, but we have to hurry. Can you remember where you were the last time you had it?"

"Must been by river. I carry rifle on back, and because always so heavy—"

"Then come on, let's go."

"Many thank, Walter, *moi Schwintuletzki*. Zwiczos-birski not forget what you do for him. One day will come, when I—"

"Don't talk, be quiet. Or the corporal will wake up."

The tall soldier threw his arms around Proska and pulled his head to his shoulder and pressed his chin against the shorter man's lank hair.

"Cut it out," Proska said, warding him off. "I'm not a girl."

"Ah, anyone can see that. But you good man."

Silently, eyes on the ground, they walked past the two birches, one on either side of them, and then moved through the tangled network of old, tough blackberry bushes to the river, passing the place where the dead Dynamite Jesus lay.

"My nose report stink," said Zwiczos.

Proska nodded and said, "Mine too. Someone must be decomposing."

"Man must stink when he turn into earth?" the tall soldier asked.

"He must, Thighbone."

"NCOs too?"

"Yes, noncommissioned officers too. It's only majors and higher that don't stink."

"So what they do?"

"Gentlemen smell. Do you know the difference between stinking and smelling?"

"Here we must turn. I have go right here, through these little bush, and then I—no, don't know difference."

"Then you don't need to know it. Knowing a lot just makes a man dizzy."

The sun stretched its legs and stepped over the horizon. It brought with it warm light and awakened a great deal of life. The sounds of the day began to wander over the marsh: burbling, chirping, peeping, rustling, crackling, croaking, quacking, creaking, gurgling. The fat waterhole belched, adders sunned themselves, a black grouse gazed wild-eyed upon his befeathered beloved, fish rose from the marshy bottoms and with open mouths goggled at heaven. Their heaven tossed them flies and exhausted beetles, and now and then a whirring butterfly—the fish looked up and nowhere else, in expectation of something that they in fact received.

Thighbone and Proska walked through the dew-laden grass, staring at the ground. The leather of their boots became soaked and soft, and their metal toe caps gleamed white. The tall soldier walked to the edge of the riverbank, unbuttoned his pants, and relieved himself. This caused him great delight, and he called out triumphantly, "Walter! Look here! I piss in his house. Hoo, he will wonder why back fin suddenly warm. Surprise for breakfast, watch out!"

"Are you nuts?" Proska asked him grumpily. "Who are you talking about?"

The tall soldier buttoned up his pants again and said, "I mean Mister Pike. Satan! Always get away. Smarter and stronger than us, I think."

"Knock it off and help me find your gun!"

They searched up and down the section of the riverbank where Zwiczos insisted he had been, but they didn't find his rifle. The higher the temperature rose, the more nervous and impatient Proska became. He stopped searching and looked alternately in the direction of the Fortress and at his watch. When they saw the bridge, the railroad embankment's steel continuation, rise up in the distance, Proska stood still and declared, in an unyielding tone, "Enough of this. We're not going to find the thing. Let's go back now."

"*O moi bosä*," Thighbone whimpered. "Corporal crank telephone and—"

"He won't crank anything, I promise you."

"But phone right there on box, Walter."

"I'm telling you, Stehauf won't be making any telephone calls. The line is out of order."

"How you know this? You do cut yourself, *snick snick*?" He made a scissoring gesture with two fingers and winked at Proska.

"Come on, man. If Stehauf gets salty, I'll give him something to gripe about."

The two men took the shortest way back to the Fortress. The sun, now diagonally overhead, burned down on them, a torrid challenge. The wind in the willows woke up and stretched, and high time too, for the first clouds were already visible over the horizon. With an effort, the wind arose and went to work.

Proska and Zwiczos left the little mixed-growth forest, bypassed Stani's grave, and were about to approach the Fortress from the side when they came to a hard stop as though rammed into the earth. Proska dropped his rifle and raised his hands; the tall soldier felt a booming and buzzing in the back of his head. He got weak in the knees, and saliva filled his mouth. When he too raised his hands, they were shaking. He wasn't capable of uttering a curse. Proska's chin was twitching at regular intervals, as though he were being struck heavily and with equal regularity on the nape of his neck. He felt his tongue swelling and thought his heart was trying to get away from him, as a gelding once got away from his brother-in-law Rogalski. The soldiers had neither the courage nor the presence of mind to act, to confront the situation the way they had probably imagined doing from time to time— in less dangerous moments, of course. Behind their Fortress, with the soundlessness of the heat and the suddenness of a clock stopping, a good dozen civilians had appeared, most of them older men—some had faces that looked like maps of the Andes Mountains— and these men, unspeaking, were holding Russian submachine guns in their big sunburned hands and aiming the weapons at the two German soldiers. They all stood there like that for a while, motionless, facing one another, and then the oldest member of the group broke away and went up to Proska.

"Come," the old man said curtly. "You too," he said to Thighbone.

He picked up Proska's rifle and threw it to a man who caught it and leaned it against the wooden wall of the fortress. In front of the bench, Willi and the artiste were standing, also with their hands up.

"There!" said the old man.

The soldiers formed a line; ten leveled gun barrels guaranteed that the captives made no false moves. The old man called one of his comrades to his side and held a whispered conversation with him, spitting repeatedly as they talked. He had a broad, energetic face, and the upper part of his left ear was missing. His hair was black and thick; at least a week's growth of beard covered his chin and throat. As the two men whispered, the old man jerked his thumb several times in Proska's direction, finally nodded, and—after the comrade he'd been speaking with had disappeared into the mixed-growth forest—turned again to the soldiers.

"You, here," he ordered Proska, "and you"—he addressed Thighbone—"here too. Corporal and fat soldier, there. *Kto*—" He interrupted himself and focused his little eyes on Thighbone, who had muttered something to Proska as they stepped out of line.

Gesturing to a giant civilian in whose hands the submachine gun lay like a child's toy, the old man pointed to the tall soldier and said softly, "*Daj!*"

The giant, dressed only in a collarless shirt and a pair of pants, shifted his gun to one hand, ambled calmly over to Zwiczosbirski, and abruptly smashed his fist against the tall soldier's face with such force that he fell groaning to the ground. Proska made a movement, but when he saw that the old man was looking at him and the big strong fellow hadn't budged, as though awaiting another "*Daj*," he held still.

"Who speaks Polish or Russian?" the old man asked sternly.

"He does," said Willi, pointing to Zwiczos, who was laboriously getting back on his feet. The tall soldier spat out blood and saliva and shook his head hard, as though throwing off the pain.

"*Ty rozumiesz po polsku?*" the old man asked.

Thighbone nodded.

Then there was a sound of excited clucking, and Alma, her claws curled, fluttered down from one of the two birches, landed smoothly in the midst of the men, ran a few steps, stopped, and looked around in confusion. The hen ruffled her feathers and jerked her head back and forth, and while all the men stared at her, she started scratching and pecking in the grass. Melon pursed his lips and called to her: "*Cheep, cheep, cheep*, Alma! *Poot, poot.*"

Alma raised her head, listened attentively, and then went on scratching.

"*Coo, coo,*" the fat artiste piped, his hands in the air.

But the hen failed to obey the voice of her fire-swallowing master. The old man made a hasty, impatient sign to the giant civilian and ordered, "*Dawaj! Szybko!*"

The giant laid his submachine gun on the ground and approached the chicken, stretching out one hand. "*Poost, poost, poost,*" said he. Every time the big man said "*Poost,*" Melon thought he felt a darning needle being thrust into his butt. The chicken raised her head again and to the astonishment of all flew to the civilian's outstretched hand, hopped onto his shoulder, then onto his head, and then onto his other shoulder. There Alma stopped and sat, a shudder went through her body, and a small, greenish-white mass fell onto the giant's back.

All the civilians laughed.

The old man shouted in his rusty-sounding voice: "*Szybko!*"

The giant immediately grabbed at the hen, but at that very moment she gave a hard push, launching herself off his shoulder—he could feel her claws in his flesh—and flew clucking back to the birch in which she had previously been sitting unnoticed.

The civilians laughed, and their gun barrels waggled.

Zwiczosbirski wiped the blood off his chin with a handkerchief. He thrust a thumb and an index finger into his mouth and felt around for loose teeth. Corporal Stehauf smiled out of cowardice and fear. The furious giant bent down, grabbed his submachine gun, and walked to the foot of the birch tree where Alma was perched, looking down curiously.

The giant took aim; the chicken eyed him as though from a great distance.

"*Szybko!*" the old man shouted again.

The gigantic civilian pulled the trigger, and as the shots echoed, Alma fell from the tree like a stone and landed with a thud in the grass. Her feet twitched once, twice, and then she lay still. Melon shut his eyes; his hopes seemed to be lying on the ground with the dead chicken. He swayed slightly, and his face changed color.

Willi observed him in amazement and then broke into a hoarse laugh. The coughing fit that followed obliged him to lower his hands.

"Hey!" the old man shouted.

Stehauf obeyed.

The old man loudly counted the four soldiers: "*Jeden, dwa, trzy, cztery.*"

With the tears from his coughing fit still standing in his eyes, the corporal said, "We're still two short."

"Hmm. *Co on chce?*" the old man asked, turning to Thighbone.

"He says . . . two men . . . still missing," said Thighbone in a crushed voice.

"He has no need to tell us that, we know it! All of you, keep your mouths shut, understand? Whoever speaks or moves will be shot. You will be taken away one by one . . . Proska?"

"Present," said the assistant.

"You will be last."

Three civilians led the corporal away; after a little while, three more took Melon, and after they had disappeared, Zwiczosbirski was likewise led into the mixed-growth forest. Proska pricked up his ears, because he was sure he'd hear gunfire soon, but no shot shattered the warm morning air.

Only the old man and Proska remained. The gigantic civilian, as he passed the dead chicken, had leaned down and picked her up. The grass where she had lain was dark red.

To Proska's astonishment, the old man, the last civilian guarding him, slung his submachine gun over his shoulder and then went away too. The assistant watched him leave like a capricious apparition but didn't dare lower his hands. He had the distinct impression that he was being observed from somewhere, and he was possessed of sufficient instinct to tell himself that putting his hands down could mean death. The watcher or watchers might well be waiting for him to do just that.

He was standing with his face to the alder bridge and his back to the Fortress. He was about to decide on a time limit for standing there like that when he was addressed, from behind, by his first name. A woman's voice had called, "Walter!" He knew he'd heard it, even though fright shot up like a flame into his brain.

He spun around in a flash.

Wanda was standing in the entrance to the so-called Fortress, her legs planted wide apart, her face deadly serious, her mouth determined. She was holding a submachine gun and pointing it at Proska's chest.

"Squirrel," he stammered confusedly, letting his hands fall to his sides.

"Hands up!" she ordered, the expression on her face unchanged.

The confused man obeyed her command.

"Come here," she said. "Come right here in front of me. I want to see your eyes close up. I'm sure you won't take offense." As she spoke, she hardly opened her mouth. She was wearing pants made of dark blue cloth and an undyed, tight woolen pullover that revealed more than it concealed. Her hair was stuffed under a cap whose worn visor she'd flipped up. Between her somewhat too short pants and her shoes, her legs were partly visible.

When Proska stood in front of her, she pressed the mouth of her gun barrel into his chest and said, "The safety catch is off. If you lower your hands, I'll pull the trigger."

He was so dismayed by her transformed face that he didn't dare to contravene her orders. He was convinced she'd fire at him the moment he failed to do what she commanded.

"You," she said softly.

Proska stared at her.

"Take off your jacket," she ordered.

He hesitated a little but did what he was told.

"The shirt too . . . And now come closer."

She pushed the black muzzle into his naked flesh so hard that he staggered a couple of steps backward. His arms shook as sweat ran out of his armpits and over his loins. The thick vein in his forehead swelled, and his feet burned as they had rarely done before in his life. He could feel the strength of the sun on the nape of his neck.

"Go ahead and shoot," he murmured in a daze.

"Why so fast?" she asked.

"What is it you want from me? Why do I have to stay here? Did you send the others away so you could torment me in peace?"

"I want to teach you something," she said.

"How to hate you?"

"Hate and love have the same mother . . . I want to teach you a feeling. You have to learn what it feels like when the weapon points its finger at you.

Look, my gun is pointing at you. It could just as well be pointing at one of your comrades, but apparently it didn't want that. I think it has something special planned just for you."

"What the hell's all this? Pull the trigger and stop the playacting. Thank God, Wolfgang—"

"He's fine," she said, interrupting him. "He didn't get a chance to send you his greetings, but—"

"He's alive?"

"He's alive, and he's not doing bad, as I just told you."

"So what do you want from me, Wanda?"

"You shot my brother, not long after we said goodbye, you and I. I heard the shots in the distance. He was hit by more than twenty bullets. We found him on a hill, next to some blackberry bushes . . . You must have done it."

"Your brother?" he asked.

"Yes, my brother." She pressed the muzzle deeper into his chest.

Proska stammered, "I did . . . shoot a man . . . that's true. And it was . . . on the day . . . when we . . . were together . . . that's true. I remember it clearly . . . very clearly . . . I was furious . . . at him."

"Why?" Wanda asked curtly.

"He was walking so . . . carelessly . . . as if there was no war on . . . He had a look . . . at a blackberry bush . . . and he was wearing a flower . . . a yellow flower . . . your brother. Was he your brother?"

"Yes."

"My God . . . I didn't know . . . How could I . . . have known? You . . . never told me. I kept wishing he'd stop walking, your brother . . . I thought . . . go back, go back . . . is what I thought. But he kept coming . . . coming toward me . . . I had to shoot, Wanda, otherwise he would have seen me and . . . my God . . . if I had only known . . . he was your brother . . ."

"Be quiet," she commanded. "And get dressed."

He did so while she looked out over the marsh. Then he placed himself in front of her again and put his hands up.

"I'm not going to shoot you," she said.

"What *do* you intend to do with me? Come on, pull the trigger. Can't you see I'm waiting for it?"

She looked at the ground and saw that a spider was making a desperate effort to get past her shoe. She raised her foot and waited until the arachnid was inside the Fortress.

"Go away," she said. "Go where I can't see you ever again. Leave me alone, hurry up, disappear! Go into the marsh or wherever you want. Just away from me!"

While Proska was descending the hill from the Fortress, the girl turned her face away from him and sobbed. Before crossing the alder bridge, he looked back at her, and when he saw that she'd taken off her cap and laid her forehead against the wooden wall, he wavered for a moment. *Shall I go back? Is she waiting for me? No. I have to go, I can't stay here.*

He walked on, becoming smaller and smaller, and when he turned the green corner of the mixed-growth forest, a civilian came toward him and ordered him to put up his hands.

· NINE ·

Proska did what the civilian had ordered him to do: he walked on ahead, made no effort to turn around, and obeyed the other's commands calmly and stoically. When the civilian told him to go right, he went right, without any ulterior motive, without checking the escape possibilities that such an opportunity offered. There were a number of tricks he could have used to bamboozle his captor, a surly, lanky youth, but on the other hand, he knew doing something like that would make no sense.

They moved along in silence over the soft ground. The civilian seemed to want to drive Proska into the river, for he was taking him in exactly the same direction from which a pure, refreshing smell, the smell of the river, was wafting. The lanky lad stank of rotgut. He was blind in his left eye; he didn't need to shut it when he took aim. His submachine gun chafed against his jacket.

Proska came to a halt on the riverbank and gazed at the water, and in the water, he could see his face and the sky. Then, over his shoulder, a head appeared; it was the partisan, furtively scrutinizing his own reflection.

"You," he said.

Proska turned his head to the side. "What is it?"

"Keep going along riverbank."

"What are you going to do with me?"

The lanky lad grinned and said nothing. He circled around Proska like a sheepdog circling his flock, never taking his one healthy eye off him.

"I'm thirsty," the assistant said.

The partisan pointed at the river. "There," he said. "Plenty water. Drink."

Proska lay down on the riverbank, supported his upper body on his arms, and drank. His arms shook with the effort; he closed his eyes, inhaling and exhaling hard between the cooling drafts. The water was nearly tasteless.

Suddenly, he felt a boot on the back of his neck, a boot that was pressing him down. He let himself fall to one side, wetting his shoulder. The civilian stood over him and signed to him to stand up. "You! Enough drink. We go on."

As Proska got to his feet, the partisan automatically recoiled a few steps. It was a completely instinctive move whose purpose was to gain enough distance for an overall view, and enough time to act if he had to. The sound of shooting came from the mixed-growth forest. The little explosions, following one another in rapid succession, were like drum rolls that definitively awakened the marsh. Frightened birds darted from their hiding places, spraying out of the treetops like black sparks. The river flowed by, green and placid. It wasn't beating against its banks.

"Keep going," the lanky partisan said, even though Proska hadn't stopped at all. The command was a preventive measure, and Proska kept walking ahead of him, walking with a heavy head, his hands behind his back, his body bent slightly forward. The railroad bridge became visible in the distance. The struts securing the supporting arches gleamed dully. The two men headed for the bridge. As they climbed up the railroad embankment, some gravel stones shifted and crunched under their feet. A signal hanging as though from a gallows indicated the track was clear. No arriving trains were expected.

"Keep going," the guard ordered when Proska slowed his pace. He was hungry. Had he smoked a cigarette now, he would have got dizzy. He would have got dizzy without smoking too. But things hadn't gone that far yet. Currently, all he felt was a slight weakness in his knees. Proska didn't ask his civilian guard if he'd eaten anything that day; as far as he was concerned, the answer was obvious. People under guard all succumb to the same fallacy: it's obvious to them that their guards are better off than they are.

"*Stój*," the partisan ordered. They were standing in front of the station house in Tomashgrod. Much time had passed since the little building had last been whitewashed. It had only one floor. A round, affable face appeared at a window, one of those faces that delighted children run after because it looks so funny. The lips of this face were moving, and although no sound penetrated to the outside, Proska's guard seemed to understand what was being said. He gave his prisoner a push.

"Forward."

The door was opened from inside, and the face rose in the opening like a sudden moon. It was still round and full, but no longer affable. Proska's head was enveloped by a cloud of alcohol vapor.

"Come," said the moonface.

"You, go in," the other commanded.

Proska was led into a bare-walled office. This room contained four chairs, one in each corner. The seats of the chairs had been polished to a shine by the behinds of the stationmaster and his assistants. On one of the chairs sat the giant who had knocked down Zwiczos and shot Alma. The giant was chewing something and gurgling as he swallowed it. His submachine gun lay quietly under his chair.

He was tearing up a large piece of bread and throwing the chunks into his mouth, like a steel-worker shoveling coal into a furnace. Never before in his life had Proska seen such a massive guy. Moonface took a seat, and so did the man who had brought Proska in. One chair was still free, but Proska didn't have the nerve to sit on it. He stayed on his feet.

Proska was standing approximately in the middle of the room and didn't know which of the other men would speak first. Given the choice, Proska would have opted for the giant. He had the impression that the huge fellow had been born in the light of truth; he didn't believe the giant capable of dissembling, or lying, or cynicism. He was a combination of up-rightness and biceps, of honest simplicity and ursine strength.

Proska waited. The soles of his feet were burning. Impatience couldn't help him; impatience had never helped him. Proska had respect for time—an unconscious humility in regard to that dimension had characterized him even as a child. Patience as legitimate self-defense. His carotid artery twitched. He thrust his chin forward, his neck muscles tensed, and the twitching stopped.

Moonface licked a cigarette paper, the giant put his gun on his lap, and Proska's guard wasted the vision in his single eye on the window sash. Proska thought he could detect, along with the reek of schnapps, a horsy smell in the room. Could it be the giant who smelled like that? Proska looked at him appraisingly. He examined the imposing phenomenon, the enormous result of a single act of procreation. *Yes, this man might well give off the smell of a horse.*

Moonface lit his cigarette, exhaled the smoke in Proska's direction, and said unexpectedly, "Tomorrow. Not today. Early tomorrow morning, when the fog moves up the embankment. Understand?"

"No," said Proska. He thrust his hands in his pockets, already feeling a little more familiar now that a word had been spoken. All of a sudden, he could afford, he could dare, to shove his fists into his pants pockets. He was hiding his fists from his enemies, and he knew exactly why. Proska repeated, "No. I don't understand."

"Good," Moonface said. Then he banged his belly against Proska so hard that it looked as though he was trying to wound him.

"Good. Once again. Early tomorrow morning, very early, you will stand facing the railroad tracks. The others also stood facing the tracks. A man should not look at his own death. Understand?"

"Yes," said Proska. He said "yes" dryly and casually; he said "yes" as though he'd been asked to confirm whether he'd received a letter.

Moonface was smoking some pestilential tobacco. The smoke seeped into Proska's lungs and made him nauseous.

"We're going away. *Jutro.*" Two men left the room. Now the giant was still sitting in one corner, while Proska stood in another.

"You. Chair," said the giant amiably.

The assistant sat down and stretched out his legs. He leaned far back, closed his eyes, and then abruptly jumped up.

"You, chair," said his watcher, ingenuously encouraging.

Proska sat down again, hesitantly, and clutched the sides of the chair seat with both hands.

The giant shifted back and forth in his corner. He tossed a short, despairing laugh over to Proska. The assistant caught it and threw it back. They played pitch-and-catch with laughs.

"What are you people going to do with me?" Proska asked.

"Do? Doing always good. I do very much."

"With *me!*" said Proska. "Do you understand? What are you going to do with me? That's what I want to know."

"Know," the giant repeated, and then he laughed so loud that the room resounded. The door was pushed open, and in came a barefooted boy who looked around before laying a chunk of bread on the floor in front of Proska's chair. Then he ran back outside and came in again with a milk jug, which he also laid at the assistant's feet.

"Eat," said the giant. "Eat, do, know."

Proska leaned forward and picked up the bread. He ate and drank hastily. He felt his strength coming back, and when he'd finished eating and drinking, he asked, "Do you have a cigarette?"

"Here," said the giant. He reached into his pocket and stretched his closed fist toward Proska. Proska held his open hand under it, and when the giant unclenched his fist, out fell a bullet, a submachine gun cartridge.

"Do," said the giant, laughing, and after a while, "I, Bogumil."

The two men had run out of conversation. They knew nothing, or almost nothing, about each other. They shut themselves off. Neither had any reason to open up to the other. Maybe they weren't capable of doing that, or maybe they refrained out of consideration for some kind of principle.

Sleep, Proska thought, *lie down and sleep. No one can keep the hour from arriving. If you can't bear the wait, the best thing to do is to sleep the time away. That's getting off cheap. That's strategic cowardice. But sometimes it helps.*

He peered out the window. The sun had already moved past noon. It looked large, invincible, capable of anything. He wanted to smoke, and a quiet rage overcame him. What he most wanted to do was to sucker-punch the giant into unconsciousness. He squeezed the SMG cartridge, and the palm of his hand became hot and moist. *By the railroad. They're going to shoot me. Of course they are, what else are they supposed to do with me? Early tomorrow morning, they'll lead me to the embankment. Someone will take aim. I won't see who's aiming at me.*

Proska sprang to his feet, and the giant, startled out of his brooding, rose and cried, "You! Chair!"

Proska didn't heed his words. He walked to the window and looked down the tracks. Two powerful fists yanked him back. He stumbled and fell to the floor. *You, leave me in peace! If you leave me in peace, I'll leave you in peace too. What have I done to you?*

Aloud, he shouted, "What do you want from me! What have I done to you, you big ape? You just wait."

He got up from the floor, dusted off his pants, and turned back to the giant. "Don't flatter yourself, big boy. Don't think you're the strongest. There are some guys even stronger than you."

"Chair, do!" the giant ordered.

The assistant obeyed. He obeyed, because in obedience lay his last, his only possibility. Had he not obeyed, not even that would have remained to him; the giant would have blown him away with a breath.

Late in the afternoon, Proska was awakened by a song. He turned his head to the window and pricked up his ears. He'd fallen asleep while sitting on his chair, and then the song had penetrated his hearing, plucked him out of a brief, salutary unconsciousness, and thrust him into the day. His neck was stiff. He massaged it carefully, his eyes fixed on the window in expectation of the men who were singing outside. Their song, interminable and apparently happy, seemed to have but a single refrain, for Proska kept hearing the same words; and although the song gradually faded farther away, became softer and softer, and finally could no longer be heard, Proska continued to stare through the window, steadily hoping to catch a glimpse of the singers all the same. He caught no such glimpse. A woman carrying a new zinc bucket crossed the railroad tracks. She was wearing a bright blue kerchief on her head, and she too was singing, but inaudibly.

Evening twilight flowed into the bare office. The air grew cooler. Proska turned around again, and the giant nodded paternally to him. *There, you see*, his nod said, or *Now at last you understand that the world outside is not for you.*

Then he stood up and stretched his massive body and yawned. All that mute sitting had made him tired. He stamped his feet; the floorboards creaked. He grabbed his submachine gun by its short, bluish barrel and whirled it around, creating a current of air. Suddenly, he was standing in front of Proska. He smiled down at him and put a hand into one of his pockets.

"Chair," he said with childish joy, and then he reached into his pocket, jerked out a beer bottle, opened it, and set it on the floor. A stale smell of strong liquor rose from the bottle and wafted through the room. Proska didn't know how he should react.

The giant pointed to the bottle and said, "Do, do."

Proska shook his head. He couldn't drink; at that moment, just the smell of alcohol nauseated him. With the tip of his foot, he pushed the bottle away, taking great care not to overturn it. A cold shiver ran down his spine as the glass crunched over the sand on the floor.

The giant bent over, picked up the beer bottle, and returned it to its former place. As he did so, Proska could see down the neck of his shirt and observe his thickly haired chest, working at high speed. He also saw the many little black points formed by the roots of the hairs on the back of his neck, and as the giant's face was so close to his boot, Proska speculated about what would happen should he kick his guard under the chin with the boot's metal toe cap. If nothing else, at least he could then get his hands on the submachine gun, and with an SMG and two magazines in his possession, he'd be off to a pretty good start.

Bogumil must have guessed what Proska was thinking, because all at once he made a vigorous backward leap and looked suspiciously and uncertainly at his prisoner. Still in a crouch, he again gestured toward the beer bottle and said categorically, "Do!"

And when Proska refused, shaking his head, the giant released the safety catch on his submachine gun. Proska waited awhile, and nothing happened. He turned his head to the window and watched the sun dip down below the horizon. Nothing happened. Then Bogumil laid the SMG on the chair, picked up the bottle once more, approached his captive, and put the bottle in his hand. And now Proska drank. He guzzled down the acrid stuff, moved the bottle away from his mouth, belched, smacked his lips, groaned, and guzzled some more. His face became contorted. He threw his head back and guzzled. He rolled his eyes and guzzled. He felt as if hot lead were flowing down his throat, and the sounds he made were "*bah*" and "*ehh*" and "*prrr.*" On the other hand, this drinking seemed to give him pleasure the likes of which he'd never known before; he imagined that, by drinking, he was expiating some guilt, some offense, and after every swallow he gazed upon his guard, checking the expression on his face. Bogumil was tremendously pleased; all anger and suspicion had left him. His eyes were beaming with uncomplicated happiness. He was standing with his mouth half open, his chin loose, and his jaws ready to snap shut, a nutcracker waiting to be put to work.

He had won.

Then he clapped Proska on the shoulder and pulled him close and threw him onto the chair so hard that its legs creaked dangerously. Proska uttered a deranged laugh; the rotgut liquor made him insensible to pain.

"*Ty*," cried the giant, "*ty, widzisz, co ja mam*. What I have here. See what I can. What I here have. Knife, little shiny knife. Little knife can kill big man. That not good. And here, what I have here? Muscle! And now what I do with knife and muscle? You watch what I can. *Tu patrz no*, look over here, you duck feather, you look."

Bogumil bared an arm, an arm thick as a stovepipe, and flexed his biceps. He lifted his eyebrows high, made sure that Proska was looking at him, and with his other hand raised his little knife over his head. The little knife hovered almost a meter above the mound of his biceps.

One final time, the giant checked the direction the knife would take when he released it—he gazed at the sharp point and the muscle in turn—and then he smiled a superfluous, pathetic smile and opened the fingers the knife was dangling from. It dropped straight down, a flashing, triumphant exclamation point, struck the rigid biceps, bounced off, and fell to the floor. The giant straightened up, grinning, and Proska babbled, "Fabulous, I'll be damned! Bogumil, you're an artist of knife-throwing! Bravo! Standing ovation! Did you hear it? Can you swallow fire too? I knew somebody who could swallow fire. There's a whole bunch of artistes in the world, huh? They're everywhere, we've got 'em, and you've got 'em too. Got any cigarettes? Pull one out of your nose, man.

Show me what else you can do. If I don't get anything to smoke in the next hour, I'm going to die
of abstinence. Boh! You don't understand a word I'm
saying, do you? Tell me, Bogumil, are you this stupid, or are you just pretending to be this stupid? Early
tomorrow morning, I guess they're going to come
for me . . . You should have met Melon, he knows
something about fire-eating. But why am I talking so
much! Come here, little brother, I want to give you
a hug."

Proska got up, swaying a little, stretched his hands
skyward, and made a few hopeless grasping movements, as though he wanted to pull the sky down into
the office and keep it there as a witness to what he now
planned to do. With his hands up, he stumbled into
the giant and tried to catch hold of him. But Proska
never fulfilled his purpose, the big man recoiled from
him, and every time Proska got close, he received a
blow in the chest that sent him stumbling backward.

"Bogumil," Proska stammered, "come here, for
goodness' sake, let me hug you. 'Cause we are brothers,
you and me. We're dependent on each other. You're
here, because I'm here, and I'm here, because you're
here. You gave me your rotgut schnapps, we'll never
try to hurt each other again! I won't shoot you, and
you won't shoot me. Come on, this comedy is over,
why do you keep pushing me away, hey! What's the
meaning of this? I just said we were brothers. Brothers,

Bogumil. My name is Walter, brother. I'll give you my sweat liner. Everything's been in vain—Stani and Zacharias and Captain Kilian. Come here!—Ow, you mad dog. You don't care about any of that, do you? Don't you want to be my brother?"

The giant pushed him back hard. Proska slammed into the wall and fell to his knees and looked up sorrowfully. And then Bogumil spoke, serious and cold: "As soon as you get beat, you want to be brothers. We know this tune. Only when you need mercy, when your dirty life becomes dear to you, that's when you talk about brotherhood. As long as you're the masters, you shit on humility and compassion. Oh, we know this tune. You thought I was stupid. You thought I couldn't understand what you were saying. I understand everything perfectly, every word and every thought. But your thoughts are so pathetic, so slimy. I ought to break your neck. Brothers: that's what the losers always say. There's no kind of repentance in the world so repulsive and so cheap. You say brother, and everything's forgotten, right? Would you have called me brother if you had been the one with the gun? And if you'd had to guard me? You would certainly not have said such a thing. It would never have entered your mind. If you had said brother to me yesterday and tried to hug me, then I would have gone along gladly, but today I can't. I am indeed here because you're here, and you're here because I'm here, but if I wanted to, I could take you over to the embankment and shoot you down. You're dependent on me, that's true, but I've never been dependent on you. Sit in your chair, stay in your corner, and don't move, because if you should move, I could fly into a rage, and then you'd be lost. Behave as though you weren't there, that's your wisest course of action at the moment."

The giant spat and walked over to the window. Proska was instantly sober. What he'd heard he hadn't heard in a dream. The bad liquor tried to persuade him not to take Bogumil's words seriously, to let them bounce off him and so lose their penetrating effectiveness. But the gush of equanimity generated by the alcohol was too weak. Proska stayed where he was, lying against the wall, dizzy with shame, his hands raised defensively in front of his face, as if such a gesture could cancel the other's presence. He was badly frightened by the change in the giant and the way he'd spoken to him. Proska had been thoroughly taken in.

Only the breathing of the two men was audible in the room. It grew dark. The darkness came in and joined them and prevented them from looking each other in the eye. That was good. The darkness encircled their foreheads and caressed them. The darkness stepped in the way of the day's last clouds. Outside the landscape fell away, fell backward into the silence. Blackness froze the trees, and the sky covered its own tracks. There was no trace of twilight left in anyone's eye. And distance was near, distance came to everyone. As always, the moon, the yellow guard dog, was on its chain.

Footsteps sounded on the gravel stones between the railroad tracks. Soon the steps could be heard on the other side of the left-hand wall and then in the entrance. The door was opened, and a man peered in.

"*Dobra noc,*" he whispered. "*Bogu, co ty tam patrzysz? Bogu, hej.*"

Bogumil slowly turned to the door. He went out.

Proska raised his head and observed that it was dark. The voices of the people conversing in the corridor could be heard through the door. Proska couldn't distinguish the voices, but he had the feeling they were talking about him. He had no wish to leave the corner he was lying in. Here, he thought, he'd be somewhat safe from Bogumil's eyes.

And all at once someone kicked Proska, a knee grazed his ear, the toe of a boot struck him in the thigh, and he curled himself up like a caterpillar. The man who'd stumbled over him stood still and listened. Proska didn't move.

"Is someone there?" the unknown person said.

Proska jumped; he knew that voice. He stood up soundlessly and said, "Yes, someone's here."

"Walter, is that you?"

"Yes, Wolfgang."

"My God, what are you—"

"Quiet, not so loud . . . Milk Roll, my boy, come here, come on, sit down. Here, I'm standing against the wall, give me your hand. Careful! There's a chair. Be calm, otherwise he'll come right back in, that—"

"He won't come in here anymore."

"How do you know?"

"He went away."

"You saw him go?"

"Yes, he went away, and now the guy who brought me here is sitting outside. The door's locked."

"Well, where were you, Wolfgang? I looked everywhere for you. I was furious at you, because I thought you'd just picked up and left on your own. Then I even started thinking they had killed you."

"Are you drunk, Walter?"

"Was drunk! So it smells like schnapps in here? I can well believe it. That Bogumil gave me some, that . . . I had to drink it."

"Do you know where we are?"

"Of course I know where we are," Proska said.

"And do you know what they intend to do with us?"

"How could I know that?" Proska said. "They told me nothing. Do you know anything?"

"No, but I can imagine."

"And what do you imagine? The railroad embankment? Facing the railroad?"

"Maybe."

"Do you have a cigarette? A butt would be enough, Wolfgang. I'm dying for a smoke, I can barely stand it. If I thought I could get a cigarette right now, I'd let them do whatever they wanted with me. My blood's getting thick and backing up everywhere. Don't you have something? Just a few crumbs of tobacco?"

"I don't have any cigarettes," said Wolfgang, "and even if I did, I wouldn't give you any. It will be a slow process, but you're going to have to get used to the idea of becoming a nonsmoker. And here you have an excellent opportunity to do that—nobody's demanding anything of you—"

"Will you please be quiet? If I want answers like that, I can get them from myself."

Wolfgang sat down on the floor next to Proska, cocked a knee, and laid his chin on it.

"Man," Proska said after a while.

Milk Roll kept quiet.

"It's all over now, Wolfgang. This is the end. When we were going back to the Fortress, they were already there, waiting for us. Alma's dead, and as for the others—Melon, Thighbone, Stehauf, and Poppek—I don't know what's become of them. Maybe they're not alive anymore. We're still alive, you and I, but I can't figure out why. Is it a coincidence? Is it luck? Why don't you answer me? Come on, are you deaf? I'm talking to you."

"And I'm listening closely," said Wolfgang.

"You listen the way trees listen."

"That's not enough?"

"Give me a break. Let's talk about something else, like how you came here."

"Good," said Wolfgang. "I want to tell you. You'll hear the whole thing, I won't leave anything out. And when I'm finished, if you think you have to strike me dead, then you have my permission to do it. I probably won't try to defend myself."

Proska laughed. He gave Wolfgang a push and laughed. But he didn't feel very comfortable doing so.

Wolfgang said, "I ran away because I couldn't stand being with you all any longer. I could have put up with you on an individual basis, but all of you together, organized Germans with a sense of duty—that was too much for me to bear. I knew almost all of you were living in the Fortress unwillingly, and I knew you were all homesick and you hated the people who sent you there and those who were there before you. It's decent enough, I suppose, to feel hatred for one side, but if a man finds himself compelled to hate both sides, then he has to admit that he's in a dilemma of his own making. Germans take denial so far that they can stare into an abyss and consider it a danger only for others."

"Just tell me where you were," Proska interrupted him impatiently.

"Where I was? I ran away fast so you wouldn't be able to find me, so none of you could stop me. I ran straight into their arms."

"Whose?"

"You know exactly who I mean, so why ask?"

"You ran to the civilians, to the partisans."

"Yes. And the partisans brought me to an officer. He'd obviously been directing their operations for a long time. He wore a uniform and spoke German. He knew all our names, and I got the impression he felt a little sympathy for me. Of course, I wouldn't swear to that. I asked him right away if he knew anything about you, and he said you were the only one unknown to him. And by the way, he was unexpectedly friendly to me."

"So that's why he's had you locked up in here?"

"He may send someone to get me early tomorrow morning. He alluded to that . . . They're men like us, cobblers and farmers and carpenters. There are some poor wretches among them, as there are among us. And I've seen that they sometimes tremble, and that they carry around the same mass of desires that we do . . . Why aren't you saying anything now, Proska? You get a kick out of holding your tongue on this subject, is that it? You'd like to blackmail me with your silence, right? I'm a turncoat, a rat, a traitor, isn't that what you want to say? The most brutal form of sadism is the sadism of silence."

"Finish your story," Proska said.

"There's not much left to tell. I'll probably—"

Wolfgang stopped talking. A head appeared on the other side of the window. There was something oddly calm about the way the head moved, from left to right, as if someone were solemnly carrying it past the window on a pole.

"The second guard," Proska whispered. "I don't get the idea that they're indifferent to us. The other one's sitting in front of the door."

The head appeared again, soundlessly and regularly following its route.

"We'll have to get used to them . . . What were you about to say, Wolfgang?"

"He can hear me."

"Are you afraid of that skull?"

"No."

"Well, then."

"I've offered myself to them. Maybe they'll take me." Wolfgang swallowed. "Idle, passive pacifism is an impotent ghost," he said. "Anyone who constantly talks about how they're against war but is content to leave it at that and does nothing else to eliminate war belongs in the museum of pacifism. We must arrive at a form of active pacifism, and, precisely in the current case, we need to be prepared to take serious and drastic action. Nothing can be done through intellectual effort alone. If we want to achieve a festive life, we first have to accept an active life. After all, who controls the world's values? You do, you alone. Things receive and retain their value only in the spotlight of the individual consciousness. Moral motives are always individual affairs. We should finally use our strength to prepare the kind of future we can find security in one day."

Proska said, "So you've switched sides. You've done an about-face. Do you know what that means?"

"I've always chosen the path of greatest suffering."

"You're still suffering right now?"

Wolfgang looked at the disembodied head, which passed the window as though on a track, and answered, "The suffering won't ever stop, it will be with me always. But I won't need to stand in a corner if we're asked one day, you and me and all the rest, what we've done to attain the great object of our desires."

"What do you mean by the great object of our desires? A life without digestion problems?"

"Your sarcasm is cheap, Walter, but it's not infectious. What's really contagious is nationalistic resentment. That resentment is the root of German arrogance and the source of the goddamned conviction we have that we're the chosen people."

"Oh, come on."

"Do you doubt it?"

"So you've changed sides. Just like that, you've turned your back on your comrades."

"Comrades? Take it from me, there's no comrade-ship without compassion. We shouldn't waste another word on that subject."

"Listen up, you Milk Roll, you. I know you have some highly educated bees in your bonnet, but there's one thing I have to tell you: when a man makes an agreement among comrades, he keeps his word. You ran away and left me to guard the bridge alone. Didn't you think about the agreement we made? You're a Judas."

"Yes," said Wolfgang. "I'm a Judas. And I became one for your sake. I ran away because I didn't want to influence you . . . Even though now it may look like my betrayal puts the others in danger, one day it will be clear that I did what I did for their own good. You know me, Walter, and you can be certain that the step I've taken will prove more beneficial than harm-ful. I've betrayed my comrades because I feel sorry for them. And you—you can spit on me if you want, you have the right."

"If I spat on you, you'd hiss like a hot stone. You're already glowing with suffering, man. I could heat up some canned food on your cheeks."

"Then do it, if you have some." Melancholy and bitterness lay in Wolfgang's response. He wished that the night would never end, that it would stay dark from then on.

Their silence, emanating from each, crossed paths in the room; their silence brought them together at an invisible intersection.

"Walter," Wolfgang said abruptly, "be honest. If we'd been born here in this marsh, today we'd be partisans too . . . But then, haven't we always been partisans? Don't we all have a tendency to see legality in illegality? Haven't we always believed that in some situations there are two kinds of law? And that you can receive absolution in two different ways?"

"Early tomorrow morning, they'll march us over to the railroad embankment," Proska said.

"They won't shoot us."

A rhythmic, crackling fear was suddenly among them. The men sat and waited. They didn't see each other, but they knew they were close, close together under the enormous night sky, and they both felt a sense of safety. Neither made any attempt to sleep. They were dead tired, both of them, but the idea of sleeping, of stretching out their bodies and still-ing their poor, anguished thoughts—that idea failed to occur to either of them, because such an attempt would have been hopeless. Two soldiers, two lumps of life, hunkered down next to each other like pigeons perching on the hour hand of a clock in a bell tower. True, the hand did move very slowly, unnoticeably, but it moved, and the two experienced men prepared themselves to plunge, to tip over, into the Gorge of Decision. They prepared themselves to decide, the first step in any activity. They were close to each other. Before, they would have been indifferent; before, they would never have had the same feelings; but now not even their dirty gray shirts separated them. They were so close to each other that each could have taken the other for himself. Good comrades.

Late in the night, Proska began to speak. He didn't say much. He groped his way over to Wolfgang and tenderly stroked his narrow, sloping shoulders, touching him with indescribable tenderness, and then he said, "Wolfgang, we're going to stay together. You can count on me. I'll do what it takes. If you should speak to the officer tomorrow—that could happen, couldn't it?—tell him I'll help them wipe the Gang off the face of the earth. He should give me a mission, the officer should. Tell him that, Wolfgang, all right?"

· TEN ·

In the afternoon, it started to rain. The water drummed on their canvas ponchos, and they kicked their feet sharply with every step to shake the clumps of mud off their boots. Their forward progress was slow at best. They stooped as they walked; their breathing was labored. Wordlessly, they stumbled over a field, past old craters in which thin, marshy water stood. Proska behind, the officer in front. The officer was young, his face freshly shaved. The war hadn't yet fulfilled all his hopes—you could tell that by looking at him. Proska was carrying out his first mission. He had changed sides.

Hunger was tormenting them when they stopped on the rim of a hollow. They looked at each other as the muffled, leaden voice of a thunderstorm sounded behind their backs. The rain struck their faces and forced them to shut their eyes. The horizon advanced so close it almost made physical contact with them. There was a dense growth of young birch trees in the hollow, their trunks shining dully in the humid air.

"Come on," said the officer.

Circumspectly, they approached a building with a roof of reeds—a building that had pulled its reed cap down low over its forehead, as if the world were none of its concern—and the officer took a little revolver out of the holster on his belt.

In the courtyard, which was bounded on one side by the main house and on another by a ramshackle stable, stood two wheelbarrows that had been rammed together, a plow, a rusty harrow, and a low chopping block with an ax buried in it. The roof of the stable was damaged, and it was easy for rain to find its way through. The windows of the main building were out of square and smeared with whitewash on the inside. The officer pointed to the ax and said, "Grab that thing there."

Proska tried to pull the ax out of the wood, but without success. The officer, who'd been observing his efforts, walked over to the chopping block, brought his boot down heavily on the ax haft, and jumped back to avoid being struck by the whirling tool.

"Pick up the ax and come with me. I think we'll find some hams here. Old chimneys are never empty."

The officer pushed open the door, which had been left slightly ajar; it squealed on its hinges and banged against a wall. Spiderwebs were ripped apart, and dust swirled up from the hall, which was only about twice the size of the bottom of a coffin. A torn, dark blue jacket hung on a nail, its pockets turned inside out. Below the jacket, on the hard-packed mud floor, lay leaves, bread crumbs, and to-bacco shreds that seemed once to have been in the jacket's pockets. A tattered stretcher leaned upright against the wall.

"I sniff something," said the officer.

He opened one of the two doors that gave onto the hall. A concentrated stench rushed out to meet them. Proska, who was looking over the officer's shoulder, could for a time see nothing but the whitewashed windowpanes.

"Come on," said the officer tonelessly.

Proska inspected the room and suddenly uttered a low, horrified cry. He dropped the ax and defensively raised his hands in front of his face. The officer held his nose, took out his handkerchief, pushed back his cap, and wiped his damp forehead.

Until recently, the room they were standing in must have served as a makeshift operating room. Two tables stood against the wall; straps hung from their corners. Those straps were used to lash down the wounded who needed to be operated on quickly. The screams of pain and the whimpers seemed still to be hovering under the ceiling beams.

Proska cried, "There, in the corner! There's an amputated foot, and two hands, and some more feet, and one of them—"

"Still has its boot on," said the officer, completing Proska's sentence. He looked, all at once, very old.

The rain drummed against the windowpanes like a tired machine gun.

In the evening, their stomachs were filled with meat. The rain had stopped. The fog, the cruel evening fog, crept over the meadows and fields and into the abandoned craters and trenches. The two men sat, full and shivering from cold, in a roadside ditch. The officer had discovered some cans and rusks in a blown-up tank. They'd eaten in silence, and then they'd smoked. And after they'd smoked, they'd trudged on, having mutely agreed to stand up simultaneously from the uprooted tree trunk on which they'd sat and fortified themselves.

The thunderstorm did not grow quiet. It was reddening the western horizon, and from time to time the soldiers turned their heads in that direction and listened to the storm.

The seconds dripped down on them, as did the minutes. There behind them, where the thunderstorm raged, shells were streaking into the earth, there trees were bursting apart, there steel was mowing life to the ground. There splinters and shards whirred through the air; there clumps of earth, hurled high, splashed down into puddles; there bodies fell over into nothingness; there, by the conveyor belt, stood death. There behind them, under the thunderstorm.

Proska thought, *Maybe Wolfgang's sleeping now. I'll see him tomorrow, when we get our midday meal. He's even younger than this officer, younger, even younger, younger. Younger? Nobody here is young anymore. They all have a job, every one of them has a job: killing and dying . . . He hasn't told me yet what's in store for us tonight. Well, there's still time . . . My footwraps are soaked through . . . I wonder what's become of Zwiczos? . . . So far, I haven't needed to shoot anyone . . . so far . . . If it comes time to defend myself, I'll defend myself. Whoever says A must say B. And I've said A . . .*

The officer jumped up. Two headlights shot their beams over the intersection. The shafts of light rose and fell, sometimes shining through the trees that flanked the road at irregular intervals.

The officer climbed out of the ditch. He placed himself on the road, legs planted wide apart, and watched the onrushing car come toward him.

He slowly raised his hand. The headlights were dimmed and then turned off completely. The automobile braked and stopped. Proska thought he could identify the almost soundless opening of a car door, and then the officer speaking to the driver.

"Come," the officer called out.

The assistant stood up, got his gun, squeezed into the back seat of the vehicle, and laid his weapon across his knees. The engine howled; the car drove on, its headlights dimmed.

Proska noticed a steel box in front of his chest. He assumed the box held some sort of radio set. When he looked at the front seat, he saw the silhouettes of two heads; the officer and the driver weren't conversing. As the automobile advanced, the thunderstorm became heavier and heavier. The air pressure made the loose windows vibrate. The driver switched off the headlights and reduced his speed. The moon, which had just arrived on the scene, stared into the auto from the side and gave the right half of Proska's face a pale luster.

All at once, the car stopped. One of the front doors was opened from outside and a head and one wide shoulder thrust themselves inside the vehicle.

"*Oj*," said the stranger when the officer whispered something to him. The two exchanged a few more words, sotto voce. Then the officer ordered, "Drive on."

Shapes flitted across the road and then disappeared again. They emerged from a roadside ditch or stepped out from behind a tree. A shadowy, spooky bustle of back-and-forth movement, like something from another world.

"Slower," the officer commanded.

Proska heard the driver down-shifting; the engine revved briefly and then started turning at a more moderate rate.

A practically square suitcase, a case for phonograph records, occupied the seat beside Proska.

A nearby explosion sent the car into a skid. A door popped open; the officer, who had almost fallen out, closed the door again. Proska was shaking. He clutched his rifle, although he knew that he couldn't use it, that it could bring him no relief. Flames shot up more and more frequently from the fields on both sides of the road. The steel, set free, sought life, sought a last breath. Soldiers gave the steel its freedom back. They gasped and called and toted and stuffed new steel down the throats of their cannon. Soldiers flung themselves onto the earth—steel-fear, steel-hope.

The officer ordered the driver to stop in front of a farmstead. With every explosion, the interior of the automobile became so bright that Proska could read the numbers on the rear sight of his assault rifle. He kept staring at the sight and didn't look outside. Above them, death roared out its greetings, heavy greetings you couldn't ignore or react casually to.

The fists of the steel turned the horizon into a carousel.

"Eleven," said the officer after a glance at his watch. The firing was now increasingly sporadic; here and there, flares went up. It became unnaturally still in hell. The whooshing noise that remained in the air even after the steel tubes had fallen silent slowly faded away. Farther off, behind the farm, a machine gun occasionally muttered, but only at long intervals, and it sounded exactly as harmless as a cicada's song.

"Into the farmyard," the officer ordered.

The driver steered the car into the yard, dodged a pump he'd been able to see only at the last moment, passed a long, empty barn, and stopped in front of a picket fence.

"This is good," said the officer.

He turned around and opened the steel box that Proska had taken for a radio set. A lever that held the lid shut snapped open. The officer manipulated knobs and buttons, scratching and buzzing could be heard, and then, above the men's heads, on the automobile's roof, a strong, regular humming began.

"Open the suitcase," said the officer softly, "and give me a record, the first one you put your hand on. There's a tiny lightbulb under the seat—can you feel it?"

"Yes."

"Then turn the thing to the right and see what the record is."

"It's called 'Come . . . into . . . My . . . Love Nest,'" said Proska, holding the record close to the electric bulb and spelling out the words.

"Give it here."

The officer laid the record in the steel box and swung the tone arm over the grooves. From a holder, he snatched a microphone, struck it with one hand several times, and blew into it, and when the noises he provoked echoed down from the roof in greatly amplified fashion, he raised the microphone to his lips and said, "Good evening!"

Proska flinched at the voice, electronically boosted to ten times its volume.

The officer went on: "Now that everything's quiet, I can greet you. Men of the Sixth Regiment: this is one of your brothers speaking! Say goodbye to the war and come over to us—or go home! What are you in civilian life? Locksmiths, tailors, carpenters, civil servants! Do you know who you're shooting at? You're shooting at locksmiths, tailors, civil servants. The uniform doesn't change the heart. Come out of your holes and throw your weapons away. Just look at the sky, at this friendly night sky. Doesn't it stir some thoughts in you? You're freezing cold, you have nothing to smoke and nothing to eat. But your regimental commander, Lieutenant Colonel von Schlachtzitz, has as much to eat and drink as he wants. In the past week, his wife in Munich has received nine packages—packages containing your cigarettes . . . Now I've said too much . . . We want to bring you a little night concert. Music will surely help you remember home better.

Lead softens the bones, music softens the heart. Here's the first record: 'Come into My Love Nest.' Good evening, and happy listening!"

The officer put the microphone back in its holder and set the needle on the edge of the disk. The record began to turn, and into the swollen, lurking silence, into the filled-to-bursting stillness of that autumn night, a phonograph droned out a pop song. The soldiers of the Sixth Regiment raised their heads up out of the mud and listened attentively. They wiped their filthy stubble with the backs of their hands, took advantage of the break to void their bladders in peace, or drew greedily on cigarette butts under the shelter of lice-infested overcoats. The men across the way knew what that was like.

Proska took out a new record while the officer spoke into the microphone. This time, his discourse was briefer; he said only, "Just so we don't get out of practice, brothers, I must advise you to put out your cigarettes. The next record is a little longer. It's a documentary recording made in God's own studio: fifteen minutes of heavy mortar fire. Best wishes for happy listening."

The driver fired a flare gun through the open window of the car. The glaring, greenish ball of light wobbled obliquely upward, stood still for a moment on high, spread a pale glow over the earth, and went out as it fell back down. Soon afterward, the fraught

silence burst, as though lanced by the rumbling artillery barrage and harsh, emphatic detonations. In
swift succession, the shells fell along the line of fire,
struck the earth, bored fiercely into it, and exploded,
flinging everything in the vicinity high in the air:
grass, branches, dirt, straw, stones, roots, water, and
soldiers. And when it wasn't whole soldiers that the
shells, with grim determination, hurled spinning
skyward, then it was pieces of soldiers, limbs, body
parts, all effortlessly torn off by the shattering iron.
With hollow thuds, fountains of earth spewed up
from the churned fields. Shrapnel, low-flying, insidious, and deft, swept the ground. And here and there
a man screamed, or gave a rattling gasp, or groaned.
All at once, one was missing a hand; another felt
blood filling his mouth; another tied off a vein; another had no chance to become aware that his face
was gone.

"The next record," said the officer. Proska handed
it to him.

"Stick together, comrades, come to us! We'll give
you time to consider while we play a new record for
the survivors of the last one. 'Alte Kameraden' is the
name of the tune. See you soon, and happy listening."

The needle ran scratchily along the thin grooves
and awakened the music etched into the shellac. The
loudspeaker blasted it out into the silence. A cool wind
suddenly arrived and carried the notes even farther.

Proska was preoccupied by his headache, which had blossomed in the back of his head and had now advanced to the left side of his forehead. He pressed his hand against his brow, but the pain wouldn't subside. He followed the torturous throbbing as it spread across the bridge of his nose and made him slightly dizzy. Proska thought, *After this record I'll ask him for permission to get out of the car for a moment . . . I can't take it anymore . . . Maria often complained about splitting headaches . . . they must run in the family . . . Why is he talking to the people so scornfully? They're our comrades, after all . . . you can't convince anyone with scorn . . . and convincing them is the very thing we're here to do . . . I've never yet found a headache tablet that did me any good . . .*

Walter Proska's thoughts had reached this point when he removed his hand from his forehead, his headache instantly forgotten.

He sat up straight and listened.

A wall, a horizon of cries was approaching them, rapidly and steadily. Muzzle flashes from the attackers' weapons lit the darkness in a thousand places. The loudspeaker was far too weak to drown out the frenzied clattering of automatic gunfire.

"Get us out of here!" the officer shouted. "Right now!"

The engine sprang to life. A submachine gun was hammering away, very close to them. Rounds howled as they penetrated the vehicle's sheet metal; two windows were blown to smithereens. When a hand grenade exploded near the picket fence, the force of the explosion could be felt inside the automobile. "They're here," the officer groaned. Proska shoved an assault rifle through the window and emptied a magazine. He received an immediate reply! Now he punched the driver in the back and said, "Let's go, for God's sake! What's wrong with this damn car?" He bent his head forward, as though that would help to increase the vehicle's speed. Shouts came from nearby. Proska heard the calls very clearly: "Keep going," they said, and "Don't stop," and "This way," and "The rats must be in the farmyard."

"What are you doing? Let's go!" Proska bawled desperately.

The car gave a jolt that was buffered by the shock absorbers, and the panting driver forced the vehicle to dodge the pump and scurry down the narrow driveway.

"Faster!" Proska cried. "They're going to block our way, and then—"

Tweee, tweee, tweee. He was interrupted by the sound of bullets striking sheet metal.

When the car reached the wide rural road, the driver accelerated. In the fields on both sides of the road, flames blazed up wildly: an artillery barrage.

Gradually, the cries ebbed away, along with the nervous chatter of the guns, and after they'd been driving for several minutes, a subdued rumbling and roaring was all that Proska could still hear. The driver was sitting behind the steering wheel like a robot, not speaking, not turning around. Proska leaned back in exhaustion. His headache began again, boring through his skull from inside. The cold night air coming through the broken window brought him no relief. The officer was slumped on his seat. He was unconcerned about the record, which was still spinning while the needle bounced around the label.

The driver stopped the car in front of a farmhouse. He and Proska got out. The officer stayed seated where he was, unmoving. Proska took a few steps away from the car and watched as the driver tried to force open the officer's door. The lock must have been damaged by gunfire or by an exploding shell.

Proska wondered why the officer didn't just slide over to the other side and get out, which was what he, Proska, would have done at once.

Then the driver managed to break the lock and open the door. The officer instantly toppled out of the automobile, struck the ground headfirst, and lay still, his position strangely contorted.

"Hey, you!" the driver called.

Proska went to him, bent over the fallen officer, and saw that he'd taken several rounds in the throat and head.

"Grab ahold," the driver said.

Together they lugged the officer into the farm-house and laid him down in the hall.

"You got any matches?"

"Yes," said Proska.

He held out the matches in the darkness and felt the other's hand take them from his fingers. A match-stick burst into flame. The driver dropped the match. It fell on the dead officer's chest.

· ELEVEN ·

It was quiet in the barn. Sometimes, to be sure, there was a rustling in the hay when a soldier turned over in his sleep, but those were the only sounds. Proska lay close to the big barn door. He was resting from his first mission. He couldn't fall asleep. On the spot where he lay, the straw was wet, so he'd had to give up the idea of using his tarp as a blanket to lie under and instead spread it over the wet straw as a pad to lie on. Through a crack diagonally above him, damp, foggy night air came streaming into the barn. If he raised his head, he could see the crack clearly, and he could detect it without raising his head by stretching out a hand and feeling the cold draft. It wasn't much warmer inside the barn than it was outside in the field. But at least they were somewhat sheltered from the rain.

So this was the life those on the other side had to endure. It was just as drab, and no better. Of course, it was in some ways better, as Proska had noticed. For example, the wounded soldiers he'd encountered were exultant, even in their pain. They knew, they had seen, that their advance was continuing, their movement ever forward. Their reinforcements called out to them jokingly as they passed. The horizon was gray, the faces were gray, the destruction was gray, and the earth was gray, but morale was high and steadily rising.

Leaves fell from those trees that were still upright. The bare branches reached skyward, clean and oddly polished-looking. Autumn. Autumn of convictions, autumn of conscience.

From the hatch of a demolished tank lying in the field behind the barn hung a hand: a signal indicating *This way to autumn*.

The barn door was gently opened and a flashlight switched on. Its jabbing beam passed Proska but stayed near him, and when at last it landed on him, it went out. Then Proska heard the sound of approaching footsteps. A soldier bent over him; it was the sentry, whom Proska was able to recognize from his Swabian dialect.

"Ya're the Prozka, no?" he asked.

"Yes. What's up?"

"Got a message for ya. Can ya come outside?"

Proska rose and followed the sentry out of the barn.

The wind assaulted them at once. Proska turned up his collar, thrust his hands in his pockets, and took a few steps in place.

"So," the sentry said, putting his mouth close to Proska's ear. He spoke to him softly, insistently, and at length; the longer he talked, the shorter his remaining time outside the barn seemed to him. When soldiers are on guard duty, even those who are generally mute become chatty. Proska, on the other hand, was growing more and more impatient as the sentry babbled on. He kept his eyes over on the spa park and lent the talker only half an ear. And then Proska went away. He left the sentry where he was and walked along the edge of the field. He bent forward as he walked, his head always a bit in front of his legs; his legs had trouble following his head. A farm lane brought him to a road, and he hurried along the road to the spa park. The trees in the park had given up their proud posture. They gave the impression that they would never recover from the plucking and hacking the artillery had especially subjected them to. Half-blown-off treetops hung like giant twig brooms over the abandoned paths, and the wild pigeons that had always been happily at home there no longer dared to return. The ruins of the health resort still smelled of smoke. The roof and two side walls had fallen in and buried the spacious dance floor and everything that had been on top of or under it. The only things still standing where they'd stood before were on a little veranda: two folding chairs with flaking white lacquer paint. For a long time now, no one had gone out there to sit on them.

Proska circled the ruins and glanced at the little veranda out of the corner of his eye. The short vein in his forehead swelled with excitement: someone was sitting on one of the folding chairs, facing away from him.

He resolutely stepped onto the veranda and said, "Hey!"

The shape rose and came toward him, as if he'd lured it with that single word.

"Walter!"

It had sounded like a soft, uncertain, affectionate call. Proska recoiled.

"Wanda!" he cried in dismay. "My God, is that really you?"

He went to her and hugged her close and took the back of her head in his big hands and pressed her head against his throat. Her hair was damp from the moist air, but he kissed it again and again.

The wind seemed to be looking for something in the ruins of the spa, knocking a tin can off a pile of stones and rushing breathlessly through cracks. Howling in disappointment, it kept climbing up a side wall that was still standing.

The man put his arm around the girl's hips and pulled the rough material of his overcoat tight against her body.

"Come," he said. "It's cold. Let's sit behind that wall. You must be freezing."

"I'm not," she said, and she let him lead her.

They sat on two dry stone slabs in the lee of the wall. Wanda drew her knees up close to her chest and trapped the bottom hem of her coat under the toes of her shoes.

"Now I'm good until tomorrow morning," she said.

"How did you manage to find me?" he asked.

"It wasn't easy."

"And how did you get here?"

"Will you come back?" she asked.

"Back where?"

"Back to me. To Tomashgrod. I've told the people there a lot about you. They're all good people. Poor people. You said once that we . . . Do you still think about that?"

"Yes, Wanda, and so we will. But I can't come back yet."

"Why not?"

"I've made a commitment, Squirrel, I've signed documents. So has Wolfgang. Now I'm on your side. The war isn't over yet. Every hour, some people have to die—decent, poor young men. If it was up to them, believe me, they'd rather live. But they can't, just because there's this Gang, this abominable Gang, that—"

"What's a 'gang'?" Wanda asked, interrupting him.

"When an evil person is too weak, he looks for other evil people. The greatest mutual understanding in the world prevails among evil people, because evil is unambiguous . . . You can argue about the truth, Wanda, or even about death, as Wolfgang said once, but evil is just evil, it can't be anything else. That's why the Gang gets along so well, and that's why not one of them has any pity for those who have to bite the dust for their sake."

"Then when will you come back to Tomashgrod?"

"When the evil ones are in the ground."

"How long will that take?"

"Nobody can predict that. But the stronger we are, the sooner they'll disappear."

"And if the evil ones are stronger than your men?"

"The evil ones are strong only on the outside. If you want to kill them, you have to strike them on the inside."

"I don't understand that."

"But you will soon."

They stopped talking; he flicked away his cigarette butt, took her hand, and rubbed it between his own warm hands. The moon broke through for a brief while and looked down glumly on the two of them. It showed itself only when the heavy, low clouds rushing across the night sky allowed it to.

After a while, Proska said, "Have you forgotten it?"

"What?"

"Your brother's bad luck . . . I saw you crying when I went away from the Fortress."

She didn't answer.

"Do you know," he asked, "what became of Poppek and the corporal?"

Wanda shook her head.

"I don't mean to torment you, Squirrel. You mustn't take offense if I ask you these questions."

She closed her eyes and ran her hand through his lank hair. The corners of her mouth twitched.

"You," she said.

"You're not crying, are you, Wanda?"

"No."

"Will you wait for me? I'll come back one day."

"Yes, Walter. I will wait. I can wait. I'll think about you every day."

"My Squirrel."

"You."

"Maybe you'll be sleeping when I come back. I won't wake you up right away, I'll go close to your bed and watch your face, and all at once you'll feel someone looking at you, you'll open your eyes, and at first you'll be surprised to see me. Then you'll smile and pull your warm arms out from under the blanket and put them around me."

"Will it be like that?"

"Yes," said he, "it'll be like that. And if you're not asleep in your bed when I come back, then maybe you'll be waiting for me in the train station in Prowursk. You'll be glad, and you'll wave to me, and I'll ask, 'Can I travel with you? Not far, only to the marshes. I can pay you if you want . . .' Then what will you say, Squirrel?"

"I'll threaten you!"

"You know what? I could get up right now and take the train with you to Tomashgrod."

"Or walk there," she said.

"I wouldn't mind walking the whole long way."

"The roads are pretty soggy . . ."

"So what? If they're wet and slippery, we can slide home."

They were holding hands tightly, as if nothing could separate them anymore and there would be no more farewells.

"Listen," she said shyly.

"Yes?"

"I've brought you some cigarettes, Walter, not very many, but all I could get in Tomashgrod. The people back home are poor, and most of them smoke their tobacco in pipes. I figured you'd be glad to get a few cigarettes, especially since you don't have any."

"Squirrel," he said, and he pressed her hand to his chest.

"Here," she said. "I sewed the cigarettes into a piece of tarp. At first I was just going to give them to the sentry."

He laid his head on her lap and stared into the darkness.

"Squirrel?" he asked after a while.

"Yes?"

"Maybe we'll have a baby or two, later?"

"No. We'll have a baby soon, Walter."

He said, "I'm sure it won't be long before I come back."

She rested her hand on his head and said, "We'll have a baby sooner than that. I came here to tell you. I asked many people about you, and you weren't easy to find. The baby will come at the end of winter. The people in Tomashgrod found out about it before you did . . . Are you sad now because we're going to have a baby so soon? Why don't you say something?"

She touched his face here and there with her fingers.

Proska sat up and stammered, "I knew it, I was waiting for you to tell me. If I could, I'd go home with you today, right now. If only . . . Now the wait won't be so hard for you. I'll be with you, even when

I'm not there. If you knew how happy I am! We'll see each other again tomorrow, Wanda, won't we? Maybe we'll stay in the barn for a whole week . . . You're different from before, I hardly recognize you. Why is that?"

"You," she said. "Aren't you cold? You don't have an overcoat on."

"I'm not cold," he said.

"You're liable to get sick."

"No. That doesn't happen so fast with me, I'm tough. Will you stay here, Wanda? Can you? Maybe just one day?"

"Yes, Walter."

"And we'll see each other tomorrow?"

"Yes."

"Here at the spa?"

"Wherever you want, Walter. If you say I should come here, I'll come here, and if you want us to meet somewhere else, I'll go there."

"How was your trip? Was it hard?"

"Not hard. Lots of soldiers helped me."

"Later," Proska said, "we'll go on a long journey together, but not on foot."

"Where to?" she asked softly.

"To Sybba. It's a village. I'm sure you have no idea where Sybba is. It's not very big, it sits between a lake and an old pine forest. The lake's called the Lycksee, and the forest is the Sybba Forest. We'll go there,

Wanda. We'll go to my brother-in-law's place. His name is Kurt Rogalski, he's a farmer, and something of a landowner. My sister Maria is his wife. You'll like her. And from Sybba we'll take the train to Magdeburg. I have an uncle who lives there, my father's brother. He works for the savings bank there. Do you know what a savings bank is?"

They were sitting close together, warming each other. They fell silent, and their silence was enough for them. The other's presence satisfied every wish; Walter and Wanda felt a deep, simple contentment, and their satisfaction—a holiday, a period of repose, hard to obtain and hard to possess—rooted itself in their hearts. In the distance, they could hear the drone of a single airplane: regular, monotonic, a modern lullaby.

"I can't stay here much longer," said Proska. She stretched out her legs and started to get up.

"Stay a little longer," he said. "I have time for one more cigarette."

He smoked the cigarette to the end, and then they stood up and embraced, and he took her by the hand and led her through the ruins of the health resort, over the little veranda with the forgotten chairs and through the deserted park.

"Will you come tomorrow, Wanda?"

"Yes."

"At eight?"

"Yes, if you want."

"And will you find a place where you can sleep?"

"I've already got one."

"That's good, then."

He embraced her and kissed her, waved to her, and went away.

When he was gone, she returned to the ruined spa, sat down where the two of them had been sitting shortly before, caught the bottom hem of her overcoat under the tips of her shoes, and laid her chin on her knee.

Proska passed the sentry wordlessly, carefully opened the barn door, and lay down on his tarp. He fell asleep fast. After two hours, he was awakened again. A truck was waiting for him with its engine running.

· TWELVE ·

The sharpshooters were nervous. They didn't look through their telescopic sights but rather braced their chests against the edge of the trench and wiggled their fingers in their gloves and their toes in their boots, and some of them shut their left eyes tight and tried to make out a target amid the rigid branches of the bushes. From day to day, the sharpshooters counted for less and less, every day they lost a bit of significance, and they were no longer asked, as they used to be in former days, about their kill tally. Their rifle butts were without question thoroughly notched, but those were old notches, they weren't even shiny anymore. There was no sharpshooter who didn't long for a return to the varied and entertaining days of static combat, and from time to time some of them would make use of the pauses between attacks to rhapsodize about the past with reciprocal memories of "fun targets." The Siberian sharpshooters were good. Proska knew them because, previously, he'd had to face them. Now, however, he was in their midst; as special adviser to their commander, he could observe them up close, and he was surprised by their modesty and by their strangely innocent faces. Every now and then he imagined they were secretly drawing a bead on him, and sometimes he turned around expecting to discover the mouth of a rifle with a telescopic sight pointed in his direction, but he invariably found only an indulgent smile or an inscrutable look. Had it not been for the daily attacks—attacks that brought them farther and farther west—Proska would have had no source of new strength and confidence. But things kept moving forward, and the fact of their steady advance seemed, in retrospect, to validate his decision in a very demonstrative fashion, and that fact, moreover, appeared to confirm that he was on the side of the just, for the just—Proska thought—always succeed in the end. He mentally calculated how long the Gang could hold out, and how much longer it would be, in the worst case, until he was free again. Proska was prepared to face the consequences of his decision. But he hadn't yet pointed his automatic weapon at his former comrades in arms.

Over on the other side, they still had no clue. Forty minutes!

Those on the attacking side had submitted themselves to the hands of the clock, to those lean, pedantic functionaries of time. They had synchronized their watches.

Forty minutes.

Wait, be patient, obey. See how the dial records every second, authenticates, stamps, and signs it. One second of life, certified by the minute hand's tiny movement. No drop of time falls outside the measuring cup, nothing gets lost. Time can never be outwitted.

Twenty-one . . . twenty-two . . . twenty-three . . .

Time—what is it? A jackdaw that nests in the old tower clock? A cock with red-rimmed, angry eyes?

A patient, turbid river?

Proska pulled out his pocket watch.

He reflected: *When the shell goes in over there, jump up. Thirty steps down to the stream, spring over it, hit the dirt. After the shell explodes, they'll stick their heads and their weapons up over the edge of their trench. Empty a magazine, rapid fire, get up, move forward. Stay calm. On the slope, get down again. No cover. Play dead. If no farther advance is possible, lie there like a corpse, don't move.*

"How much longer?" Wolfgang asked.

"Twenty-five minutes."

Such minutes have to be endured individually; they're minutes when men are cruelly alone; expelled from the musty cellar of collectivity, they think only for themselves. Suddenly, everyone would like to have a watch, they'd like to keep an eye on the dial as the hands go about their business; they'd like to count along, to be certain the watch isn't fooling them. The minute hand plays on their nerves; they urge it on: faster, faster. *But that makes no impression on you. You're incorruptible. I can offer you whatever I want. You have no nerves. You don't go slower, you don't go faster. Hellish calm.*

"Wolfgang?"

"What?"

"If we get stopped, I'm going to throw myself down and play dead. As long as it's daylight, we won't get out of this valley alive."

"Yes."

"Are you cold?"

"Yes."

"You see that peninsula over there? We used to call it Wittko."

"Why are you telling me this?"

"Beyond Wittko is Sybba, and Sybba's where my brother-in-law and my sister Maria live."

"Ah."

Sixteen minutes.

The snow glistened bluishly. The oblivious sun pulled up over the horizon.

From time to time, there was some isolated, irregular shooting from the troops on the other side, who fired as though trying to distract themselves. Proska laid his pocket watch on the edge of the trench.

"Do you plan to leave it there?" Wolfgang asked.

"Yes, but only for fifteen minutes."

"And then?"

"Then I'll put it back in my pocket."

. . .

Five minutes.

The men were silent, waiting for the liberating signal, the firing of the first shell, the first impact. Then they would heave themselves up off the ground, a short, powerful thrust, and charge down the slope, trampling the still-unscathed snow cover. They closed their eyes, ground their teeth, felt that no one could help them, that they were alone. Proska watched the small patch of snow he was breathing on start to melt. The shimmering, frozen surface grew loose, brittle, sank deeper and deeper with each exhalation, and finally caved in.

Propelled by the long-awaited and yet surprisingly sudden artillery onslaught, the men leaped up and looked over at the opposing line of trenches, where snow, frozen chunks of earth, and pieces of wood were spinning and plunging around as though in a whirlwind. They opened their mouths, and their cries exploded amid the exploding shells, which were now landing in quick succession.

Proska jumped over a frozen brook. He rammed a fresh magazine into his rifle and emptied it into the parapet of the trench. Then he snatched two egg-shaped hand grenades from his bag, shifted his weight to one leg, and prepared to advance. As in a fever, he saw the man who had been the first to climb the slope wildly firing his submachine gun in all directions. Suddenly, the man dropped his gun, clutched at his chest with both hands, collapsed, and rolled back down the incline, rolled down to Proska's feet. The assistant tripped over him and fell headlong to the ground.

Go on, go on, don't stay on the ground, you could be forgotten, go on, forward. Why do you have eyes in the front of your head, Proska? Two hand grenades, one at a time, index finger in the pull-ring, turn, yank. One fast, one slow, the second hand will not be influenced as it moves around the dial. Conform to the unit's tempo. Someone's lying next to me, red snow where he collapsed, line of red drops, treasure hunt, Maria, his face is still warm, Wolfgang's letter.

Proska heard a groan. It came from the man he'd stumbled over. He crawled to him and lay close beside him. He could feel the warmth in the fallen man's body.

"Where are you hit?"

The wounded man remained silent.

Proska poked him in the thigh and repeated, "Where are you hit, man? I'll bring you to the rear."

He straightened up and looked around.

The snow in front of him sprayed high in the air. Proska immediately threw himself down again. He couldn't count the brown clumps that lay on the snow like big, fantastic molehills. He heard no more cries, and he knew that the strength he and the others had summoned up, the nervous torment they'd suffered during the long wait, had all been pointless and futile. The objective had not been reached. Otherwise he'd have been able to straighten up without bullets immediately striking the ground around him.

Proska made a second attempt. His intention was to spring up and beat a retreat at top speed, without stopping until he reached safety. But when his back rose above the wounded man, Proska felt for a second as though he'd been scratched with the sharp lid of a tin can.

The wounded man gasped for breath.

"I can't help you. How can I get you out of here? If I do so much as move—haven't you noticed that they shoot at every movement? Play dead, lie still. If they counterattack, that won't do any good either, we'll just freeze to death here, you and me. Don't keep groaning so much—they might hear you, and if they hear you, they'll shoot, you understand? We have to play dead. I can't help you . . . My God, there you go, groaning again. Be quiet, I tell you. Don't be so careless. Swallow your pain and be quiet, otherwise . . ."

Heavy gray clouds pushed their way in front of the sun. The sky looked as though it would start snowing soon. Proska carefully thrust each hand into its opposite sleeve and massaged his fingers. He turned his head to the side, hoping he'd be able to see his own trench. But he didn't have enough of an angle.

The wounded man lay on his back, babbling to himself.

"Please be quiet," Proska implored him.

"Who . . . are . . . you?"

"Why do you want to know?"

"Tell me . . . your . . . name."

"Proska. Do you think knowing my name will relieve your pain?"

"I'm . . . going . . . to die."

"When it gets dark, I'll bring you back."

"When it gets dark . . . I'll be . . . dead. Can't you . . . carry me back . . . right away?"

"No."

"I'll . . . remember . . . your . . . name."

"If I stand up, they'll see me and . . ."

"Why . . . is it . . . so cold?"

It cost the wounded man a great effort to force the words out.

"I can't give you my coat," said Proska. "If I move, they'll immediately start shooting."

"Who . . . will . . . shoot?"

"Don't ask so many questions. And lower your voice."

"I have . . . to know, Proska . . . when it starts . . . getting dark . . . I'll be dead."

"Talking's wearing you out. You have to be quiet so you can regain your strength."

"Do you . . . know . . . this area?"

"Yes. I'm from around here."

"They got me . . . twice." The wounded man groaned. "Proska?"

"What do you want?"

"What . . . time . . . is it?"

"It must be about ten-thirty. I have a pocket watch, but I can't take it out."

"Why . . . not?"

"Because I'd have to move."

"You don't . . . need to . . . be afraid . . . Proska . . . You can . . . go ahead . . . and move . . . you're lying . . . behind me . . . If they . . . shoot . . . they'll hit . . . me . . . Don't you think . . . I make a good . . . bullet shield? Eh?"

"Be quiet," Proska ordered. "If you don't settle down right now, I'll settle you down."

The other began to babble something that Proska didn't understand.

After a while, the wounded soldier said, "You . . . you *will* . . . bring me back . . . won't you? . . . You won't . . . leave me . . . lying here? . . . You can't . . .

do that . . . I'm from Schmiedeberg . . . Do you . . .
know Schmiedeberg?"

"No," said Proska.

"My wife . . . still lives there . . . with our . . .
Christel . . . She was four . . . at Christmas . . . she had
to get . . . two presents . . . on December 24 . . . one
for her birthday . . . and one for—"

The snow next to Proska sprayed high in the air.

"Shut your mouth."

"What's the matter?" the wounded man whimpered. He was in great pain.

"They're shooting at us," said Proska.

The wounded soldier whimpered and started beg-
ging again. "Can't you . . . take out . . . your watch?"

"Why should I? It's ten-thirty. Don't you understand me when I talk to you?"

"Yes, but . . . I want . . . to know . . . the exact
time."

"Why, for God's sake?"

"So I can . . . figure out . . . how long . . . I
have . . . before night comes . . . When it's here . . . I'll
be . . . dead."

Around noon, it snowed. Fat flakes tumbled down
to earth and covered up the fantastic molehills.
The wounded soldier murmured to himself. Proska
thought he was humming a tune. Eventually, he grew

silent and the thick flakes covered him. Proska felt the cold moving up his legs; his face, on the other hand, was hot and getting hotter. It seemed to him that his bodily warmth was retreating from the advancing cold and now concentrating in his face. His lips swelled, and the blood in his short forehead vein pulsed more rapidly. He was tired, and had he not been so painfully hungry, he would have fallen asleep, in spite of the danger that entailed. The shooting had stopped.

Proska found that the layer of snow on his back was getting thicker and heavier, yet not so heavy that it could keep him from standing up. He thought about Wolfgang, about the letter he was carrying in his pocket, and about the wounded soldier, who hadn't even turned over on his stomach when it began to snow. Proska also thought about tall Zwiczosbirski. Wanda too emerged from the shrouded consciousness of his memory, wearing her little green dress, the belt drawn tight around her hourglass waist. He imagined she was sitting on a wall close to him, and for several seconds, he seemed to be holding her hand. Proska was suddenly astonished to realize that he'd made no effort to write to her or at least to inquire as to what rules and possibilities applied to him in this regard, and he resolved to do that at his next opportunity. He scolded himself for not having done it sooner, for having been so negligent, for having left Wanda in uncertainty for such a long time.

As night began to fall, Proska heard approaching footsteps.

Two men, conversing.

One of them said softly, "There must be two more over there."

The other replied, "Sometimes they just play dead and let themselves get buried in snow. They learned that from the Mongols. They can lie under snow without moving for twenty-four hours, and it doesn't do them any harm."

"My bladder wouldn't go along with the plan."

Proska held his breath. He could hear that the voices were directly above him. The footsteps stopped. He thought, *If they find me now—the hand grenade—if they grab me—pull the ring—maybe they'll just go away.*

He could sense the two men's eyes on his back and felt a surge of warmth flooding into his legs.

One of the men scraped the snow off the wounded man, who at that moment started whimpering.

Proska had an urge to spring up, but he got control of himself and remained motionless.

"This one's still alive," said one of the men in surprise.

"Now . . . night . . . is falling . . . ," the wounded man babbled. "The dark . . . it's here . . ."

"He's delirious," the other man said.

"We'll bring him back."

"Him?"

"We're supposed to bring back everyone we find."

"Let's put him out of his misery."

"You must be nuts. You can't just shoot him. Put that pistol away! Now! We're going to carry him to the rear. The man's still alive."

"Pros-ka," the wounded soldier groaned.

"Did you understand what he said?" asked one of the men.

"No idea," the other one said. "Sounded like a name. Probably his."

"This is a turncoat."

"We're bringing him back."

The two men bent over the wounded soldier; one grabbed his feet, the other lifted him by the shoulders. Then they went away, wobbling with their burden through the deep snow.

Proska slowly raised his head. He drew up one leg and placed his hands under his chest. And then he slid over the frozen surface of the brook, rounded an un-naturally high hill under which the bodies of several men were apparently lying, and stopped to breathe only when he was already halfway up the slope to his own trench. His toes were tingling from having been frozen. *I'll rub them with snow when I get back*, he thought.

· THIRTEEN ·

When a burst of machine gun fire swept over their heads, they ducked down so far that their lips brushed the snow. A willow branch torn off by the bullets fell on Proska's neck, and he flinched as though from the lash of a whip. Now even the earth was against them: four men had been gravely wounded during the night, not by gunfire or shell fragments, but by frozen clods of earth. Every impact sent up a fountain of snow that still hung in the air after the shrapnel had gone whistling by. The craters became smaller, more defined, the walls around the edges of the craters flatter.

"Now!" Proska shouted. He jumped up, started running, charged through a stand of willow shrubs, panted as he dashed across an open space, and flung himself into a trench. Behind him, a muffled fall:

Wolfgang. The bursting shells sprang after them, implacable and threatening.

"Stay calm," said Proska. "We're practically there, only two more jumps."

Rat-tat-tat, said the machine gun again. Now it was zeroed in; the rounds made a sharp, dry sound as they struck the banked, hard-frozen earth on the edge of the trench.

"If I could only see him . . . Walter . . . I'd shoot now . . . can't you spot him? He must be behind us, at an angle—"

Wolfgang's voice was drowned out by a high-energy detonation in their immediate vicinity. Some clumps of flying mud hit them on the back—they were the harmless clumps, the ones that fell perpendicularly to earth. With the next explosion, the two men pushed themselves up off the ground and ran forward crouching. Before the machine gun began its *rat-tat-tat,* Proska looked back for Wolfgang, quickly turning around to see whether the Milk Roll had likewise jumped up and run. And in that moment, Proska stumbled, his automatic rifle flew into the snow several meters away, and his fingers dug into the white blanket. A hard pain went through his chest. He tasted snow on his tongue, and suddenly rings of fire were whirling before his eyes. Blood rushed to his ears, as though dashing for a just-discovered exit. He groaned, bent his back and his neck, and rolled onto his side. The pain was still stuck fast in his chest, right next to his heart. Trembling, Proska groped for the buttons of his overcoat, undid them, and thrust his hand through the opening. Then he drew his hand back and looked at it fearfully. The hand wasn't bloody; maybe the red stuff hadn't soaked through his jacket yet. He unbuttoned the jacket, groaning all the while, placed his fingertips on his warm chest, and felt for blood. But he found nothing. Although he could precisely identify the spot at the center of the pain, his investigations produced no further information.

Wolfgang came creeping over to him.

"Walter!" he cried.

"You have to get out of here," Proska said with an effort. "I can't walk. You'll find your way back, it's not far. Not far at all, two or three good jumps."

"What's the matter, are you hit? I still have a bandage pack with me."

"It's no use," said Proska.

"Be quiet now. Turn over, go on! I'm going to cut your overcoat open, then you'll be all right. Two or three good jumps."

The MG started its staccato hammering again, but the bullets whizzed over their heads, too high, much too high.

Wolfgang cut open the back of Proska's overcoat and then his jacket and his shirt. His skin was unscathed, no entrance wound anywhere, and no exit wound either. But Proska surely must have been hit. What path into his body had the metal slug taken?

"Where does it hurt?" asked Wolfgang.

"You have to get away, now," said Proska. "All they have to do with me is give me the coup de grâce, but if they catch you—"

"Is it here?"

Two airplanes whooshed over the village, fired, made turns so deep that their wings almost touched the ground, and vanished. The MG fell silent.

"Now we can go on," said Wolfgang.

Then Proska unexpectedly stood up and took hold of his rifle. He'd only fallen chest-first onto a sharp clod of frozen earth. Soon his pains were completely gone.

After a series of zigzag advances, they reached the village.

Behind Rogalski's shed, they stopped and discussed what they should do next. They didn't know whether Proska's brother-in-law had fled or stayed; the farm looked abandoned. Then there was the fact that they couldn't stay there long, because they'd received strict and important orders, and if those orders hadn't by chance required them to pass close to Rogalski's house, they probably wouldn't have gone there on their own initiative. Proska had been given the mission only because he knew every path and every stone in the neighborhood, and he'd taken along Milk

Roll because four eyes see more than two, and because two rifles can accomplish more than one, and because, generally speaking, two people who undertake a task have better prospects of success than only one.

A needle-sharp wind pricked their faces, their cheeks burned, and their fingers grew stiff. When they spoke, they hardly moved their lips. A bank of snow clouds hung over the horizon. Now and then the ice on the frozen lake cracked, and every time, there was a booming sound like thunder. Proska was waiting for the dog to start barking, but the dog didn't bark; surely it was curled up in its doghouse, sound asleep, lying on its chain with its head between its forepaws. Or maybe Rogalski had taken the dog away with him. The two soldiers couldn't be seen behind the shed, but they couldn't see anything either.

"Now what?" Wolfgang asked. "Do you intend to stay here?"

"We'll go into the yard from the back."

They circled the shed. The farmyard door creaked when Proska opened it. Wolfgang was standing right behind him.

At that moment, a shot was fired, and the echo resounded in the farmyard. They didn't know where the shot had come from. Proska cried, "Get down!" and both of them lay in the snow. They scrutinized the windows and the dormers. The shot must have come from there, they thought.

"We have to get to the barn, Wolfgang. You go first. When you reach it, I'll follow."

While Milk Roll sprang to his feet and headed for the barn, making long, bounding strides, Proska stared at the dormers. A second shot rang out, and the report banged against the barn, ricocheted over to the woodshed, and from there to the farmhouse. In Proska's ears the reverberations produced a high, clear, persisting buzz, and he opened his mouth so the buzzing would disappear.

The bullet struck Wolfgang in midstride, dealing him a short, sharp blow and knocking him backward. His arm described a swift circle, his legs bent at the knees.

Proska had watched as though paralyzed. Now he took his eyes off Wolfgang and scanned the house, and he noticed the entrance door slowly move and saw a shotgun barrel peep out, just above the cold cement floor, pointing at him. Desperately and instinctively, Proska jerked the butt of his automatic rifle to his shoulder, aimed at the door through which he had so often, in former days, entered the house, and pulled the trigger.

Everything went black before his eyes.

The force of the rounds had flung the door open. Fresh wooden splinters shone in the clear air.

After a while, Proska raised his head and looked over to the house. A man was lying on the cement entryway; the bullets had reached him through the wood.

Proska jumped up and ran to Wolfgang, lifted him up, and carried him to the barn. He set him down so that his back was leaning against the planks of the barn wall. Proska knelt beside his wounded comrade.

"Wolfgang, my God, what is it, damn, what's wrong with you? Can't you hear me? Say something." As he spoke, his big, ruddy hands were fiddling around on Wolfgang's chest while he tried to hold up the unconscious man's constantly drooping head. A wave of heat surged up into Proska's own skull. "Hey!" he cried. "Why don't you answer me?"

Proska clapped both hands to his forehead, and Wolfgang abruptly toppled sideways. Proska felt a strangling sensation in his throat, and it seemed to him as though all his saliva had flooded his mouth at once. He straightened up Wolfgang's body again. "Talk to me, Wolfgang, answer me, open your eyes." He tenderly caressed his friend's cheeks and failed to notice that the front of his overcoat, the part over his chest, was turning darker. The assistant shook Wolfgang by the shoulders, so that his head jerked back and forth, and cried, "Why don't you answer me? Why are you acting like this? Tell me what's wrong!"

Wolfgang's eyes were shut, his face tense and contorted, as if he were enduring pain. His arms hung down limp; no more breath issued from his mouth.

Proska threw himself on the snow next to Wolfgang and clasped his legs. Proska's back heaved; the man was sobbing.

And after a while, he grew completely calm; he got to his feet and dragged Wolfgang over the snow-covered ground. He hauled him to the edge of the field and then a good distance into it. At last he laid him down with great care, as if there were still something left in him to destroy. Then he knelt heavily beside him.

"Goodbye, Wolfgang. Goodbye, my friend."

Proska slowly ran his fingers over Wolfgang's forehead, left him where he was, and went anxiously back to the farmyard.

Mistrustful and hesitant, he pushed open the door to the farmhouse, and then he saw that the man his bullets had riddled through the door was his brother-in-law Rogalski.

Proska stood there as if a burning beam had just crashed to the floor a few centimeters in front of him. Intense heat surged up into his face, suddenly dazing him. He stretched out one hand and groped for the wall. The wall supported him. It did not leave him in the lurch, he could lean on it, it didn't collapse under his touch—which, had it happened at that moment, wouldn't have surprised him.

These too are unexpected fruits of conscience, Proska.

We're better at hitting the closest targets, we tend to miss the ones that are far away. But we're made for distance, and if we want to reach far enough, we have to overcome what's near, we disregard it like day-blind owls. Now what will you do?

Proska stared at the man on the floor; then he pushed himself off the wall and tottered into the house.

"Maria!" he called hoarsely. "Maria? Where are you? Maria!"

When he got no answer, he went out to the entry-way, pushing Rogalski's shotgun aside with his boot. He headed for the barn, opened the door, and listened.

"Maria!" he called, "Are you here? Are you hid-ing? It's me, Walter!"

He was about to go out again when there was a rustling sound in the straw.

"Maria?"

A woman appeared atop a mound of straw and gazed fearfully down on Proska.

"Well, come on," he said tonelessly.

She slid down and hesitantly approached him.

"Are you afraid of me?" he asked, making an at-tempt to smile. Neither of them held out a hand to the other.

"What was all that shooting?" she asked, distraught.

He said, "That was a careless thing to do, hiding in the straw. If the barn had caught fire, you would've burned up."

"My God, where have you come from, Walter? What happened? Shots were fired in the yard, several shots. I heard them very clearly. Was it you?"

"We don't have much time," he said.

"Have you talked to Kurt?"

"Yes."

"Where is he?"

"Gone."

"Gone?"

"He's safe."

"Without me?"

"He's waiting for you."

"Let me run into the house."

"No, don't, stay here. You have very little time. I'll show you how to reach safety. We have to go to Barany Cove."

"And Kurt?"

"He's there too. You'll see him soon, come on."

"But what about my things, Walter? I'm all packed and ready. It happened so suddenly, you know? I had just made goose confit—the jars are still in the cellar."

"Come on now, fast," Proska ordered sternly. "If we delay even a minute more, we'll be too late."

He seized Maria by the wrist and pulled her after him.

He pulled her over the snow-covered field and through a pine forest, unspeaking, his facial features unchanged. His tight grip made her groan, but he didn't let her go. Maria had given up asking him questions. She was afraid of her grimly determined brother. They reached a road and followed it.

When they heard the clatter of an approaching engine, Proska drew Maria behind a tree trunk. Not far from them, they spotted a truck that had apparently been stuck in the snow on a side road and was now trying to climb up to the higher, wider road on whose shoulder Proska and Maria were standing. Proska attentively studied the soldiers, who were busy sticking branches and cardboard under the truck's free-spinning rear wheels, and then he said, "All right, now you go over to them. They'll take you with them. We'll meet again soon. Go now."

"What about you?" Maria asked.

"I'll be along later."

She gaped at him in amazement, turned, and left him. He moved to a different lookout position and waited, and after a short while, the truck, banging and bumping, heaved itself onto the road and drove away. Maria was standing on the box in the back, strenuously gazing toward the spot where, not long before, Proska had stood.

After the vehicle was out of sight, Proska slumped to the ground. He gradually comprehended what had taken place. An excruciating headache went to work inside his forehead.

Out of here . . . out of this country . . . out of this world . . . abandoned, alone . . . this can't go on . . . Why doesn't the world hold its breath? . . . Why do the crows fly over the field? . . . Doesn't anyone understand what just happened? . . . So there's no moment when life could take a break . . . just for once, out of respect? . . . Why are you all so indifferent, so patient, so cynical? Don't you feel something, anything? . . . Are you so insensible to my pain? . . . Does my torment not strike you speechless? . . . Am I nothing, then? . . . Must it all go unnoticed? . . . Why don't you stop your hearts? . . . Is my pain so little your own?

Proska staggered backward. Heavy clouds hovered above him; it began to snow. Light snowflakes landed on his hand and melted.

He walked down the road, which didn't fork. He entrusted himself to it, and it took him along. The fresh rabbit tracks were gradually obliterated. Proska took a fleeting glance at the sky. It was a dull metallic color and held a lot of snow, ready to fall.

Proska didn't look back anymore. He kept his eyes pointed ahead of him. And ahead of him lay the steely horizon, which he was helping to expand, toward the west, toward the reddening sunset. One day that steel wall would collapse, it would disperse like fog in the busy hands of the wind—one day.

For now, however, men still supported it, men still drove it resolutely forward. Would it never end?

· FOURTEEN ·

"Na *zdrowie*, cheers, or something like that!" said Proska. He swayed as he walked over to the two soldiers and handed each of them a glass, and then they drank. And after they had drunk, the soldiers—both Mongols—sat down on the bed, and Proska sat on a chair. He pulled the chair close to the edge of the bed, so that their knees were almost touching. Outside, under the window, the truck the soldiers had brought Proska in waited with its engine idling. The room was big, the walls freshly papered; the bed looked a little lost in one corner, the floor was shiny, and the chairs were new and uncomfortable. They forced the sitter to sit up straight.

Proska fished some cigarettes out of a wooden case and offered them around. One soldier refused, the other accepted. They smoked and drank, and then both soldiers suddenly stood up from the bed and left without a word of farewell. Proska hurried over to the window and watched the two clamber into the truck, which then drove off.

He stayed at the window awhile longer, hoping they'd come back. At last, he turned away, weary and disappointed, and lay down on the bed. He registered the warmth the Mongols had left behind on the bedspread. The window was open, and an optimistic spring climbed in. A delicate song wafted up from a hedge; the courageous bird was earthy-brown and very small.

This was the end Proska had been looking forward to with increasing eagerness of late. The Gang had disappeared, melted in the fire of justice; they were on the other side of the mountain, as they say in Georgia. Over the miserable, scorched landscape of the war, narrow columns of smoke rose into the air, signs of a past conflagration, signs of a present calm. The wall of steel and fire had collapsed, and among the survivors, a strange illness was spreading: guilt pangs.

Smashed tanks lay in fields; in ditches alongside railroad tracks, mighty locomotives with eviscerated bellies rested; and many roads had no more protection on either side, for the houses that had shielded them with their cruelly precise facades had broken apart under the embittered blows of the bombs.

Proska tried to fall asleep. He was lying on his side, his right arm almost fully extended. His respiration was powerful and regular; his breath struck the freshly papered wall, scattered, and spread through the room. His right arm gradually grew heavy, the blood accumulated in one place. Because his right temple was resting on his upper arm, a buildup developed, a little dam blocking the circulation of the red fluid. Proska flung himself onto his back and exhaled loudly. It was broad daylight outside. He unbuttoned his shirt, and when he put his hand through the opening and touched his chest, he could feel that it was clammy. So was his forehead, and so were his back and his behind.

I have to go to sleep, Proska thought. *I've waited years for this moment. To sleep, to go under, to tip out of consciousness . . . Everything's over now. I could get a reply from Wanda in two weeks. From her, from her! How changed she seemed that last time, in the ruins of the spa . . . Why did the Mongols leave so fast? They knew me, after all . . . Wanda will come, she'll come here to me. Wanda.*

He rolled onto his left side, because he was used to sleeping on one side or the other. He felt his heart hammering indignantly against his elbow, refusing to put up with being compressed.

"This won't work," he said half aloud to himself, and he imagined he saw the words swimming around like little buoys in the room. Groaning, he turned again onto his back, snorted, flexed his thigh muscles, let his fist fall against the wall, and moved his eyelids. His desperation was sublimely pointless.

He sat up halfway, took a nonsensical look around, and threw himself back on the bed so hard that the springs squealed. He raised an arm and made grasping movements in the empty air. Then he cautiously laid a hand on his forehead. He could feel the pulse in his left temple throbbing against his fingertips. *It's no good. I've forgotten how to sleep this way. I'll just have to get used to it again.*

Proska rose and stood at the open window, his feet planted wide apart. There was an air current that cooled off his hot body. The afternoon was enveloping the front yard and the street in solitude.

He thought of himself as abandoned; he believed he was alone in the world. Proska, conscience's assistant, felt pity for himself. By roundabout ways, he came to the conclusion that this day was a Sunday. Tomorrow he would enter his office for the first time, he'd take up the position he'd been offered without any effort on his part. He recalled the last conversation he'd had before being discharged. Colonel Swerdlow, a young, intellectual officer, had summoned him. When Proska arrived, Swerdlow had scurried over to him on his thin little legs, greeted him amiably, and led him by the arm to a chair. Then he'd offered him a cigarette. Behind his desk, the colonel didn't look so frail. He seemed to grow out of the polished wood, and the massive, pawlike, carved feet of the table supported him a little as well.

"Show me the documents," said the colonel.

Proska opened a breast pocket and took out some papers. "Here," he said, laying everything he'd had in his pocket on the table.

The colonel didn't touch the documents, nor did he read them; he merely pushed them uninterestedly to one side and put a ruler on them to hold them in place.

"Are these all the papers you've got?"

"Yes."

The colonel spoke accent-free German. But he spoke very softly, and Proska had to lean pretty far toward him if he wanted to understand every word. The colonel's face scarcely changed as he spoke. He refrained from emphasizing individual words with gestures.

"If these are all of them, then that's good," he said.

Proska stood up. As far as he was concerned, their business was at an end. He made briskly for the door.

"Don't go, Proska. I have something to say to you. Sit back down and listen closely." The colonel crushed out his cigarette and murmured, "Every power on earth is inclined to protect itself. One kind of self-protection consists in setting up outposts in places that are at risk. Such outposts function as breakwaters or lightning rods or membranes. You yourself know how important they are. In the era of reason, if you don't have outposts, you're sunk. You understand me so far?"

"Yes," said Proska.

"Then that's good . . . You fought on our side."

"Yes."

"The war is over now."

"Yes."

"But the need to fight—to fight in a somewhat different way, of course—isn't over. Within the socialist society, nothing stands still. Standstills exist only in the bourgeois world, and that's why every member of the bourgeoisie suffers from sphincter cramps. Do you follow me?"

Proska nodded.

The colonel marked a pause, fastidiously scratched his long head, and tried in vain to press his black, close-clipped hair down against his skull. In the end, he renounced this effort with a scant smile and said, "You have proved yourself, Proska, you've shown that you're not a sentimental traditionalist. In general, a revolutionary state has no need to thank any given individual, for by the very fact of his cooperation, such an individual has received a guarantee for the future. In your special case, however, I want to say that we acknowledge a certain appreciation. You will receive your discharge from us today. We need men like you in our zone. We have big plans for you. Now you are to pack your things and come back to me with them. You'll be assigned an office, and you'll live in a room that's already been prepared for you.

But go now. Later, I'll give you the necessary instructions . . . Have you understood everything I've said?"

"Yes," said Proska, and then he stood up.

He'd received the necessary instructions; he'd also received new identity documents and, to his surprise, a selection of canteen items, and after he'd taken his leave of Colonel Swerdlow, the two Mongol soldiers had come to fetch him and bring him to his future apartment.

The Sunday silence lured him outside—clearly, the two soldiers weren't coming back, so why should he wait for them?

Proska closed the window, gave his clothes a cursory adjustment, and walked out to the front garden. He turned around and observed the house he'd been brought to. He liked it, certainly, but he had the feeling the proprietor could appear before him at any moment and ask what he was doing there and what gave him the right to move about so blithely on someone else's property. Speculating about the owner was surely idle, but Proska couldn't get used to his new situation so quickly, and therefore he instinctively ducked down below every window and went to great pains to walk past in such a way that nobody inside could see him. Once, to be sure, he let himself go, he got careless and strutted bolt upright to the middle of a window, and then, in a fit of defiance, he turned his head toward the house and even stared through the glass pane. For the first time, he saw his own room from outside: the bed, cowering in one corner like a flat, gray animal, and the rigid chairs, and in front of the bed, the wooden chest that held his belongings. He smiled cautiously and continued his reconnaissance. He didn't know who—besides himself—lived in this house; naturally, he would have been glad to find out, and had he noticed someone at one window or another, he would also have been prepared to strike up an acquaintance, but he saw nothing that might have led him to conclude that the house in question was occupied by anyone other than him. This, it turned out, was the sole result of his reconnaissance, but it was quite enough for him; the certainty gave him satisfaction. Had he not had this certainty, he would probably have left the garden gate open; now, however, he pulled the little gate closed almost pedantically, nor did he refrain from sliding home the useless bolt, which anyone could have easily reached.

Proska walked down the street. In the distance, he'd spotted two old women trying to cross the road diagonally. Apparently, their progress was slow at best, for Proska, striding toward them, had covered a considerable distance while the women had gone only a few steps. Proska picked up his pace; his intention was to greet the ladies, introduce himself, and then ask them some questions. He felt an urgent need to talk with people, and he walked faster and faster in order to intercept the two before they reached the single undamaged house that seemed to be their goal. When he was almost within hailing distance, they greatly increased their speed, and just as he was taking a deep breath and opening his mouth to call, the unexpectedly nimble old women, their black skirts flying behind them, sprang into the entrance.

Proska hastened after them—he wasn't going to give up his plan so easily—but when he reached the entryway, he found it empty. He determined to hide in a wall niche and wait. He suspected that behind their apartment door—he could see it from his post— the women were laughing themselves breathless. He almost thought he could hear their heartbeats.

The stairwell, which received light only through a little window patched with cardboard, smelled strongly of boiled cabbage. Proska lurked in the niche, his head against the tiled wall, the words ready to leap from his tongue. Nothing happened; the apartment door stayed shut.

Maybe they're not listening after all . . . why would they . . . I didn't do anything to them . . . but people don't run away for no reason . . . still, nobody here knows me . . . they ran from me . . . what am I doing in this building?

Someone inside seemed to be fiddling with the door. Proska, startled, pressed his body hard against the wall. Then he watched while a child, a little girl with a serious face, stepped out onto the landing, looked back, and nodded, as though receiving a final instruction. Then the girl, who was carrying a doll, came to the wall niche and knelt down quite close to Proska.

The child hadn't noticed him yet. She held the doll at arm's length, turned it this way and that in the meager light, and started to give it a stern talking-to. Proska squinted down at the child. He dared not turn his head, because he was afraid the little girl would discover him and take fright.

"Be good and stand there," said the girl to the doll. "You mustn't fall over now. If you fall over, you're going to get it. First one leg, and then—"

The doll fell over onto the cement floor; its head hit the metal strip on the edge of one of the steps.

"See what happens when you disobey? So let's try again. First one leg—"

The doll fell over again, and the girl uttered an angry little scream, turned up the doll's tiny checkered skirt, exposed its minuscule panties, and spanked its behind with two fingers. Proska smiled to himself and breathed a bit less warily.

"Come on," said the girl. "For the last time. If you won't be good, I don't want you anymore. I'll find myself another doll. I have to say, you're not very nice."

Taking great care, the little girl spread the doll's legs, let it go, and . . . stood up in mute rage. The doll had fallen over again. The child looked down on it contemptuously and moved closer to it, centimeter by centimeter. Then she suddenly raised a foot and brought it down on the doll's head. There was a sharp crack. That crack was too much for Proska. He groaned, came charging out of the wall niche, gave the little girl a slight shove, raced down the few steps, and regained the street. He slowed down only after turning into a side alley.

He looked behind him several times, and after he'd made certain he wasn't being followed, he continued at a leisurely pace, assessing the damage the buildings had suffered, casting a glance over a garden fence here and there, and sometimes—just in passing—gazing into windows. Since the sun was now cheerfully sitting on his back, and since he was enjoying his walk, his inner comrade started feeling merry and demanded a song. And Proska warbled a tune to himself. *Ah, yes.* His legs weren't heavy, no straps were compressing his shoulders, and there was nothing in his hands. Nothing. He warbled to himself: "Ro-hose Ma-rie." *My God, am I in a good mood, or what?* All the meat-processing factories were closed. "Cuddlin', kissin', I've been missin'." *What a day. Flex those thighs, flex those calves . . . Ah, yes.* He warbled to himself, "Come a-gain-gain-gain," "God's no older than thirty, and he wears a woolen tie," "When I come, when I come, I will certainly be there."

A saxophone tugged at his sleeve—a tune played by a saxophone, of course. *Well, say. Where are you hiding, marvel of holes and keys?* Proska came to a stop. Without realizing it, he'd been walking for hours. "I'll be there soon," the darkness said.

Proska entered the bar and went straight through to the dance hall. The saxophone had seduced him. The dance floor was almost square. The orchestra was playing a slow fox-trot, and eight or so couples were dancing. The room smelled of hay and tobacco and sweat. A waiter cried, "Coming through!" and once again, "Coming through!" and skillfully balanced a tray of beers all the way to the tables. "One-eighty. And you, that comes to, wait, stop, you're paying for both? Then three-sixty, please."

Proska waited. He had nothing in his hands, and his hands were used to having something in them. Something that weighed around four kilograms. He slipped his hands into his pockets. And when the orchestra had ended the slow fox-trot, he observed that five of the men who were leaving the dance floor likewise thrust their hands into their pockets. He felt drawn to them, and he sensed that they also felt drawn to him. Apparently, they knew one another—from somewhere. But where? He had no idea.

"Will you please move away from the door?" said the waiter to Proska. "Sit at one of the tables. There's no shortage of chairs—plenty of room for you. Do you want something to drink?"

"Yes, a beer. A lager."

As Proska was squeezing past the occupied tables, he gave a sudden start and fixed his eyes on a young woman. She wore a leaf-green dress with a narrow belt around her hourglass waist. He closed his eyes as though in a daze, he trembled, he stood as stiff as a clothes pole among the tables.

Wanda, he thought. *Wanda, Wanda. Here? That's not possible. Wanda, now, dancing, here?*

With his eyes closed, he took two little steps, and his thigh bumped into the edge of a table.

"Hey, watch where you're going, man, you're not blind! You almost knocked over the beer glasses. You've got plenty of room!"

Proska emerged from his thoughts and looked at her. She paid him no attention. Who was she, anyway? He didn't know her at all. Maybe she looked something like Wanda. Something like, no more. The orchestra played a fox-trot. The girl danced with a one-armed man. He held her tight, you had to give him that. He never lost his grip on her.

Now Proska no longer felt like sitting at one of the tables. He slowly left the bar, and as he was leaving, he said to the waiter, "No beer for me."

The waiter nodded.

While still a good distance away, Proska spotted a light on the upper floor of the house he now called home. Either someone had already been living up there before his arrival, or someone had taken advantage of his absence and moved in fast. The bolt on the garden gate was not shot; Proska remembered that he had shot it. He entered his room, undressed in the dark, and after waiting for a longish time in the vain hope of hearing voices or the sound of footsteps overhead, he fell asleep. That night, he didn't dream.

· FIFTEEN ·

In the beginning, Proska's office colleagues changed very quickly. There was a constant, soundless coming and going; people would appear and do their job for a period of time, and then an immense shadow would fall on them from one side or another and they would disappear overnight. Only Proska remained. He was allowed to remain. When he came out from behind his double doors in the evening, he'd go up to every person in the office and very conscientiously say goodbye, because he didn't know whether he'd find them there the following day. He didn't have the power to do anything about that, he didn't even know who was responsible for those changes, but they happened, and therefore someone must have decreed them. Proska gradually acquired a knack for identifying who would be the next to go; the people concerned bore their fate on their faces unmistakably, like a stigma. Only very seldom did Proska's forecasts turn out to be wrong. And when he did get one wrong, he'd assume not that his prophecy had been mistaken, but that the bureau in charge of making personnel changes had revoked its decision at the last minute. On what grounds, he of course had no idea. He wasn't indifferent to knowing, but he saw no possibility of finding out. Sometimes he thought that the colonel had a hand in this; however, there was no proof of his involvement. Proska sat behind his double doors and pondered. He racked his brains with the most remarkable hypotheses, but his fickle cogitations bore no fruit. Nothing corroborated them, and his anxiety grew. His anxiety grew, even though he himself had nothing to complain about. The double doors warned him whenever anyone tried to pass through them, so that he never had any fear of being disturbed. When he heard the first handle turning, he changed the expression on his face and cleared his desk of everything not connected to his work, and in this way he was forearmed at all times.

The people who brought Proska a document to sign or asked him to take a look at a case eschewed any attempt at familiarity, they remained impassively humble in his presence until he made his decision, and they didn't allow themselves to proffer any helpful advice, which he never expected anyway. When he was alone again, he began to brood, he thought despairingly about Wanda, he kept wondering why she hadn't answered any of the many letters he'd sent her since their last meeting. He reflected on the possibility that a child of his was alive in the world, and he tried to imagine what that child looked like. Proska thought himself back to the marsh; a stealthy longing for the Fortress and the old river overcame him. *Wolfgang, Zwiczosbirski, Maria . . . if Maria knew . . . if she found out I killed Rogalski . . . she'll find out sooner or later, if she hasn't already . . . the past isn't all that merciful . . . it comes back . . . it'll shine a light on my secret one day . . . everything's stored somewhere . . . the words we spoke in the rain, our movements, our looks, our thoughts, everything . . . there's no depth so deep that time couldn't bring it back up to the surface . . . Sit and breathe and wait . . . breathe . . . wait . . . almost all the people have been replaced . . . they'll replace me too . . . and then what happens? . . . They can't just let me go . . . Why do they favor one person and let the other disappear? . . . On Thursday they arrested Mospfleger because he was in a bar soliciting for the conscientious objectors' organization . . . This morning Jupp was missing . . . I bade him a proper farewell last night . . . Maybe they're intercepting my letters to Wanda? . . . Outposts, the colonel said . . .*

Proska suddenly decided to pull open a drawer and toss into it everything that was on his desk.

He threw his scarf around his neck, pulled on his overcoat, and opened the double doors. The people in the outer office looked up in surprise; they'd never seen Proska behave that way; they found his grim determination unsettling, and they started frenetically rummaging through the papers they had in front of them. It was the first time he'd ever left the office during working hours. They were aware of his recent past, and they respected him for it. But none of them knew what it was that he actually did behind those double doors; they had absolutely no idea what kind of role he played, for he neither participated in training sessions nor showed up at meetings or demonstrations. Naturally, they sometimes wondered why he nevertheless stayed on. The only explanation they could come up with was his past.

"Kunkel," said Proska. "You sit by the telephone. And if the phone rings, then you pick up the receiver and say I'll be back soon."

"Very well," said Kunkel. "I have two more documents for you to sign—"

"Later," said Proska. "We'll do all that later."

And he left the office.

Benches were ranged on both sides of the long, tiled corridor, and on the benches sat people waiting their turn to enter Proska's department; and when he walked past them, his upper body bent forward, his footsteps echoing, their murmured conversations died out, and he was the focus of all eyes. Those individuals were dependent on him, and they seemed to suspect that this was the case. The flying skirts of his overcoat occasionally grazed someone's knee or snatched another's breath from his mouth. Proska turned to no one. Up until then, his outer office had spared him all direct contact. He'd never walked down the fully occupied corridor before, and at that moment, he vowed to deal in future with the waiting supplicants himself. To be sure, doing so would prevent him from getting as wrapped up in his thoughts as heretofore, but on the other hand, he knew he could use some distraction.

As Proska briefly paused on the stairs to button his overcoat, he heard the murmuring—an anonymous trickle—start up again in the corridor. It struck his ear like distant drumming. He sprang down the stairs, strode past giant posters, loyalty ribbons, and pithy admonitions, turned his head away as he passed the porter's glass cage, and stepped out to the street.

Outside, rain was falling. Proska turned up his coat collar and walked across a deserted square.

It was a cold and gloomy autumn afternoon. The sun hadn't shown its face for several days. The air was oddly heavy; his lungs seemed reluctant to take it in. A cloud of haze usually hung over the factories for only a while before being dispersed by the wind, but now the haze was obstinately squatting on the city. It got into your pores, your nostrils; you could taste it on your tongue.

Proska walked through the public gardens. Not a human in sight. He slowed his pace, and someone who didn't know him might have assumed that he was trying to go in two directions at once, for he trotted forward a few meters and then made a tight loop that brought him back to a spot not too distant from his starting point. He continued in this way until the gardens were behind him, and by then he was already at the train station. *The colonel will be at his friendliest if I come to see him right before he gets off . . . now is too early, I might disturb him in the middle of some important work . . . hope he's not vacationing somewhere on Lake Ladoga at this very minute . . . actually, I think he lives there . . . it'll be best for me to get to his office in an hour or so . . . no earlier . . . under no circumstances should I get there earlier.*

There were a strikingly disproportionate number of women in the station, many of them holding children by the hand. They looked up at the clock and then out at the platform. The platform was wet with many puddles, which the rain was gradually enlarging. With the exception of the railroad employee at the ticket window and an old man supporting himself with a cane, Proska was the only man in the concourse. He stuck a cigarette between his lips and lit it, and when he did, everyone looked at him. He pretended not to notice, walked over to a red poster, and feigned reading the black words. This, he hoped, would make the people spare him their looks; but he could feel those looks burning through the back of his overcoat, as sharp as before. Then he turned around and asked the woman standing nearest to him, "Why are you all waiting here? Is this some kind of meeting? Why aren't you in your houses at this time of day? Your men will want their dinner when they get home from work. Me, I'd let my wife know . . ." His voice became unsure, thin. He realized that his clumsy bonhomie was out of place. But how was he to retreat now? The old man was blinking at him suspiciously, the ticket puncher craned his neck for a better view, and the other women inconspicuously crowded forward and surrounded Proska in an open circle.

Then a voice called out from under a sliding window: "It's coming! Sangsdorf just called it in!"

The women pricked up their ears as though electrified, and then they and their children surged noisily through the barrier. The old man hobbled onto the platform behind them.

"What's going on here?" Proska asked the ticket puncher.

"Go on out, pal, and you'll see what's goin' on."

"It almost looks as though He's coming in person."

"Who you talkin' about?" the employee asked.

But Proska was already past him and on the platform. He jerked his head in the direction everyone was staring in. He was here, after all, and whatever it was that the others were waiting for, he figured he might as well wait for it too. He was ready. The women's hypnotized staring communicated itself to him. He fixed his eyes on a sharp bend in the railroad embankment, beyond which the dully gleaming double line of steel tracks disappeared. The looming surprise, it seemed, would come from there. Looming, like a threat? He leaned against a Berlin optometrist's enamel sign that read IF IT'S THE EYES, GO TO RUHNKE. The rain left him in peace there. The barriers at the level crossing weren't down yet. A horse-drawn carriage rattled over the roadbed, slowly, the driver exhibiting the proverbial patience of his profession. The horses rhythmically bobbed their great heads, never once taking their eyes off the road in front of them. The carriage had barely reached the other side when a warning bell sounded; with every note, the barriers came down a little lower. Proska watched them settle into the forked supports and bounce up and down a few times until they finally lay still.

And then the train came. The locomotive barreled around the curve at such a surprising speed that some of the people waiting began to tremble and cry out in frightened amazement. The engine chugged closer, its iron forehead bowed like a steer's. It was pulling twenty-six freight cars, reddish boxes bolted shut. The women grew reckless and positioned themselves close to the rails, some of them so unthinkingly that the locomotive would certainly strike them if they didn't move before it pulled in.

"Get back, everybody get back, away from the rails!" the ticket puncher cried. He moved along the edge of the platform, pushing the women back. The fireman leaned out over the rim of the engine's tender. Soon there would be something to see. He got impatient and stamped on a piece of coal with his boot heel. The train stopped and was immediately besieged by the women.

The sliding doors of the freight cars rolled open, and a cluster of humanity formed around every opening. Children called out, women called out, innumerable calls resounded through the rain. Men clambered down from the freight cars and turned their heads, a little surprised and incredulous, when they heard a call meant for them. And then, without speaking, they let themselves be embraced and kissed and led away. Their faces were hollow, their eyes absent and sunken. Some were discovered while they were still in the freight cars, retrieving their tin cups from the nails they hung on. In such cases, the men were literally yanked off the train and assailed with the uninhibited joy of reunion. Several women walked rapidly up and down the platform, their eyes desperately seeking men who had been supposed to arrive and yet were not there.

Proska very attentively took in everything that was happening. *So there they are . . . they held out to the end for the Gang . . . and now it's gone, and the poor dogs are still suffering . . . maybe some of them would have done what I did, if they'd only had the opportunity . . . strength isn't so important, but opportunity . . . the old guy with the cane seems to have spotted his son . . . hold on to it, for God's sake, keep that stick in your hand, it's your friend . . . without it, you're finished . . . it's not just an ornament . . . you see, you almost fell . . . there, that's better, like that . . . and there's the ticket puncher, feet planted wide apart, spine bent forward . . . he wants to see some sights too . . . the fellow's enjoying himself.*

At this point, Proska's thoughts stopped. They shut down abruptly, as though crushed by a heavy weight. Before him stood a long, tall man, a man carrying a cotton jacket over his shoulder and, in one hand, a cardboard box. Proska wouldn't have noticed the man if he hadn't stopped in front of him. On his head sat a fur cap, a shabby, weather-beaten thing. His face was emaciated by the past, and a shred of heaven swam in his expressionless eyes. The wind was lashing him like a whip, pressing the material of his pants against his scrawny thighs and calves and pushing his legs apart. He leaned back slightly, as if he found in the wind something that could support him. The man looked like a bent nail, and he was staring and staring at Proska. His gaze made Proska feel cold inside; he gripped the coins in his pocket and rubbed them together. He'd moved away from the enamel sign.

There was no more feeling in the soles of his feet. He had the sensation that he'd come upon himself unexpectedly, as though he'd never known himself before in his life and had gone to the station by chance, unaware of his existence and surprised to find that he could exist at all. He had the sensation that he, Proska, had been withholding himself from himself all the livelong time, and that now, as never before, he was approaching himself, ready to say, "Hello, Proska," and "How are you doing?" He also had the sensation that he hadn't needed to breathe in the past and was discovering only now that breathing was an absolute necessity.

Proska stepped closer to the scrawny man, who was watching him unmoving. But the moment Proska took a step forward, the other took a step back; these steps were repeated four times. Apparently the scrawny man didn't want Proska to come any nearer. Proska gave up and stood still, because he realized what he was doing was futile, because the other was retreating from him with such calm seriousness, and because Proska could see in the other's emaciated face his readiness to back away from him, if necessary, to the end of the world. Many of those in the crowd who had found one another were streaming out of the station, and the ticket puncher hastened to detach the chain he'd put up between his little house and a barrier. Eventually, even those who had waited and hoped in vain left the platform; however, they didn't go away completely, but rather occupied a position behind the picket fence next to the station and stared hard at the empty train.

Proska's hand was ready, and if the other had extended his own into the space between them, Proska's would have reached the middle first. But the other did no such thing. He just stood there, leaning slightly on the wind, and hypnotized Proska with his presence. Proska couldn't take this for very long; he began to reason with himself, and thought that the best way to overcome such situations was by speaking, if only a single word. What was tormenting him and petrifying him was the uncertainly that lay in silence, and he sought a way to break that silence; for then, he told himself, it would be easier for him to cope with the apparition of the other. And he raised one hand and made a trivializing gesture in the scrawny man's direction, as if to say, *What's with the shark look? That's not like you*, and in the very same second, Proska said, "Zwiczos, for heaven's sake! Where have you been?"

He actually asked that question: Where have you been? Nothing else occurred to him. His imagination had shrunk under Thighbone's eyes, withered by that merciless stare, which seemed to have seen through him a long time ago. The sensation of being seen through inhibited him fearfully. But now that the first word had been spoken, he wanted to assess its effect.

"Thighbone," he added, "how did you wind up here? Why are you looking at me like that? Come here, for heaven's sake, I won't do you anything. Are you afraid of me?"

Whereupon Zwiczosbirski silently turned away from him, circled him carefully, as though he were taboo, and walked into the station without looking back at him. Proska pursed his lips and jingled the coins in his pocket.

The ticket puncher approached him from behind and said, "Whatcha waitin' for? There ain't no one left."

· SIXTEEN ·

I've been expecting you for some time now," said
the colonel. "Frankly, I often wonder why it's so
hard for you to find your way to me. Sit here by
the desk."

"How did you know I intended to come and see
you?" asked Proska. His surprise was so great that he
forgot to sit down.

"That's not important," Colonel Swerdlow answered. "And even if I told you, it wouldn't help you
any."

"But you can't suspect what I have in mind."

"We don't suspect it, that's true, but we know it."

"Then you know why I'm here."

"I know why, but just so you won't doubt our
willingness to listen to you, go ahead and tell me!"

Swerdlow started to clean his fingernails with a
pocketknife. The surface of his desk was empty;

apparently, the colonel had been on the point of leaving his office. However, he didn't give the impression that Proska's visit was keeping him from doing other things. He even seemed happy that Proska had finally come to him.

"Come, sit down, Proska, and tell me what's on your mind. Do you want to take off your overcoat?"

"No."

"But why not? Your coat can dry while you're here. Maybe it won't dry completely, but at least enough to look like it's dry. Besides, you can speak more freely with your coat off."

"I'll keep it on," said Proska. He sat down and laid the skirts of his coat over his knees.

"You don't have much to say to me, right?"

"Yes."

"You've come here to make a demand?"

"Yes," Proska repeated. "I've come here to demand an explanation."

The knife scratched away under the colonel's fingernails.

"There," said the colonel after a while. He folded the knife shut and threw it onto his desk. "One must do that from time to time." He smiled and went on: "Tradition collects like black dirt under your fingernails, and because it accumulates fast and nobody wants to put up with it, you have to dig it out every now and then . . . Do you know why monkeys don't make any progress? Because they haven't yet discovered the revolutionary significance of hygiene. If they had, they'd be in a completely different position today . . . But I don't want to bore you with dull pleasantries. Right now, you look as if you've never laughed in your life. What have you come to tell me?"

"You already know."

"You seem to be distressed by the fact that I know something you consider your exclusive knowledge. Believe me, it's the only way to conduct a revolution without risk. If we didn't know what the rest of you know, if we had no clue about what you want, then we could lay ourselves on the stove and let Grandma stuff us. Why have we revalued the individual consciousness in favor of the collective consciousness? Why have we given ourselves so much trouble to creep inside your ganglia? Why have we drilled into your lives like worms burrowing into the earth? Why have we denied ourselves and slept and sweated beside you under a single blanket? Because we recognized that the revolution can succeed only under one condition. And this condition requires us to know what the rest of you know, requires us to be aware that our knowledge has value only if we've discovered what knowledge you all are carrying around inside your skulls. Whoever's not prepared to sleep with the masses and to remain cold during the consummation in order to record their reactions—whoever can't do that is sunk without hope."

Proska said, "None of that interests me."

"I know these things don't interest you," said the colonel. "And the truth is, there's no need for you to worry about them either. You're a misfit, Proska, and you can consider yourself lucky to be one. Because if you weren't a misfit, we surely wouldn't have forgiven you so many times. But we need men like you . . . You're probably wondering why I'm speaking to you so frankly, right?"

"No."

"So you're not wondering?"

"I'm wondering, but about something else," said Proska. He pressed his fingers against the edge of the desk so hard that the knuckles turned white.

"You're wondering why the people in your office change so often, is that it?"

"Yes," Proska said loudly. "You and the others in charge, you disappear everyone who doesn't suit you. One morning people just don't come to work, and nobody knows what's become of them. What do you do with the people who don't suit you, huh?" He thought of Zwiczos and clenched his teeth and looked Swerdlow hard in the face. "How can we keep working with these constant changes?"

The colonel opened and closed his knife and ran his tongue over his upper teeth. "Calm down. The changes correspond exactly to the dynamic principle of progress. Stale water tastes bad. What would you rather drink from, a stagnant pond or a mountain stream? You see what I mean."

Proska was shaking. He bounded to his feet and said, "You people on top, you drill your way into us, that's true, but once you're inside, you inject poison into our bloodstream and devour us from within. I've watched you long enough to know. I see where you want to take us. You can't fool me."

Swerdlow gave him a narrow-eyed, scrutinizing look and said calmly, "Don't get so worked up. We haven't transferred you anywhere. Which is how you can tell that we trust you. And in fact, we trust you even though you don't come to any meetings or participate in any indoctrination sessions. And yet you of all people could sure use some indoctrination. Then you'd understand why the engine must be cleaned."

"Why was Mospfleger arrested?" Proska asked coldly.

"For sufficient reasons."

"For what reasons?"

"Have you accepted the fact that we know more than you?"

Proska said nothing.

The colonel went on: "So you have accepted it. Is it unthinkable that we knew more than you in Mospfleger's case too? To breathe is not to judge, Proska; breathing is indeed a prerequisite for judging, but only one prerequisite out of many. Since you're apparently lacking the other prerequisites, I would—if I were you—let breathing be enough and refrain from judging in this way."

"You disappeared him because he was promoting an antiwar organization."

"The setting up of any organization is a thorn in the State's side. But you be quiet now. You've already said enough. I'll be chewing on what you've told me for a good while."

The colonel got up, scurried over to the window, and pulled down the shade. Then he returned to his place behind the desk and explained, "I don't like being looked at through a window. It always makes me feel so defenseless. Can you imagine that?"

"God can see through window shades too."

"Yes, but you know, I've never yet had a feeling of defenselessness where he's concerned. When he shaped us in his image, he made a mistake. And now he's paying a stiff price, because as soon as we get in a quarrel with him, we use the abilities he gave us against him. I wouldn't like to be in his shoes. But you shouldn't talk about God at every opportunity . . . You wanted to know what we do with the people who disappear from your office?"

"I don't want to know anything else about any of you," said Proska. He stood up and went to the door. "You can all do whatever you want. I've always put my cards on the table, and I can say I—"

"Hush," the colonel interrupted him. "Be quiet now. You're tired and overexcited. You have to get some sleep. Go home, Proska. Rest up, recover from the world. Who knows what got you so upset . . . Good night."

Proska left the colonel's room without another word. A little dazed, he stopped on the first landing of the staircase, and it seemed to him as if he heard a brief, metallic click. Then he slowly continued down the stairs, passed unimpeded through the checkpoint, and reached the street. Rain was still falling, thin as threads. Proska wrapped his overcoat tight around himself and walked in some direction, any direction, if only to leave the vicinity of that building. But whichever way he turned and however fast he walked, the house didn't let go of him; sure, he could set out and head north, south, east, or west, but he couldn't get more than a certain distance away. When he stood on the farthest point, he lost the impulse to go any farther and turned back, as though he were a small particle in an electromagnetic force field and couldn't leave a strictly limited area under his own power. He decided to go to a favorite bar and get something to drink. Beer, potato schnapps, something. He was a familiar figure in the bar; even the cats knew him. Whenever he ate there, they would sit at his feet and beg, closely following the spoon as it approached his mouth. The animals carried on with their innocent shamelessness until he finally grew angry and threw some scraps on the floor. Then the cats spared him for a while and gobbled up whatever had come their way.

When Proska entered, the bar owner gave a start and led his guest to one of the rooms in the back. It was a small room with bare walls, a table and chairs in one corner, and on the table, beer; Kunkel, a man from Proska's office, was sitting on one of the chairs.

"Good evening," said Kunkel.

Proska nodded, perplexed. The innkeeper closed the door.

"What are you doing here?" Proska asked. "Do you come to this place often?"

"No."

"Are you here because of me?"

"Yes. I'm glad I've found you. There are three of us looking for you. Fabrun's waiting in front of the dairy store just down the street from your building, Kroogmann's at the train station, and I, as you see, am waiting for you here."

"What does this mean?" asked Proska. "Aren't you going to tell me why you're all lying in wait for me? What is it you want?"

Kunkel whispered, "You have to disappear."

"What?"

"You have to bugger off, as fast as you can. They're waiting for you in your apartment. I watched them go in. So far, they haven't come back out."

Proska asked, "Are you sure they're in my room, waiting for me? Other people live in that building . . . How do you know they want me?"

"Proska, you can be sure it's you they're waiting for. I don't know anybody who's more overdue than you."

"You're not giving me any news. We're all overdue, even before we get here. I'm just now coming from Swerdlow."

"So what do you want to do?"

"I have only one possibility."

Kunkel pushed a little packet across the table, seized Proska's hand, pressed it, and said, "Maybe we'll see each other again before too long. Take care."

Then, impassively, he left the room.

Before midnight, the rain suddenly stopped and the wind became weaker. Proska failed to notice any of that. The spruces in the protected plantation area were crowded close together, and when the man touched a branch, the drops of water hanging on the needles immediately sprinkled him. He made very slow progress.

The young spruces, a head taller than he was, tolerated him in their midst only with great reluctance.

In spite of the season, the air among the trees was strangely sultry. The sultry air lay dense over the earth, and when Proska, at regular intervals, ducked his head and listened, or when he dropped down on his knees to rest and held his ear to the night, then the sultriness wafted over him, and it was as if the earth blew its breath full in his face, copiously and rudely. The breath wafted over him from all sides, wherever he turned; there was no escaping it. His shirt and underpants were stuck to his body. His fingers swelled up, and there was a savage throbbing inside his temples.

Beyond the spruce plantation, a plowed field awaited him—soft, fertile soil. He jumped down into the first furrow. He could hear his heart pounding against the ground. His hand felt along the furrow's little wall, and then he raised his head, supported his upper body on his arms, and peered across the field. The moon unexpectedly slipped out, looked down, and left. All clear—no sentry for twenty meters. Proska continued on, moving from furrow to furrow. Between jumps, waiting, listening intently and waiting. In some of the furrows, water, a finger deep. Low clouds, low sky.

Proska jumped again, and on the way down, he saw that someone was already lying in the spot where he was about to land. He threw himself to one side, wrenching his body out of the direction of its fall, but he couldn't avoid the legs of the person cowering under him. Proska realized at once that this was no sentry—it was a woman. She cried out softly; Proska's boot had struck her shin.

"Quiet," Proska said in a choked voice. The woman fell silent and concentrated on looking straight ahead. Beside her lay a backpack, soaked through and covered with mud.

"Is someone out there?" Proska asked softly.

"Two of them. They cross each other just before the meadow, then they move apart again. Every three minutes."

"And?"

"They're about to come together again. When they part, that's the time."

They lay side by side in the furrow, unspeaking, and when the sentries approached their meeting point, Proska and the woman put their heads down. His face rested on her sweatpants. He felt a little less insecure than before.

Once again, the moon sprang out from behind a cloud.

"But not now," the woman whispered.

He raised his face and checked to see how much time the next cloud would need to hide the moon, but the moon had already gone in again.

The sentries came together. They conversed, carrying their carbines braced against their hips. Proska thought, *Safety catches off, ready to fire. Young people.*

He hissed, "I'll take your backpack. We'll go faster."

She answered softly, "No, I can carry it. It's not so heavy."

He sensed that she was lying to him, stretched out a hand, and grasped one of the backpack's straps. He tugged on it cautiously.

"This backpack's too heavy for you, ma'am. You can't run with it." The woman, seeing that his hand was on her property, pulled the backpack away from him and clasped it tightly, desperately, to her chest.

"I'll carry it," he whispered. "Otherwise we'll never get across."

"In that case, too bad for me," she said. "But if you take my backpack, I'll scream. I won't care about anything anymore."

"I really don't want it for myself."

"Then leave it to me."

Proska saw that he wouldn't be able to overcome the woman's distrust. She would have preferred letting the sentries catch her to letting him carry her backpack. *This is a waste of time*, he thought. *Even if I try to help her while we're running for it, she'll scream . . . let her lug the thing herself . . . the sentries . . .*

The sentries parted, marching away in opposite directions, slowly. After a few steps, the darkness had already swallowed them. In their invisible presence, however, they were bigger than ever; the two sentries suddenly became four, eight, sixteen, thirty-two. In daylight, two sentries are two sentries; in darkness, they increase and multiply.

"Now," said the woman.

"Not yet!" said Proska.

She obeyed. She stayed where she was, lying beside him but prepared to jump up, waiting for his signal.

Proska picked up a clump of earth, squeezed it in one hand, and ordered, "Go!"

And then they both sprang to their feet, ran crouching over the furrows, ready to throw themselves down at any second, splashed into standing water, slipped, pulled themselves together, went on: he in front, unencumbered by baggage, strong and resolute; she behind, desperate, reeling, her heavy backpack slung over one shoulder. When the distance between them became too great, he stopped impatiently, turned his head, and waved her forward. They reached the meadow: rotting posts and triple strands of wire. He climbed up on the top strand—the posts leaned toward him—and jumped. A screeching, rusty sound was heard. Proska pressed the bottom wire down to the ground with his foot, and with his hands he pulled up the middle strand, saying, "Come through, quick, quick."

While she was creeping through the wire fence, he turned his head alternately right and left, his eyes piercing the darkness, looking for the sentries. They must be back soon. Maybe they were already close? Maybe they were watching him and the woman as they put themselves through this hopeless torment? Proska released the strands of wire, took the woman's hand, and pulled her into the meadow. *The sentries must be just about to cross . . . we won't go much farther . . . four more steps . . . get down and lie still . . . now.*

He dropped to the ground, pulling the woman down with him. She lay half on him; her body was shaking. Her breath seeped through his clothes. He counted to ninety and relied on God. His angle of vision was too small to let him make out the place where the sentries would meet. And after he had counted to ninety, he raised his upper body, bracing himself on his arms, and panted, "Fast, across the meadow."

They traversed the meadow and reached the tall, stern forest. They went through the forest and found themselves unexpectedly standing on an embankment. The horizon grew lighter; the day promised to arrive before long. The red eye of a distant signal burned through the early morning fog. A road ran past their feet. Proska said, "Now we're all right, here's our road. We were lucky. I counted to ninety, because I thought the sentries would have to be far enough away by then. I was right. Where do you want to go?"

The woman answered, "The next village. Where my husband is. It's not far from here. He'll probably come out to meet me."

"Are you saying that because you're afraid of me?"

"No," she said. "My husband will help me carry this pack. It's his manuscripts and notes I went over to pick up. I got everything that was left."

"That's why you went to the other side?" Proska asked.

"He needs this work. He was just offered a professorship."

She spoke more and more softly, and in the end she choked and her voice fell silent. She sat on her backpack and wept.

Proska clambered down the embankment and walked to the train station. On the way, he encountered a man, and he stood in the man's path and said, "Your wife's sitting back there. Everything went fine."

The next train north left right on time.

The big locomotive came to a stop, right on time, under the glass dome of the main railroad station. The engine blew its black smoke at the transparent roof in great puffs; water streamed down its hot flanks and dripped onto the rails. A man with an oilcan went up to the locomotive, turned several caps, looked for the little funnel, found it, and raised the can.

Proska got off the train. Immediately caught up in the stream of travelers heading for the exit, he was washed up the stone steps and almost startled to find himself standing in the station's dusty hall. He was no longer wedged between warm shoulders; the stream had lost him, expelled him.

Nobody knew him, nobody wished to speak to him, nobody interested him, and no one noticed him. *Things will go on . . . I'll get a job, I'll work . . . it'll be all right . . .*

Confidence and optimism swelled in him. He strolled unhurriedly past the vendors' stands lining the concourse, reading the posted prices and the writing on cans and boxes. And then he stopped in front of a wall on which a large blackboard hung.

On the left, a poster: MURDER, and printed below: REWARD. And in addition to the poster: public announcements, warnings, appeals, requests, tips, want ads, and search notices: GREAT DANE MISSING. WHOEVER HAS . . . SILVER BRACELET LOST, THE HONEST FINDER WHO . . .

A locomotive passed through without stopping and shook the station hall. The floor vibrated, and the vibrations extended deep into Proska's body as well. With half an eye, he read the administrative and private messages. His gaze slid over the board, involuntary and purposeless. MANDATORY REGISTRATION . . . SCHOOL VACCINATIONS WILL TAKE PLACE ON . . . RAT POISON . . . SUCCESS GUARANTEED, MANY CUSTOMER TESTIMONIALS . . . INSPECTION UPON REQUEST . . . IN ACCORDANCE WITH THE

REPORT OF THE LDJ/IIIC AND THE DISTRICT COMMIT-
TEE OF THE VDB, ALL MEMBERS MUST . . .

Proska jumped suddenly, as if someone in the
clouds had called his name. A jolt like a lightning
strike surged through his body. He bent a little to one
side; all the blood withdrew from his brain; he shut
his eyes and opened them again at once. He murmured a name and turned around jerkily, fearing that
the name he'd spoken could have been overheard by
a stranger. But there was no one near him. He was
all alone in the spacious hall. An announcement was
hanging from the edge of the blackboard:

WHO CAN PROVIDE INFORMATION
REGARDING MY HUSBAND,
KURT ROGALSKI?
LAST SEEN IN SYBBA, EAST PRUSSIA.
INFORMATION REQUESTED BY
MARIA ROGALSKI,
CURRENTLY AT . . .

"Who can provide information . . . ," Proska read in
an undertone.

You, Proska, you alone. You alone know what
took place, and why. You caused what happened to
happen. There's no action that doesn't entail suffering;
you acted as you thought you had to act. You didn't
lie idle. Your conscience constantly lashed you, urging

you forward. The actions behind you are inessential. What's essential always happens up ahead . . . Your sister Maria is looking for her husband. You killed him. We were all witnesses, we all saw him put himself in your line of fire. But it was your finger that curled around the trigger, it was your shoulder that absorbed the recoil.

Maria is asking for certainty. You alone can give it to her, Proska. You must give it to her. Suffer, but don't forget to act. You don't need to write to her now—she wouldn't demand that of you. But one day you must write her, one day. When you know where you'll sleep, where you can be alone with yourself and the long days, when you know that all paths yearn to be walked to the end: then do it, Proska, do it. You will do it. You must do it. By now we know you too well to think you won't.

P roska opened his eyes and shook himself, as if trying to throw off the last drops of memory that were still clinging to him. He had needed months to find the strength to write to his sister. Now the letter lay in the mailbox over there on the other side of the street, a properly stamped confession for which the old, oblivion-seeking pharmacist had loaned him the stamps.

What will she say when she reads it? . . . And how will she answer me, if she answers me at all?

He saw the postman arrive at the mailbox, watched him open the bottom flap, observed him as he impassively let the letters fall into a waterproof canvas bag, climbed back on his bicycle, and rode away. The crossed strips of wood separating the windowpanes threw a sharp-edged shadow into the room. The swallows were flying low.

And then came a day when the postman climbed up the steep stairs to Proska's apartment. "For you," he said, and went back down.

Proska rushed to the window and, with trembling fingers, held the envelope up to the light. It was his letter to Maria! Someone had written in indelible pencil on the back of the envelope: "Undeliverable— no forwarding address. Return to Sender."

· THE TURNCOAT ·

by Günter Berg

*It's true, I often subject my characters to the pressure
of an extraordinary situation, to which they
must then react, one way or another.*

—Siegfried Lenz in an interview
with Geno Hartlaub, *Sonntagsblatt*,
December 25, 1966

ORIGIN

In February 1951, the German publishing house Hoffmann und Campe published Siegfried Lenz's first novel, *Es waren Habichte in der Luft* ("There Were Hawks in the Air"). A serialized edition of the text had previously appeared in print in the daily newspaper *Die Welt* from October 24 to November 25, 1950. Lenz had begun a traineeship at *Die Welt* in 1948; later, having been promoted to culture and entertainment editor, he'd also been given responsibility for the literary texts the paper published in serial form. His mentor and patron, Willy Haas, had provided him with this prestigious opportunity.

Lenz's debut novel did not go unnoticed and received a unanimously warm reception from literary critics and reviewers. Therefore, at the end of March 1951—shortly after the appearance of this first work—the head of Hoffmann und Campe, Dr. Rudolf

Soelter, saw no difficulty in immediately offering the promising young author a second book contract. The new novel's working title was . . . *da gibt's ein Wiedersehen* (". . . We'll Meet Again"), which is a line from the refrain of a well-known German popular song.

But before settling down to work, Siegfried Lenz and his wife Liselotte took a vacation. On April 15, 1951, they boarded the M/S *Lisboa* in Bremen for a trip to Morocco, stopping at Melilla and Tangier before arriving in Casablanca. The couple could afford to go on such an extended journey (they were abroad for several weeks) because of the handsome fee, three thousand marks, that *Die Welt* had paid Lenz for the serial rights to his first novel; moreover, he had the new contract for his second book in his pocket, and this combination of circumstances allowed him to believe in the possibility of a career as a freelance writer.

Soon after his return to Hamburg, Siegfried Lenz started working on his new book. As was his lifelong habit, he wrote the manuscript by hand, and Lilo Lenz typed it up, with several carbon copies. The first draft of the novel, in twelve chapters (Version I), was ready by the end of summer 1951. By the autumn of that year, the certainty that they had discovered a serious young author encouraged Hoffmann und Campe to bring the typescript, still designated by its working title, . . . *da gibt's ein Wiedersehen*, to the attention of the editorial staffs at various newspapers. At this early stage, and in the absence of a complete text, it's possible that the publisher sent out only the first chapters as a *pars pro toto*, because the staffs at *Die Zeit* in Hamburg, at *Die Neue Zeitung* in Munich, and at the *Frankfurter Allgemeine Zeitung*, in their responses, all concentrated on the "partisan story" in the beginning of the novel (Chapters 2–8) and completely ignored the "turncoat story."

In any case, there was a noteworthy mention of Lenz's novel project in a substantial article on new books about the Second World War that was published in the weekly newspaper *Die Zeit* on November 8, 1951. "The atmosphere of the Russian campaign, the winter snowstorms, the houses in the villages, lying like black points in the white void, the burning summer sun, the mosquitoes, the dust of the provisional roads, the shots fired by partisans hidden in treetops—all this will feel oppressively close if you read Siegfried Lenz's novel . . . *da gibt's ein Wiedersehen*, shortly to be published by Hoffmann & Campe." The author of this long piece was Paul Hühnerfeld, who had already given Lenz's first novel, *Es waren Habichte in der Luft*, a brief but friendly review in the May 10, 1951 edition of the same paper, and who now, six months later, had no doubt that Hoffmann und Campe would soon be publishing the young author's new novel.

Hühnerfeld called his article "The Pros and Cons of Witness Statements: Authors between Reporting and Literature—the Dilemma of German Books about the Eastern Front." On the whole, he's disappointed by what he sees as little more than "detailed descriptions of what war is like" in the novels he's chosen for discussion. Only in Lenz's text does he acknowledge a power of literary penetration that goes beyond mere description: "This book doesn't aspire to be an eyewitness account, but perhaps it does reveal poetic ambitions. And thus this author gets closer than the others to evoking what war is really like."

Hoffmann und Campe solicited several expert editors' opinions and in the end asked the Germanist and folklorist Dr. Otto Görner, in Karlsruhe, to take over the editorial responsibilities for the first draft (Version I) of Lenz's text. A meeting was arranged and took place around the same time as *Die Zeit* published the article that first mentioned Lenz's new novel project; therefore, editorial work began only after the review appeared. Görner was apparently as impressed by the force of the novel—"which grabs the reader by the neck"—as Paul Hühnerfeld of *Die Zeit* had been. After having met the author in person in Hamburg, Görner wrote him a detailed letter, indicating his fundamental approval of the novel while suggesting some corrections and indicating passages where he thought sharpening or greater emphasis was needed. In closing, he wrote, "I am sure, my dear Herr Lenz, that you will take these considerations of mine as they are meant to be taken and not as pedantry. They address only matters of technique and craft. And please allow me to use this opportunity to tell you once again how much I enjoyed our conversation at Hoffmann und Campe's offices" (Otto Görner to Siegfried Lenz, November 13, 1951).

In all probability, it was immediately after the conversation in the publishing house and the reception of Görner's follow-up letter that Lenz started to work on revising Version I, which he completed around the beginning of 1952. In a rapid run-through, the author tightened the first or "partisan" section of the novel, cut dialogue, and lightly polished passages here and there. But the second part, the "turncoat" section, received a thorough revision; Lenz wrote some entirely new chapters and divided up others (see below, "Text/Versions").

The result of this assiduous reworking was a second draft of the novel, in sixteen chapters. The author had often considered calling his work *The Turncoat*; now he wrote that title in his own hand on the cover of the manuscript. He probably submitted this second draft (Version II) to his publisher in January 1952.

In a letter sent to Otto Görner in November 1951, the *Neue Zeitung* had already declined first serial rights to the novel. Some time later, the *Frankfurter Allge-meine Zeitung* did the same; the editor responsible for the decision was Herbert Nette, who expressed regret for it to the author himself and gave as his reason for rejecting Lenz's book the newspaper's recent serialization of Rolf Schroers's novel *Die Feuerschwelle* ("The Fire Threshold"). According to Nette's self-justification, the *FAZ* had published, "not long ago, another war novel. While it's true that this novel, by Rolf Schroers, takes place in Italy, it also, like yours, depicts a partisan milieu. And so it is that for thoroughly banal reasons of content, we cannot consider publishing your novel at any point in the foreseeable future" (Herbert Nette to Siegfried Lenz, January 22, 1952).

During the course of these weeks, the "reasons of content" cited by the *FAZ* editor appear to have led to a revised assessment of the *Turncoat* project in the publishing house as well. Be that as it may, the editor Otto Görner's initially well-meaning if somewhat pedantic opinion of the story's narrative power gave way to a profound skepticism, which he expounded upon in a detailed letter to Lenz. The overall tenor of this piece of writing suggests that it was based on a reader's report that Görner had prepared for Hoffmann und Campe; in this report, he'd pronounced his judgment on the revision of the novel and therefore on Lenz's second and final version.

In his first letter to Lenz, the reader's tone had been respectful as he acknowledged the young author's accomplishment, but now Görner seemed to arrogate to himself a position of authority in regard to the youthful writer, who was half his age. And apparently, Görner also wanted to demonstrate his energetically held views to the publisher. Görner begins this second letter by accusing Lenz of failing to make some suggested emendations to his text, changes that "had been recommended for very sound reasons." Görner's intentions become substantially clearer in the middle section of his letter: "An exciting and distinctive writing style is not sufficient. Whatever the circumstances, the author must jump the hurdles that come with his subject. I suggest that he provide us with a lucid outline of a new draft of his novel. Without such a plan, further work on the text is pointless. The author must compel himself to consider seriously, once and for all, the possibilities inherent in his material." These suggestions are evidently meant more for the publisher than for the writer to whom the letter is addressed and who, no doubt, must now feel that in working on his text he has "perhaps relied all too greatly on the atmosphere of comradely understanding," as Görner conjectures.

You can sense the panic of the publisher's chosen reader when he comes to the essential point, which the substantial revision of the manuscript has now made clearly apparent: ". . . the novel should in fact be called *The Turncoat*—and that is an impossible title. Such a novel could have been published in 1946. But it's a well-known fact that these days, everyone wants to ignore the past . . . You could do yourself immeasurable damage, and in this case, your good relations with the radio and the press won't be of any help to you. We're not giving you this advice because we're academic know-it-alls, but because we know our times, because we know the developments that are taking place, and because experience has taught us that a novel can start off well and still become a literary disaster."

And because Görner, on closer inspection, considers a novel in which deserters from the German Wehrmacht go over to the Red Army simply unimaginable in the political climate of the Adenauer period and in view of the ominously hardening relations between the Western powers and the Eastern Bloc, he proposes to Lenz that he should totally rework his material and reimagine his characters. Görner particularly insists that the author must give Proska, the turncoat, a "positive" antagonist to balance his conduct and make it appear more outlandish. And in order to keep anything else from going awry, the reader writes, "Make yourself an outline for how you're going to proceed, and organize your material well. Write up this outline for us, let's say 3–4 pages with keywords and brief sentences. And then, once we reach a mutual agreement, follow your outline step by step and turn it into a narrative."

And with this, the novel for which Lenz had signed a contract was basically rejected. And in a mixture of threat and broad hint, the official reader added, "My dear Herr Lenz, don't consider making some sort of angry gesture and deciding to write a new book."

Lenz's response is quite clear and the attitude he displays quite admirable, considering the number of months he'd spent working on this important second novel.

Siegfried Lenz
Hamburg 13 Isestr. 88

Hamburg, January 24, 1952

Dear Dr. Görner,
Thank you for your detailed letter, to which I would like to respond as follows:
You consider the second version of my manuscript a failure. On this point I have nothing to say, except that I completely respect your judgment.

Siegfried L e n z
Hamburg 13 Jsestr. 88.

Hamburg, d. 24.1.52.

Lieber Herr Dr. Görner,

ich danke Ihnen für den ausführlichen Brief und möchte
Ihnen dazu Folgendes schreiben:

Sie halten die zweite Fassung meines Manuskripts für nicht geglückt.
Dazu habe ich nur zu sagen, daß ich Ihr Urteil in jeder Weise
respektiere.
Sie werfen mir vor, ich hätte es an hinreichendem Arbeit und den
nötigen Denkbemühungen fehlen lassen. Das ist gewiß nicht der Fall.
Ich persönlich muß gemeinhin mehr Mühe und qualvolle Geduld an eine
einzige "Zwischen"-Seite wenden als an acht Seiten fortlaufenden
Textes,- und ich habe dies getan. Daß Ihnen die dazu erfundene Handlung - besonders im Hinblick auf mögliche Folgen nach einer Publika-
tion des Manuskripts - zu wenig durchdacht erscheint, beweist mir:
daß ich der Intuition beim Schreiben selbst den "Rücken kehren" muß;
daß ich eine ständige Selbstkontrolle beim Schreiben brauche, und
daß ich schließlich dieses Manuskript ohne Rücksicht auf meine
Grenzen begonnen habe. Der Sprung über die Hürde ist mir nicht geglückt und wird mir nicht glücken. Die Hürde war nicht für mich
gebaut. Ich habe durchaus ernsthaft über die Möglichkeiten meines
Stoffes nachgedacht; ich fand nur meine Möglichkeiten, und wie es
sich herausstellte, reichen sie nicht aus.
Sie werfen mir vor, ich hätte Ihr Vertrauen mißbraucht und ver-
sucht, Sie hereinzulegen. Dieser Vorwurf trifft mich, wie Sie ver-
stehen werden, schwer, und ich bin geneigt, ihn als unwillentliche
Kränkung aufzufassen. Was hätte ich mir von solch einem Versuch
versprechen sollen ? Außerdem haben Sie sich mit der Feststellung,
ich hätte Sie hereinlegen wollen, begnügt; denn eine Erklärung,
womit oder wodurch ich das zu erreichen trachtete, haben Sie nicht
gegeben. In Ihrem ersten, wohlmeinenden Brief forderten Sie mich auf
die Gedanken, die Sie sich über den Fortlauf der Handlung gemacht
hatten, auf ihre Annehmbarkeit hin nachzudenken. Ich habe sie nachgedacht, lieber Herr Dr. Görner, aber ich habe sie nicht insgesamt
akzeptieren können, weil sie meinen Möglichkeiten teilweise zuwider-
liefen. Ich kann mir nicht denken, daß Sie in dieser zwangsläufigen
Unterlassung einen zureichenden Grund sehen, um mir einen Vertrauens-
bruch vorzuwerfen.
Sie werfen mir vor, daß meine Bearbeitung fast nichts ergeben hätte.
Ich glaubte, an der Figur Proska gegen den Schluß hin bereits zu-
viel geändert zu haben. Ich gebe allerdings zu, daß der Schreibende
die Reflexe seiner Figuren nur auf sehr kurze Entfernung gleichsam
durch Facettenaugen sieht.
Sie schreiben mir, ich sollte keine wütende Geste machen. Wozu sollte ich Sie machen, lieber Herr Dr. Görner, zumal sie mir in keiner
Weise hülfe ? Ich habe lange über Ihren Brief nachgedacht, ich habe
ihn wieder und wieder gelesen, ich habe auch darüber geschlafen und
ich möchte Ihnen nun mit Besonnenheit und völlig leidenschaftslos
sagen, daß ich diesen Roman nicht schreiben werde; und zwar werde
ich ihn nicht schreiben, weil ich ihn nicht schreiben **kann.**

Ich werde diese Arbeit als eine unerläßliche Übung ansehen, als das geziemende Training, das ja schließlich die conditio sine qua non für einen jungen Schriftsteller ist. Ich bin überzeugt, daß ich manches gelernt habe, was ich ohne diese Anstrengung nicht gelernt hätte ! Den besten, wenn auch schwer erkennbaren Zins bringen uns die mißglückten Versuche. Vielleicht werde ich Ihnen in zwei oder drei Jahren ein neues Manuskript zeigen dürfen, ein Manuskript das besser und ein wenig reifer ist.

Einstweilen danke ich Ihnen sehr herzlich für die Mühewaltung, für Ihre Teilnahme und die vielen guten Ratschläge

                    und bleibe mit den besten Grüßen

                              Ihr

                              S. 4.

P.S.
Ich schicke Herrn Soelter,
in dessen Namen Ihr Brief an mich
ja auch geschrieben war, eine
Durchschrift meines Antwortbriefes.

You reproach me for not having worked hard enough and for not having made the necessary mental effort. That is certainly not the case. As a general rule, I personally have to take more trouble and to expend more agonizing patience on a single "transitional" page than on eight pages of continuous text—and that's what I've done. The fact that the plot I've come up with strikes you as insufficiently thought through, especially as regarding the possible consequences of publishing the manuscript, demonstrates to me that when I write, I must "turn my back" on intuition, that I need to practice ceaseless self-control when I write, and lastly that I began this manuscript without regard for my limitations. I didn't succeed in jumping the hurdles, nor will I ever. Those hurdles were not built for me. I gave quite serious thought to the possibilities offered by my material; I found only my possibilities, and as it turns out, they're not sufficient.

You reproach me for having abused your trust and attempted to trick you. This reproach, as you will understand, deeply wounds me, and I'm inclined to take it as an involuntary offense. What might I have expected to gain from such an attempt? Besides, you are content merely to state that I tried to trick you, for you give no explanation of how or by what means I endeavored to accomplish that end. In your first, benevolent letter, you asked me to reflect upon your suggestions for the further development of the plot and

to see whether I would deem them acceptable. *I have
so reflected, dear Dr. Görner, but I've been unable to
accept all of them, because some of them run counter to
my possibilities.* I cannot believe that you see in these
inevitable omissions sufficient reason to accuse me of a
breach of trust.

You reproach me because my reworking of
the manuscript has led, you say, to almost no
improvement. Toward the end, I believed I had
already made too many changes to the character
Proska. However, I admit that the writer sees his
characters' reflections only from a very short distance
away and with many facets, like looking through
compound eyes.

You write that I should make no angry gesture.
Why would I do that, dear Dr. Görner, especially
seeing that it could in no way help me? I've given a
lot of thought to your letter, I've read and reread it
over and over, I've also slept on it, and now I'd like
to say to you, calmly, deliberately, and completely
dispassionately, that I will never write this novel, and
that I won't write it because I can't write it.

I shall look on this work as an indispensable
exercise, as proper training, which in the end is the
conditio sine qua non for every young writer. I'm
convinced that I've learned a great many things I
wouldn't have learned without making this effort! It's
our failed attempts that pay the greatest dividends,

even though they may be hard to recognize at first. Perhaps, in two or three years, I may venture to show you a new manuscript, a manuscript that's better and a little more mature.

In the meantime, I offer you my heartfelt thanks for your trouble, for your interest, and for all the good advice.

With my best regards,
yours sincerely,

S. Lenz

P.S. I'm sending Herr Soelter, in whose name you wrote the letter to me, a carbon copy of this reply.

Eventually, and to avoid further burdening the relationship between author and publisher, there was a pro forma understanding that the novel, shorn of its incriminating "turncoat" section, would be published as a novella at some later, more auspicious time. As the years passed, this compromise, which seemed highly unlikely to succeed anyway, faded from memory: the publishing director of Hoffmann und Campe, Rudolf Soelter, died in 1953; the reader, Otto Görner, died two years later. And so in the end, Lenz laid the entire business to rest, looked ahead rather than behind, and turned to fresh literary projects. In 1953, his novel *Duell mit dem Schatten* ("Duel with the Shadow") appeared and has been considered his second book ever since. Only two years after that, in 1955, his short-story collection *So zärtlich war Suleyken* ("So Tender Was Suleyken") followed. This book's enormous success also definitively consigned to oblivion whatever remained of the disagreements beween publisher and author during their ill-fated collaboration on *The Turncoat*. Siegfried Lenz remained loyal to the Hamburg publishing house Hoffmann und Campe for the rest of his life.

TEXT/VERSIONS

Lenz probably began the first draft of his second novel at the end of May 1951, after his return from his African trip. Writing by hand, he filled a large-format notebook with Chapters 1–8 and the beginning of Chapter 9. Then, having run out of room, he turned to the same notebook in which he'd written his first novel, *Es waren Habichte in der Luft*, and completed the second novel (from the end of Chapter 9 through Chapter 12) on the pages that had been left blank.

Making at least two carbon copies on her typewriter, Liselotte Lenz gradually produced the initial typescript of the novel, whose handwritten draft exhibits only a few corrections, additions, and deletions. This typescript of the new novel (Version I: twelve chapters, 276 numbered pages, and two carbon copies, in the Siegfried Lenz Literary Estate in the German Literary Archive in Marbach am Neckar) reached the publisher's hands probably by early autumn 1951 and certainly by October of that year. This version was the basis of the judgment pronounced by Dr. Otto Görner on November 10, 1951, on the occasion of his meeting with Lenz in Hoffmann und Campe's offices at 41 Harvestehuder Weg in Hamburg, within walking distance of the apartment on 88 Isestrasse where Lenz and his wife lived in those days.

Immediately after this conversation at the publishing house and the encouraging letter Dr. Görner, the publisher's reader, subsequently sent him, Lenz began the revision of his novel. To this end, he divided the second carbon copy of the novel into two parts and very heavily revised Chapters 9 through 12. In the course of the revision, those four chapters became the final eight chapters (9–16) of the current edition, but the novel didn't get significantly longer. The newly written ninth chapter greatly helps to illuminate the author's intentions in making these revisions, which resulted in Version II of his text. Lenz first wrote the new chapter in his *Habichte* notebook, in which he'd already written the final chapters of Version I.

This new Chapter 9 (pages 217–242 in the present volume) serves as the hinge between the first or "partisan" section of the novel and its second or "turncoat" section; during the course of the night described here, Proska encounters his comrade Milk Roll, and following a conversation, Proska decides to change sides, as his friend has already done. Milk Roll and Proska are both prisoners of war in this chapter, waiting to be executed (at dawn, they've been told); Lenz thus places his principal character in a state of emergency, where he must choose either extinction or treason, because the single alternative to certain death is to join the struggle against "the Gang" (as he calls Germany's rulers) on the side of the enemy.

Chapter 10 remained essentially the same. Proska accompanies a former German officer, also a deserter and in charge of frontline propaganda for the Soviets, on his final mission. The new Chapter 11—with, at its center, a last meeting between Proska and his lover, Wanda—is mainly based on parts of the old Chapter 9.

Events during the Soviet Army's westward advance had been Lenz's focus in Chapter 11 of Version I; now he divided those events into two chapters. In Chapter 12 (pages 270–282 in the present volume), Proska appears as an adviser to a Soviet battlefront commander in combat with his, Proska's, former comrades; in Chapter 13 (pages 283–294), the Red Army's westward progress takes Proska to his homeland in East Prussia. At Proska's sister Maria's farm near the East Prussian town of Sybba, immediately adjacent to Lyck, things start moving fast and tragedy ensues, both for Proska's comrade Milk Roll and for his brother-in-law, Rogalski. As readers of the novel will know, Lenz depicted those tragic developments in Chapter 13 of his revised version, but he had already included them in his first version.

The closing episodes, set in the Soviet Occupied Zone in Germany after the war, were originally part of a single chapter; the revised version expands them to three entire chapters (14–16). Lenz used parts of his original Chapter 12, the final chapter of Version I, in the closing chapter (16) of Version II. By contrast, Chapters 14 and 15 of the second version were newly written. Wanda appears once again, but only in the form of a hallucination unmistakably attributable to Proska's longing for his "Squirrel."

In these last chapters, which include both rewritten and new material, Lenz gave his depiction of life in the Soviet Occupied Zone after the end of the war not only increased volume but also notably greater depth. He portrays the suffocating constrictions of the totalitarian power structures in the SOZ, with their all-pervasive system of spying, ideological indoctrination, and control over individual lives, more effectively and in greater detail in the second, revised version of his novel.

In a scene that Lenz incorporated into his closing chapter (16), Proska makes a last-minute escape from apparently imminent arrest by fleeing the Soviet zone to the West. This scene, like others, was totally new, written by Lenz for inclusion in the revised version of his novel.

While the revisions of the first part (Chapters 1–8) were made by hand, all at one go, on the second carbon copy of Version I of Lenz's text, the substantial additions, rearrangements, and new divisions of the chapters in the second part made it absolutely necessary to produce a new typescript containing Chapters 9–16.

The basis of the present edition is the complete typescript of Version II that Lenz kept in a single folder. This typescript comprises the corrected Chapters 1–8, taken from a carbon copy of the Version I typescript, and the substantially newly written and heavily revised Chapters 9–16 (Version II typescript).

This edition preserves the orthographical choices made by the author; only small faults in punctuation and orthography due to writing or typing errors have been silently corrected.

Six months before his death in October 2014, Siegfried Lenz entrusted his personal archive to the German Literary Archive in Marbach am Neckar. The items in Lenz's archive included both the manuscript and the typescript of his hitherto unpublished second novel, which was discovered only when the materials were being examined and organized.

The novel was published in Germany in 2016 to great success and acclaim, both from the general reading public and from literary critics. Since then, *The Turncoat* has been translated into fourteen languages. A film version of Lenz's novel premiered on German television in April 2020.

ABOUT THE TITLE

The publishing contract of March 1951 states the new novel's working title as . . . *da gibt's ein Wiedersehen* (". . . We'll Meet Again"). This title alludes to the old soldier's song *"Nun geht's ans Abschiednehmen"* ("Now We Must Say Farewell"), which was written by Hugo Zuschneid (1861–1932). The lines Lenz had in mind when he chose his working title—*"In der Heimat, in der Heimat, / da gibt's ein Wiedersehen"* ("In the homeland, in the homeland, we'll meet again")—are part of the song's refrain.

During the work on his book, Lenz considered another title: *Der Sumpf* ("The Marsh"). This refers to the first part of the novel (Chapters 2 through 8), which deals with the partisans' war against the Germans. The brigades of the Soviet resistance chiefly carried out their attacks and acts of sabotage from bases in the impenetrable forests and marshlands of

Belarus and Ukraine, in which the soldiers of the German Wehrmacht showed themselves to be hopelessly overmatched.

In the course of the heavy revisions and additions made in the second half of the novel (Chapters 9–16 in the present volume), the "turncoat story" was given more and more weight relative to the "partisan story" set in the Russian marshlands, on what was from a German viewpoint the Eastern front. And so the further progress of Lenz's novel made him feel increasingly justified in his later choice of a title, which he first proposed in his negotiations with the publishing house. In the end, he himself gave his second novel the title *Der Überläufer* ("The Turncoat"), writing it in his own hand on the folder containing the second, revised version, along with a subtitle that may be translated as "Death Does the Music."

LIFE AND WORKS

Life

Siegfried Lenz, the son of a customs official, was born on March 17, 1926, in Lyck, a small city in the Masurian region of what was then East Prussia. After graduating from high school in 1943, Lenz was drafted, age seventeen, into the German navy. Shortly before the end of the Second World War, he deserted and was taken prisoner by the British, who employed him as an interpreter.

After the war, he attended the University of Hamburg before interrupting his studies to accept an internship at the German daily newspaper *Die Welt*, where he eventually became an editor (1950–1951). While at *Die Welt*, he met his future wife, Liselotte ("Lilo"), whom he married in 1949. Their union lasted until Liselotte's death some fifty-seven years later, in 2006. From 1951 on, beginning with the success of his first book, *Es waren Habichte in der Luft* ("There Were Hawks in the Air"), Lenz lived as a freelance author in Hamburg, where he died at the age of eighty-eight on October 7, 2014.

Works

Siegfried Lenz was a prolific writer whose enormous output included fiction (novels, novellas, short stories), plays for the theater, radio plays, essays, and journalism. The following chronological list contains only those titles—all of them fiction—that have been translated into English, beginning with *The Turncoat*.

1951   *Der Überläufer*, Lenz's second book, written in 1951 but not published until 2016 (English: *The Turncoat*)
1960   *Das Feuerschiff*, a short-story collection (English: *The Lightship*)
1968   *Deutschstunde*, a novel (English: *The German Lesson*)
1973   *Das Vorbild*, a novel (English: *An Exemplary Life*)
1978   *Heimatmuseum*, a novel (English: *The Heritage*)
1985   *Exerzierplatz*, a novel (English: *Training Ground*)
2006   *Die Erzählungen*, Lenz's collected stories,

published in one volume on the occasion of his eightieth birthday. Twenty-six of these stories, about a third of the total, appear in English in *The Selected Stories of Siegfried Lenz*.

2008   *Schweigeminute*, a novella (English: *Stella* in the United States, *A Minute's Silence* in the United Kingdom)

© Siegfried Lenz Stiftung

SIEGFRIED LENZ, born in Lyck in East Prussia in 1926, is one of the most important and widely read writers in postwar and present-day European literature. During World War II he deserted the German army and was briefly held as a prisoner of war. He published twelve novels, including *The German Lesson*, and produced several collections of short stories, essays, and plays. His works have won numerous prizes, including the Goethe Prize and the German Booksellers' Peace Prize.

JOHN CULLEN is the translator of many books from Spanish, French, German, and Italian, including Susanna Tamaro's *Follow Your Heart*, Philippe Claudel's *Brodeck*, Carla Guelfenbein's *In the Distance with You*, Juli Zeh's *Empty Hearts*, Patrick Modiano's *Villa Triste*, and Kamel Daoud's *The Meursault Investigation*. He lives on the Shoreline in southern Connecticut.

⚎ OTHER PRESS

You might also enjoy these titles from our list:

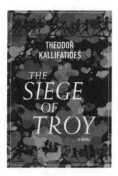

THE SIEGE OF TROY by Theodore Kallifatides

In this perceptive retelling of *The Iliad,* a young Greek teacher draws on the enduring power of myth to help her students cope with the terrors of Nazi occupation.

"A unique retelling of *The Iliad*...This is a wonderful novel." —*Boston Globe,* Most Anticipated Books of the Season

NEVER ANYONE BUT YOU by Rupert Thomson

NAMED A BEST BOOK OF THE YEAR BY *THE GUARDIAN, THE OBSERVER,* AND *SYDNEY MORNING HERALD*

A literary tour de force that traces the real-life love affair of two extraordinary women, recreating the surrealist movement in Paris and the horrors of war.

"There's so much sheer moxie, prismatic identity, pleasure, and danger in these lives...the scenes are tense, particular, and embodied...wonderfully peculiar." —*New York Times Book Review*

THE SECOND WINTER by Craig Larsen

A cinematic novel that, in its vivid portrayal of a family struggling to survive the German occupation of Denmark, captures a savage moment in history and exposes the violence and want inherent in a father's love.

"A great historical novel, a touching family saga, and a noir wartime thriller all rolled into one terrific narrative."
—Lee Child, *New York Times* bestselling author

Additionally recommended:

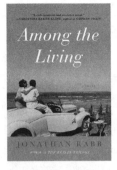

AMONG THE LIVING by Jonathan Rabb

A moving novel about a Holocaust survivor's unconventional journey back to a new normal in 1940s Savannah, Georgia.

"Jonathan Rabb is one of my favorite writers, a highly gifted heart-wise storyteller if ever there was one. From its first pages, *Among the Living* carries you into a particular time and setting…What a powerful, moving book." —David McCullough, Pulitzer Prize and National Book Award–winning author, and recipient of the Presidential Medal of Freedom

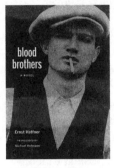

BLOOD BROTHERS by Ernst Haffner
Translated by Michael Hofmann

Originally published in 1932 and banned by the Nazis, *Blood Brothers* follows a gang of young boys bound together by unwritten rules and mutual loyalty.

"[R]emarkable…*Blood Brothers* is an enthralling and significant novel, authentic in its gritty documentary detail, dispassionate yet empathic in its characterization and starkly objective in its portrayal of Berlin's pre-Nazi social underbelly." —*Financial Times*

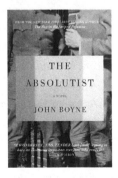

THE ABSOLUTIST by John Boyne

From the bestselling author of *The Heart's Invisible Furies* comes a devastating tale of passion, jealousy, heroism, and betrayal set in one of the most gruesome trenches of France.

"A novel of immeasurable sadness, in a league with Graham Greene's *The End of the Affair*. John Boyne is very, very good at portraying the destructive power of a painfully kept secret." —John Irving

■ OTHER PRESS   *www.otherpress.com*